CHRISTINE BESZE

BADCOCK TOUR 2:
ACOX SISTER CRUISE

Badcock Tour 2: A Coxsister Cruise

Copyright © 2018 Christine Besze

All rights reserved

No part of this publication may be reproduced, stored in a retrieval system, or transmitted, in any form or by any means without the prior written permission of the copyright owner.

This book is a work of fiction. Names, characters, places and incidents are the product of the author's imagination or are used fictitiously, and any resemblance to any actual persons living or dead, events or locales are entirely coincidental.

Editing: Heather Ross for Heather's Red Pen Editing Service

Interior Formatting & Design: T.E. Black Designs; www.teblackdesigns.com

Cover Design: Hang Le; www.byhangle.com

Shit's about to get a lot crazier, much dirtier, and a hell of a lot wetter!

A NOTE FROM THE AUTHOR

IF YOU'VE READ THE WARNING and still are up for the ride thank you for taking a chance on these wild ladies. This is an over the top, slapstick comedy. It does not follow the traditional one hero, one heroine format. It's centered around the three main female characters. If that's not something you're interested in reading then I suggest you turn back now.

These three women are wild, crazy, awkward and a bit immature, but they also have big hearts. They embrace each other for who they are, flaws and all. To me that's one of the best gifts about friendship and I wanted to celebrate that through these amazing, strong characters. It was important for me to show that the world can sometimes be a scary place and as long as you have your girls at your back, everything will be just fine.

With that being said, if you're still reading welcome to the cockride that is Badcock Tour 2: A Coxsister Cruise. Please keep your hands, feet, and all other foreign objects at the ready for this crazy ass ride. Once again, I will repeat this book is not for those who don't enjoy laughing, dicks, sex toys, lube, or any other inappropriate over the top humor and shenanigans. If you're still reading, then congratulations. You are ready to go balls deep on this cocksister train. Keep a box of kleenex handy and your martini glass full.

Thank you again, for being brave enough to dive into something that's different and go on an another adventure with these three crazy chicks. I hope you enjoy.

Cocksisters before misters!

For all of my Cocksisters and Cockmisters!

THANK YOU FOR STAYING ON THE CRAZY TRAIN AND ENJOYING THE RIDE WITH ME, WHEREVER IT LEADS.

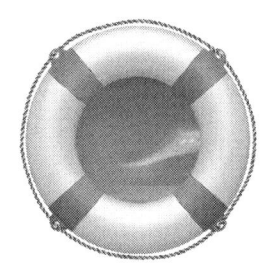

1

THE SALT OF THE OCEAN skates across my olive skin, awakening every part of my inner slut. Even the soft breeze blowing against the bottom of my purple sundress has my thighs clenching. There's just something about this kickass view that causes a girl to crave two things: alcohol and dick, neither of which I can have at the moment, but that is something I will be rectifying ASAP. I limp past customs towards the end of the dock. My foot catches on a rope causing me to stumble a few steps before I finally catch my balance.

"I can't wait to get this fucking thing off." I motion down to the eyesore currently strapped to my leg.

"It's not that bad." Jodi, my favorite filthy Brit, comes to stand on my left. Her yellow babydoll dress sways against the wind as she shrugs. She's trying to be helpful, but there's nothing positive about this.

"Not that bad? It's sweaty as fuck in this June heat and I look like a limp dick trying to get laid." Not to mention it's itching like a motherfucker.

"How does a limp dick get laid?" Darcie stops on my right and puts her hands on her hips. She's wearing a baby blue sundress with pockets that Jodi and I convinced her to put on. She thinks it's because it brings out the blue in her eyes, which it does, but it's not the only reason. It hugs her large boobs and gives just the right amount of cleavage to get us free drinks later.

"They don't, Darce. They flop around," I raise my arm and dangle it out in front of me like a wild elephant trunk to emphasize my point, "never quite reaching their destination, and look like a sad puppy in the window that never gets taken home."

"That's just…" She pauses for a second, no doubt searching for the right response. "Sad."

"Yup." I nod in agreement then my ADHD kicks in and all is forgotten. My hazel eyes glance over Darcie's head to take in the view. Sometimes, it pays to be the tallest friend in the group. My craptastic day is definitely turning around. A smile breaks across my face as I stare at the enormous ship in front of us. "Look at the size of this bitch!" I may shout louder than necessary, but to be fair I'm as excited as a dog with two cocks and don't fucking care. I'm going to be on a ship full of seamen with my girls. What's better than that?

Jodi and Darcie gasp next to me, and judging by the looks on their faces, their thoughts are mirroring my own.

"Flick my flaps and buy me a poodle. We get to spend eight days on this massive twat?" Jodi's British accent makes even the dirtiest shit sound sophisticated and I love it.

"It's huge." Darcie freezes. It's like she's finally seen an uncut dick for the first time and as if she knows my next thought she elbows me. "Yes, I know. That's what she said."

I laugh and nudge her in the side. "It's scary how well you know me. It's like we share the same twisted mind."

"That's what over two decades of friendship does to you." Darcie winks.

"You got that right, Cocksister." I laugh as we continue walking along the dock towards the beast we'll be calling home for the next week.

We only make it a few feet onto the ship when Darcie's screams stop us in our tracks. I twist to the side in time to see her swatting at the air around the knot of messy blonde hair on top of her head. She looks like a mental patient having a private party for one.

"Problem, luv?" Jodi tilts her blonde head and gives her the same curious stare that's on my face.

"Seagulls are attacking me," Darcie yells so loudly, people stop to stare at us. I shrug off their stares because this shit never bothers me, and focus on Darcie and her current meltdown. If people want to look at us like we're crazy, let them. I mean we actually are bat shit crazy so it's not like they're wrong.

"Seagulls aren't that big, Darce." I stare back at her, waiting for whatever maneuver she'll try next . "You look like you're trying to swat the Cockness Monster away."

"These fuckers probably are just as big." Her whole body is crouched and ready to attack the next 'seagull' that dive bombs her ass. She maybe be short, but she's feisty as hell.

"You sure Carter didn't leave another cum catcher in your hair?" Jodi leans in and starts picking through the nest that is Darcie's hair.

"Yes, I'm sure." Darcie sighs and backs away from Jodi. "I even counted the condoms this time."

On that note, I shrug and keep walking. Luckily, we make it inside the elevators before Darcie has another 'attack'.

From the time we step inside the elevator until the time we're exiting, the three of us can barely contain our excitement. I'm surprised Jodi isn't fanning her face with her underwear and Darcie hasn't shit herself.

At least it isn't too long of a walk to our room from the elevator. I don't think we could wait much longer to explore our own space. We burst through our room and our jaws drop. I'm so excited I don't even shut the door behind us as I stare.

"This room is the tits." Jodi's blue eyes are taking in every inch of the room with fascination, and I don't blame her. The room is fucking epic.

There's a huge ass black, wrought iron, four-poster bed against a tan wall along the right side of the room with a rope of chain draping over the headboard. A white comforter and a mountain of hooker red pillows rest on top. On either side of the bed are two small beige end tables with a red ceramic lamp on each, and on top of the right one is one of those radio/alarm clock combos. In front of us, matching curtains are draped along the sides of a set of sliding glass doors, which go from floor to ceiling and lead out to a balcony. I haven't even walked out there yet, but I can already tell it's a kickass view.

Following the same color scheme are a set of red chairs and a small round wooden table resting against a bright as fuck white wall. Off to the side of those are a couple of doors. I'm pretty sure one leads to the bathroom, but I'm not sure about the other one.

Jodi's face lights up as she does a backwards dive onto the bed. She lands with a soft squeak, and of course I have to join in on the fun, bum leg be damned. I put the weight on my good foot and push off. As I land on my back, Jodi and I let out a deep sigh. It sounds like we've just had a big O, and the truth is I could from the comfort of this mattress alone.

"The bed sounds comfortable?" Darcie teases.

"It's the dog's balls." Jodi sighs.

I feel something underneath my back and reach behind me. When I pull it out, I almost snort. "Look, Darce. They even have red towels shaped like penises." I dangle the towel in front of her.

Darcie shakes her head and glances around. I know that look. It's one that says she's overthinking something…again. "What's wrong, Darce?"

"I'm no mathematician, but there's one bed and three of us." She folds her arm across her chest and sighs, causing her ginormous boobs to come up to her neck. "I love you both, but I'm not sharing a bed with either one of you. We're thirty-five years old, which is too old for a sleepover in the same bed. Not to mention I'll wake up with who knows what in my ass."

"That was one time. And I was pissed as a fart." Jodi shrugs and plays with the material of the comforter.

"Even if you were that drunk, most people keep their cucumbers in the fridge not their bed." Darcie was just as drunk as we were because she clearly forgot the whole conversation we had afterwards, so being the good friend I am I kindly remind her.

"When they don't use it to eat, they do." I wait the couple of seconds it takes for her to understand what I'm really trying to tell her. When the light bulb finally goes off and she does, Darcie's mouth opens and closes a few times like a fish gasping for oxygen. It takes another second for her to quit looking like she wants to cram a dildo down our throats and kill us in our sleep before she can even begin to speak.

Then her whole body freezes. "You hear that?"

"Hear what?" I cock my head to the side and listen. Silence.

"I don't hear anything." Jodi shakes her head.

"There it goes again," Darcie persists, but this time I do hear it. It's a very faint chirping and easy to miss if one isn't paying attention.

"I hear it now." I whip my head around trying to figure out what the hell it is.

Jodi scans the room like a hunter on the prowl. "Where's it coming from?"

"I don't know." I shake my head and search the room for the source. Jodi mirrors my movement and walks back towards the bathroom. We only get a few steps in before Darcie's screaming again.

"It's in my hair!" She starts smacking the shit out of her own head as she runs towards the door.

Of course, she's only irritating the winged thing more. The faint chirping has now turned into full-blown screeching, which is killing my ears.

Jodi rushes over to try to get whatever the hell is in her hair out. I limp over as fast as I can and attempt to help, but it's stuck. Between Darcie freaking out and the bird flapping around, it's damn near impossible.

"We can't get a hold of it with you moving like a wild banshee." Every time I get my hand anywhere close she moves.

"I'm trying," Darcie mumbles under her mound of hair. During the struggle, her hair has fallen out of her knot and all over her face. She resembles a blonde Cousin It.

"Oh, bugger. It's really in there." Jodi holds Darcie in a weird type of headlock so I can get a better grip. Her hair has wrapped around its foot and I have to work quick or the poor little guy will lose it. I'm not sure if it's a male or female, but since it's being a nuisance, we'll go with male. I loosen him just enough that we can free him easily when we reach the door.

"Move towards the doorway. That way when I get him free we can throw him out and shut the door." In a soft tone I coax Darcie to follow my lead. My hand is still tangled in her hair, holding the bird in place so it takes a bit of finesse and timing to perfect a rhythm before we can move all together.

The three of us start to scoot, one slow step at a time, towards the front of the room, careful not to disturb it. I almost get my hand around the ball of feathers when the little fucker moves again—definitely male. This time Darcie doesn't hold back her panic and takes off towards the doorway at a run. I hobble after her as best I can with my boot, but it's no use. At least Jodi's able to keep up the pace with her. Darcie's hair is blocking her view, so she trips over her own feet and almost takes us down with her. Jodi and I land near a wall, but Darcie falls right outside the open doorway. I glance up and have to do a double take to make sure what I'm seeing is really happening. And it is. It really is.

Darcie's on the ground with the bottom of her dress up around the middle of her back, revealing her navy blue thong and firm ass cheeks, which are in need of a serious tan. There's also an extra pair of legs on either side of hers. But, it's where her face is that has my mouth dropping open in shock. It's buried in some guy's crotch.

She jerks back as fast as she can, and sits there in a daze. Jodi and I climb to our feet and hurry over to check on her. All of the blood must have rushed to her face because she's dog dick red.

"Oopsie." I prop a hand under her armpit while Jodi grabs the other side and together we help her up to her feet. She still looks a bit dazed at what just happened. "You okay, Darce?" It takes a few attempts at calling her name before she comes back down to planet Earth with the rest of us.

"I'm fine." The slight hiccup in her voice contradicts her words.

"You sure?" I'm not buying her tough girl act at all.

"Because you just facebanged his balls." Jodi watches her every movement, not sure if she's going to freak out or pass out.

Darcie nods and at that moment the little fucking bird manages to break free, fly out of her hair and down the hallway, leaving us in stunned silence for a few beats.

Groaning draws my attention back to the guy who has crawled up to a sitting position with his head hanging between his legs. Darcie's face must have done a number on his balls if he's still sitting there.

"Let me help you up." I reach out, grab his hand, and pull him to his feet. The second his hand touches mine, my whole body tingles. He must have monthly manicures because he has the softest hands. Lack of dick has my mind running wild with all sorts of dirty images of where he can rub those long smooth fingers.

When he stands, I drop my hand before I come on the spot. If he's getting me this worked up with a simple touch then it's been too damn long for me. I do a quick sweep of him from head to toe, and holy shit. He's dressed in an all white uniform that hugs his muscular, tatted arms. Judging by the lines around his deep brown eyes he's about mid-thirties. He also has no hair anywhere—and by anywhere I mean from the top of his head and maybe even down to his balls. I'm talking no eyebrows or even eyelashes. He resembles a walking penis. It's the damnedest thing. I continue on with my inspection and the world stops when I do a cockgaze. He has one of the biggest seam beasts I've ever seen. It doesn't help that his white pants look a few sizes too small, causing it to look a bit like a strangled monkey fighting to break free.

The sound of a throat clearing cuts into my thoughts, alerting me to the fact I may have been staring much longer than I thought at his trouser snake.

"Sorry about that..." I let my sentence hang as I do a quick glance at his nametag. "E. Rection?"

Jodi and Darcie snicker behind me. I suck in a breath and do my best not to laugh in front of his face. I thought we had it bad with our last names, poor bastard.

"You can call me Eric." He grins, revealing yellow stained teeth. Shit! And he started off so promising. I don't want his mouth butter on my lady bread or I'll wind up with a yeast infection.

"Okay then. What brings you to our room, Eric?" I take the time to enunciate his name and not think of the lethal weapon he's carrying around in his pants.

"I have luggage for a—" He looks down at a tag on a cart, which up until now has blended into the background. "Lisa Cox, Darcie Badcock, and a Jodi Cummings?"

"That's us." I step back out of the doorway to allow him entry to our room.

"I also brought a bucket of complimentary Champagne for our lucky winners." He rolls the cart through the door wearing a close-mouthed smile.

At the mention of alcohol, Jodi's ready to marry the guy. "Right this way, luv." She motions for him to set the champagne right in front of her.

He does as she asks and sets it in the center of the room. Then he turns and stares over at me. "Can I help you ladies with anything else?"

"Well, Eric, we do have a slight problem." Darcie puts her hands on her hips and taps her foot. Facebang into his balls forgotten, she's gone into serious mode.

"What's that?" He never breaks eye contact with her while he waits for her answer. I really wish I could tell what he's thinking while staring at her, but it's hard to tell without his eyebrows. It's like staring back at one of my vibrators, shiny and smooth but no signs of life.

"Well, there are three of us and one bed." Darcie's eyebrows shoot up to her forehead at the thought.

"Oh." Eric frowns. Or at least I think he does. Then he walks over to the door next to the bathroom and opens it up. "You do know you have adjoining rooms? There are two more beds in here." He jerks his head towards the closed doorway.

"Fuck me in the ass with an anchor! You've just made my day." Darcie walks over, kisses his cheek, and runs into the other room to check it out.

Jodi and I snort. Sometimes it doesn't take much to make Darcie happy.

Eric stares at her for a second like she's the mayor of crazy town before walking back by the cart and turning his attention to me. "Anything else?"

"Nope. We're good. Thanks." I press my lips together in a small smile.

He nods and leaves without another word.

I shut the door behind him and hobble over towards the big bed. Once my ass hits the mattress, I sigh. My mind is already in vacation mode.

Darcie comes running back into the room wearing a huge grin. "I'm so happy right now. How are you liking the bed?"

"It's feels like I'm floating on a cloud of cocks." I relax my weight deeper into the mattress and check the bounciness of the bed. I need to make sure it can handle all of the fun I have planned for it.

"Did you already pick your bed, luv?" Jodi asks as she grabs her bag off the cart.

"Yup." Darcie bounces on her feet looking ready to explode from excitement.

"You two are sharing?" I motion a finger between them.

"We are." Darcie nods. "You won the trip so we figure it's only fair that you get the big bed."

"Thanks, you guys." Them giving me the bed is a nice surprise. I mean, I was planning on begging for it, but now I don't have to.

"What are Cocksisters for?" Jodi smiles and then heads into the other room.

Darcie moves to do the same when her phone rings. She takes it out of her pocket, and judging by the way she twists her lips, I can guess who it is.

"Carter the cock slayer?" I tease.

"It is." She grabs her bag and rushes off to her room.

Watching her go reminds me that I better check in with my family, too. I take out my cell and hit the number. It only rings a couple of times before they answer.

"Home of the twelve inch Cox. How hard can I ride you?" My brother's deep voice is like a bad case of blue balls, painful.

"*Pendejo*! Cut the shit, Dusty, and put Ma on the phone." He may be younger by a couple of years, but I swear he must have been slammed in the head by too much dick in the womb.

"No can do. She's busy—as in her and dad disappeared in the back, I'm guessing for a nooner and no way in hell am I going back there. I still need therapy from the last time I caught them going at it. Ma tried to tell me they were wrestling."

"Ugh! Thanks for the visual, jackass." Leave it to my brother to kill my cockbuzz. "Just have her call me back." I don't say 'when she's done', even though both of us are thinking it because it's implied, and I hang up.

Jodi runs back into the room and straight for the Champagne bucket. Darcie strolls back in wearing an 'I just got fucked' grin.

"You have phone sex with Carter?" I tease, but damn am I a little envious.

"Maybe." Darcie's blushing, so I know something dirty happened. Then Jodi grabs our attention.

"Flick my flaps and buy me a hot dog! Let's get wankered!" She grabs the Champagne bottle, props it between her legs, and attempts to pop the cork. Darcie and I watch in fascination as she yanks up on it giving us one hell of an image.

"I can't wait to get my cockrides on." I bite my lip at the thought. Going days without dick is killing me. No woman should ever have to go without.

"Same here, luv." Jodi's still attempting to pry the cork out of the bottle, but from my angle it's looks more like she's jerking it off. "Bugger, this fucker's on here tight."

"What about Logan?" Darcie's attention is focused on me when she really should be paying attention to Jodi. It's like a train wreck waiting to happen.

"What about him?" I shrug and do my best to keep my voice neutral. Last thing I want is to be reminded of what a lying cuntsicle he is. "He was just a pit stop on the cocktrain to orgasmville."

"Still had to suck when he just left like he did without any explanation." Darcie comes to sit next to me on the bed.

I shrug and clear my throat to fight off the emotions wanting to break through. I'm not giving Logan anymore of my time. "It did, but on this trip I'll be the one doing all of the sucking."

"Yes! That arsehole Ryder is a memory. I'm ready for some bum fun with a bloke or five." Jodi does another hard pull on the cork, causing her to become short of breath. Her knuckles are white as she continues to fight with it.

I'm getting tired just watching her. "Want some help, Jo?"

"No. I've got this bitch." She grunts, does one final pull, and it shoots off like a cannon, ricocheting off the table and the side wall. Then it comes our way.

"Duck, Darce." I grab her head and shove the both of us down as it flies right past our heads, breaking the lamp next to the bed.

"Bugger." Jodi's mouth hangs open. "You twats okay?"

"We're good." I nod.

"This trip is certainly off to an interesting start." Darcie laughs.

"Stick with me, Cocksister. It's only going to get better." I grin because when the three of us are together, anything is possible.

Jodi hands us each a drink. "It is."

We clink our glasses together and I give a little toast. "To our Coxsister Cruise."

Before we can take a sip, a horn blares, killing our ears. Then the floor beneath us rocks back and forth as the ship starts to sail away from the port. The movement is so unexpected, it causes us to lose our balance and knocks us on our asses. Champagne spills all over us, and the floor. It only adds to the craziness that has been our day so far. The three of us break out into hysterical laughter. This trip is going to kick ass.

I hold my empty glass up, stare at them, and grin. "Here's to being wild and free like an STD!"

2

AFTER OUR CHAMPAGNE MISHAP, WE decided to clean up and hit the pool, which is why I'm now slipping on the bikini I bought for Ireland and never had a chance to wear. It's a bright peach color that looks perfect against my olive skin. The top has a bit of fringe to give the appearance of bigger tits, and since my chest isn't anywhere close to Darcie's size, I need all the help I can get. The bottoms hang low on my hips, but cover all the important areas. A smile spreads across my face. I haven't felt this sexy in a long time. All is good and I'm ready to go on a cock hunt. Then I look down and scream.

"What's wrong?" Darcie rushes into my room in her blue string bikini. I really need to remember to lock the connecting room door.

Jodi follows right behind her in a purple bikini, holding up an umbrella like she's ready to cut a bitch. I don't know where she got it and I'm not going to ask. At least it isn't open; we don't need any more bad luck. "Whose arse do I have to kick?"

"No one. I'm fine." Jodi and Darcie stare at me unconvinced, so I feel the need to explain further. "It's this fucking thing." I motion down towards the damn boot on my leg. Darcie's blonde eyebrows pull together as she gnaws on her bottom lip. I know that look. She's done it since we were kids. "Stop feeling guilty."

"It's my fault. I'm the one who shot you." Her voice catches as her eyes begin to water. No way. Fuck that. My best friend is not going to carry any guilt for what happened. She saved our asses.

"It was an accident, Darce." My tone is calm and soothing as I hold her gaze. "And it could have been worse."

"Yeah, you could have gotten her right in the muff flaps." Both of our heads whip over to Jodi as she sets the umbrella down. That's a new one, but Darcie and I just go with the flow that is our Jo.

"Exactly. If anyone's to blame it's the nugget-sized devil, Dixon," I remind Darcie. "He's the one who kidnapped and tried to kill us."

Her lips twist to the side as she wipes her cheeks. "I guess you guys are right."

"Of course we are." I squeeze her shoulder and brush past her to grab my bag.

"Yeah, such a shame a huge knob was wasted on a such an evil little thing. Not your fault at all, luv," Jodi adds from behind me.

I put my sunglasses on and spin back around to face the both of them. "Now, let's get our tan on while we cockgaze."

"Cockgaze?" I don't miss Darcie's questioning tone.

"It's like stargazing, but with willies," Jodi explains as I shrug, and we walk towards the door. Sometimes it's like Jodi and I share the same brain. It's fucking awesome.

"I swear I'm going to need a cocktionary to understand half the shit you both come up with." Darcie rolls her eyes while shaking her head.

"I like that. Good one, Darce." I nudge her in the side before shutting and locking the door to my room.

The hallway is pretty empty as we stroll along to the elevators. Even when we're inside we're the only three occupying it.

The lights and noise of other passengers hit us in the face like a wild dick the second we exit the elevator. The inside of this ship is huge. There's white marble flooring everywhere. Accents of gold line the stairs, railings, and walls. In the center of the ceiling there's a huge crystal chandelier. More gold inlays add some fancy contrast to the white ceiling. Signs for different restaurants, bars, clubs, and shops are lined along the walls. There is even a tanning salon and spa. We'll for sure be checking them all out later.

"Wow," Darcie gasps.

"You've got that right." My lips spread into an eager smile. We hit the jackpot winning this trip.

"It's the tits," Jodi shouts, causing people to stop and stare like she's offering free blow jobs. It happens to us a lot for some reason, so we just ignore them and move on.

We continue walking in an excited daze. There's so much to see one could spend an entire day just walking around.

When we make it to the pool, we're able to snag three blue lounge chairs next to each other. We set our stuff down and spread out our towels. The second my back touches the chair, I let out a deep sigh. Sun and fun with my girls is the best.

"Can you put some sunblock on me, Jo?" I hear Darcie ask as she lies down on her stomach.

"Sure thing, luv." Jodi squirts way too much into her hand and begins to rub it on Darcie's back. There's so much it's leaving a thick white coating that looks like jizz on Darcie's skin. Jodi even starts finger painting shapes with it. She's lost in what she's doing and enjoying it, so I let them be and focus on the scenery.

There are a few couples in the spa and some men swimming in the pool. Other than them, it's all women in the lounge chairs, which is unusual. My nose wrinkles.

"What's wrong?" Darcie props up on her elbows and stares back at me.

"Are we at a clambake?" I slide my sunglasses down the bridge of my nose to get a better look, and nope. I'm not imagining it. The majority of us are female.

"Yeah, what's with the flap fest?" Jodi talks out of the side of her mouth like she's whispering, but in reality she's talking so loud the woman to the right of us turns and smiles.

"It's quite the view, isn't it?" The woman asks. She's gorgeous. She has chestnut brown hair thrown into a messy bun on top of her head.

The large, round leopard print sunglasses give off a classic pin-up vibe, while her matching barely there string bikini is a sexy as hell contrast.

"It's different." It's the best way to explain what I'm seeing at the moment.

"I'm Tre." Her lips spread into a wide grin.

"Lisa." I point to myself, and then the girls. "Darcie and Jodi."

She waves and smiles at them before turning her attention back to me. "Is this your first one of these cruises?"

"It sure is. We won it from a contest I entered." I can't help the grin on my face. Entering a giveaway from an Irish sex shop was an impulsive thing to do, but it sure paid off for us.

"Really?" Her eyebrows rise to her forehead.

"Yup. We were shopping, I saw the entry form and figured, why not? We won, and now here we are." I wave my hand around the ship.

"Wow. You're pretty lucky." She tips her head, studying me.

"Thanks. I'm sure hoping I do get lucky on here." And I fucking better. I need penetration and I need it yesterday.

She laughs. "Something tells me you just might."

Wet feet slapping against concrete hits us, as a woman in what should be considered blue dental floss instead of a string bikini approaches us. Her body works it just right and good for her. She's also just as gorgeous as Tre. She has shoulder length brown hair, big bright blue eyes, and plump lips that Tre is eyeing the shit out of like they're candy.

"Hey, beautiful." Dental floss hottie bends down and locks lips with Tre. I'm talking full on tongue action. They're going at it so hard I'm getting a little worked up myself. I might need to pull out Henry and self-serve later. When they finally separate, I have to take a deep breath to calm my overheated body.

"You two are muff mates?" Jodi gestures with her finger between the two of them, while Darcie continues to stare with her mouth open. She's as mesmerized by them as I am.

Tre holds Jodi's gaze and tilts her head to the side, studying her for a few seconds. "Umm, yes?" She pats the brunette on the ass. "This is my girlfriend, Kate."

"Hello." Kate waves and her accent comes through, making her even more damn attractive.

"You an Australian bird?" Jodi's fawning all over her.

"Yep. I'm from Southern Australia." She nods, as water droplets drip off of her skin. I'm not into chicks, but I will be the first to admit if I ever wanted to try a clam chop it would be hers. "You're a Pom?"

"I am." Jodi nods. "These are my Cocksisters, Darcie and Lisa." She points to each of us in turn.

Kate's plump lips purse in confusion. "Cocksisters?"

"It's the sisterhood of cock lovers," I explain.

"I hate to break it to ya, mate, but I don't reckon that word means what you think." She cocks her head to the side. "It's Sheilas who've ridden the same cock."

Not another one. What is it with people being so damn literal?

"My definition is better." I shrug and watch the droplets of water drip off her perfect body. Her blue eyes dart between the three of us, she gives a slight nod, and then turns her attention back to her girlfriend.

Tre hands her a towel to dry off and she even manages to make that look erotic. I'm seriously starting to question my sexuality. Once she's dry, she tosses the towel aside and lies down next to Tre, her whole body tangling with hers.

I watch them cuddle and it makes me envious. I'm dying for some action with anything that has a pulse. "I need some vitamin D."

"You're already lying out in the sun." Darcie's neck cranes as she looks over at me from behind her sunglasses.

"I meant dick, Darce. I haven't taken a proper trip to pound town in so long I'm beginning to feel dickorexic. Henry can only satisfy me so many times. I miss feeling the twitch of an actual cock inside of me." I gesture towards my lower lips.

"Yes. My flaps haven't been touched in so long they might get stuck together." Jodi nods her head so fast the ball of blonde on top of her head bobs back and forth.

"Oh." Darcie's lips purse into an 'o' as she studies the both of us. I'm sure she wants to say more, but thinks better of it and puts her head back down.

With that, our conversation dies and we lie there getting our tan on. I'm not sure what the point of Darcie trying to tan her back is when it's covered in a thick layer of sunblock, but I've learned some things are better not to question. I shut my eyes for a brief second before my day takes a nosedive into shit town.

"Here we are, Ms. Felterbush." A nasally voice has my head whipping around so fast I damn near get whiplash. "And I didn't forget about you, Ms. Wyderbox." Everything inside me clenches and not in a good way. Please let him just be a look alike. My heart drops to my stomach when I see a very familiar phallic shaped mole on his cheek.

Fucking hell! I scrunch down lower in my lounge chair and attempt to blend in.

"What are you doing?" Darcie leans up on her elbows and gives me a sideways glance.

"I'm trying to become invisible," I whisper, this time in an actual hushed tone.

Jodi is, of course, oblivious to what I'm doing, and screams, "Isn't that Justin?" I put my finger up to my mouth to silence her, but it's too late.

A shadow appears above me. "Coxy? Is that you?"

Busted. I have no choice but to glance up at him. I'm just happy my eyes are hidden behind my glasses. I'm greeted by familiar hazel eyes, a long crooked nose, a prominent pointy chin and a head full of curly dark hair. He looks exactly the same since high school. The only difference is the porn star mustache he's sporting.

"Justin." My voice comes out in a high pitch. "Hey. What are you doing here?" I glance down to his interesting attire. He's wearing what can only be described as a black leather banana hammock. Then I glance at his empty tray. "You work here? Last I heard you were working on Wall Street?"

"No. It was Ball Street as an exotic dancer." He laughs, drawing my attention to the curly ends of his mustache, which are wiggling with the movement.

"How's Eden?" Losing touch with her is the only thing I regret out of this situation.

"My sister's doing good. She's a big CEO of her own company." His eyes light up as he talks about her accomplishment.

"Wow. What's the name of the company?" While I'm proud to hear about my former friend doing so well, I can feel the gazes of my Cocksisters burning holes into the side of my face.

"Dangles. It's a male version of the other place. She's getting ready to open the newest location in Las Vegas soon." He stands up straighter as he drops that tidbit of info.

"Good for her."

"What have you been up to?" Justin toys with the ends of his mustache as he gives me his undivided attention.

"I'm still running my family's bar." Why does that sound lame when I say it out loud?

"But, she has amazing plans to open her own place." Darcie comes to my rescue.

"Always knew you were smart and sexy, Coxy." He smiles and I just nod my head. Besides the fact that I can't stop staring at his Chester the molester mustache, I have nothing to add to this conversation. The whole exchange is awkward.

"Good to see you again, Darcie." Justin turns his saccharine smile on her, but his eyes aren't leaving her ass.

A touch of pink colors Darcie's cheeks as she grins. "You remember me?" Most of our class does. There weren't too many high school girls rocking a chest the size of hers.

"Of course I do. I've seen all your films. You still writing?"

Darcie's smile falls for a brief second, but she's able to plaster it back on before he notices. "I'm no longer writing adult films. Now, I'm working on a how to book."

"Cool." Our conversation turns stale and we stare at each other in uncomfortable silence until Justin knocks himself back to reality. "Can I get you anything to drink?"

"Um, sure. I'll have an Adios Motherfucker on the rocks." One would hope my drink choice would be a subtle hint, but Justin was never very smart.

Justin nods as his gaze moves in Darcie and Jodi's direction. "And for you ladies?"

"I'll have an Angel's Tit." Jodi claps her hands in excitement. She loves her alcohol and I don't blame her one bit.

"Make mine a Bendover Shirly." Darcie smiles, but Justin misses it because his gaze is now honed in on her ass. It's a good thing she's on her stomach. If he got a look at her good-sized rack, he'd probably pop right out of his Speedo. Some things never change.

Justin nods his head and saunters off, not taking his gaze off Darcie's ass until the last possible second. When he passes me, I'm treated to a quick glimpse of his bare backside.

"Oh, bloody hell. You can see his arse." Jodi gasps and the three of us lose it, laughing so hard we have tears.

"Thanks for saving me. I saw him and went stupid." Seeing him was so unexpected it threw me off my game.

Darcie taps my leg with the tip of her toe. "Don't mention it. You should be proud of what you do." It seems only yesterday I said something similar to her. "I write porn, you make kick ass drinks and Jodi is a successful entrepreneur with her promotion company. We are three badasses." Darcie smiles.

"Absolutely, luv! Lit Lickers has been booming and working on an American gig." Jodi smiles. These two always know what to say to make me feel better.

"So, that was *the* Justin?" Darcie changes the subject, fishing for more info.

"It was." I nod and want to curl in on myself.

"The bloke who broke your muff seal?" Jodi's jaw drops as she finally connects the dots.

"Don't remind me." That night is something I've tried for years not to think about.

Darcie's blue eyes grow wide as it dawns on her, and she flips over onto her back to stare at me. "Justin Bush?"

"One and the same." Images are fighting to penetrate my brain, but I'm doing my damndest to keep them out.

"Was he that bad?" Darcie doesn't know the half of it.

I cringe as the memories surface of us in the back of his mom's car, my legs scrunched up against the headliner because they had nowhere else to go in such a small space. "Awful."

"The way he was eyeing you, I think he wants another go, luv." Jodi's words make my vag want to crawl inside itself.

"No way in hell. I'll pass." I snort.

"You sure? I mean you said you needed some vitamin D." Darcie pushes Jodi's point and it's a good thing I know she's fucking with me or I'd throw her ass in the pool.

"I do, but it will not be another pounding session with Justin. First times are supposed to suck for girls. I get that, but he said I was moist. Moist! What am I? A fucking cake?" The people near us stop and stare. I guess I said that louder than I thought. Oopsie.

Tre and Kate's laughter break though, reminding me of their presence.

"That's one reason I'm glad I'm a sushi sister." Tre holds her drink out to me in a toast of support.

"It doesn't sound too terrible." Darcie's always trying to be the voice of reason. I love her for it, I do, but this is not one of those times.

"Not too terrible? We were in the back of his mom's Pinto—the car not the bean. Imagine these pressed against the headliner of that tiny ass car." I smack the sides of my thighs and gesture towards my legs. Being tall sometimes isn't all it's cracked up to be. "After spending a good twenty minutes finding where to put his dick, he was a two pump chump. Then he zips up his pants and asks if I'm hungry. He took me to a drive-thru for a burger and then took me home."

"Damn." Darcie shakes her head. "And I thought my first time was bad. He got it in my ass the first try by mistake."

"Please tell me you had him wash or wrap it before he finally found the target. Because chocotacos are a big fat no." Some things are just no-go zones, and besides backdoor entry, that's one of them.

Darcie nods. "I made Stewie put a new condom on. Three tries later, he finally got it in. By that time, I was so tired of shouting 'wrong hole!', I lost my voice and had to lie there mute."

Jodi and I glance at each other to make sure we're both thinking the same thing and we are. We lose it laughing.

Darcie's face scrunches together. "What's so funny?"

Jodi does a hand gesture towards her ass. "He was trying to get into the stink before the pink, luv."

"Yup, he was playing dumb so he could do your ass, Darce." My eyes water as pain develops along my side. I haven't laughed this hard in a long time.

Darcie looks like she's about two seconds away from finding Stewie and cutting off his dick, so Jodi keeps the conversation going to distract her.

"At least Justin fed you after. Both of mine slipped out and went back to the buffet, leaving me to find my knickers alone in the dark."

It takes a bit for her words to register and when they do I'm about ready to shit myself. "Wait a minute. You slept with more than one your first time?"

Jodi opens her mouth to answer, but Justin picks that moment to appear with our drinks. "Here you are, ladies." He hands each of us our drinks, wearing a goofy ass grin behind his creepy mustache and that damn leather thong. A quick cockgaze reveals his package is just as small as I remember. "If I can do anything else for you ladies don't hesitate to ask." His teeth sink into his bottom lip as his gaze holds mine, making his intentions pretty damn clear. Fucking hell. Jodi was right.

I press my lips together into a tight smile. "Thanks."

"Anytime." He winks and walks off to help another guest.

"Told ya. The bloke wants in your sausage wallet." Jodi gestures her drink towards Justin's retreating backside, spilling some of her drink in the process.

"Yeah, not happening." A heavy sigh leaves me. The last thing I want to think about is Justin, so I take a small sip of my drink and try to remember what we were talking about before he interrupted us. It only takes a second for it to come back to me. "Okay spill. Who popped your cork?"

"Oh you know, just some blokes I met at a party." Jodi stares off at the guys in the spa and mumbles, "I am cheesed off they ruined my purple dress, though."

Images of her in a purple dress come rushing back to me and things are starting to click together. I spit, shooting blue liquor all over my tits. "You slept with Dusty and my cousin George?" Her blue eyes bug out of her head and I'm positive I'm right, but I need to make sure. "When was this?"

"I don't remember. I think it was at some party we went to with you. It was like a wedding or something." Jodi sips on her drink and stares back at me.

I suck in a gulp of air as the shit finally comes full circle and I can't deny I'm right. "You were the three screwing in the coat closet at my cousin Carmen's quinceañera!"

"It was a buffet theme and all you can eat." Jodi shrugs.

"For food, not muffs." My head whips towards Darcie. "Did you know about this?"

"No way. I would have tried to talk some sense into her." Her hands go up in defense. She's going into mom mode and trying to control the crazy ass bitches that are Jodi and I.

"And boy is Dusty hung like a horse." Jodi grins, as if she's picturing my brother's dick.

I cover my ears and try to block out any thoughts of my brother in a sexual capacity. "I don't want to hear about my brother's sexscapades. It's just wrong."

Jodi shrugs and sips on her drink. She freezes mid-sip and shouts, "Willies!"

My gaze follows her finger and I about shit myself. A group of older men are entering the pool and they're free dangling. "That's something you don't see every day."

"Why aren't they wearing swimming trunks?" Darcie gasps, but doesn't cover her eyes.

"You think those sausages shrink with age or do they sag like our tits?" Jodi brings up a very good point. I almost wish I thought of it.

"That one kind of curves." My head slants to the side for a better look.

"It's like a question mark, only smaller." Darcie's head tilts to match the position of mine.

We can't help but stare in fascination. It's not every day we see one shaped so uniquely. My hands itch to slap it and I feel like a cat wanting to slap at the string dangling in front of it like a toy. Before I can do just that, my stomach growls and I decide our best bet is to leave in search of sustenance. "Thanks to the preview of this little weenie roast, I'm hungry for dinner." I maneuver myself to my feet and grab my bag before looking over at them. "How about you two?"

"Yes." Darcie nods and stands.

"I could go for some toad in the hole." Jodi grins and gathers her stuff.

I turn to wave goodbye to our new friends, the scissor sisters, and grab my stuff. When I spin back around and take my first step, there's a small puddle of water on the ground I don't see until it's too late. The boot on my foot slips out from underneath me and like a well-lubricated dick, I slip, falling right into Darcie. I reach out to grab for her and keep her from falling inside the pool, but she's all lathered up with sunblock and I can't get a good grip on her. My fingers slip and down she goes with a giant splash into the pool.

It feels like time slows down for us because everyone at the pool stops what they're doing and glances our way. Then a couple of the free danglers decide to jump in and try to save her.

Before they can reach her, Darcie shoots back up. When she breaks the surface, her bathing suit top has fallen and her girls are out on full display for the entire area to see.

I gasp and say the only thing one can in this situation. "Oopsie."

3

After the pool incident, Jodi and I helped Darcie out and went inside, openly staring at the free-swinging dicks along the way. I have no shame in dickgazing. If it's out and dangling in front of me, hells yeah I'm gonna look. We made it back to our rooms without any further issues and decided to shower before heading off to dinner.

Once I've slipped into my skintight black dress, I meet them in their room. It's set up very similar to mine with the same red and tan color scheme. The only difference is there are two beds instead of one, and one small night table with a lamp separating them. It's cute, but the beds are way too small for any kind of fuckery.

"What took you so long?" Darcie's sitting on one of the beds, leaning back against her hands. She's wearing a form fitting gold dress that shows off her girls and I'm pretty sure it took some serious coercing from Jodi.

"I had to shave my leg." My hand gestures to the now smooth skin on my good leg. "And since it's about the size of you," I wave a hand in her direction, "it takes a while." Sometimes I really hate being tall.

"You only shaved one?" Darcie stares down at my legs.

"I can't really shave this one." I extend my foot, drawing attention to my boot.

"How does that work?" Jodi stares, no doubt conjuring up a mental image of my naked-self trying to shave my good leg.

"I had to wrap it in plastic." And what a pain in the ass that was.

"A cocksock for your foot?" Jodi smirks as she leans against the bed to slide on her shoe. Both she and Darcie are dressed in heels, but since I'm Amazon size and wearing a damn boot on my foot, I'm in one very cute flat. I can't wait to be able to wear two shoes again.

"Sort of." I prop my back against the wall and cross my arms over my chest.

"Sometimes, I'm so glad I'm nugget-size." Darcie shakes her head and slips the strap of her purse over her shoulder as she stands. The movement is slow and awkward, but I think nothing of it.

"Yeah, well don't ask me to reach things for you anytime soon then." I tease, as I follow them out the door.

We head into the hall and towards the elevator, when I notice Darcie moving like a drunk duck. "Why are you walking like that?"

"Like what?" She winces, as we step into the elevator. This time there are two other couples inside with us, but my attention is focused on Darcie. She won't make eye contact with me and that's a dead giveaway there's an awesome story behind this, so being the good friend I am, I keep at her until she spills.

"Like you've just been fucked by Cockzilla?" My voice echoes inside the small space and I can feel the stares of the couples behind us. Oopsie.

Jodi tilts her head to study Darcie's movements. "You are walking like your flaps are swollen."

Blood creeps into Darcie's cheeks as she gives us her infamous death glare. I can only imagine the shit that's running through her head right now.

A few beats of silence go by and I'm about ready to push for more when the elevator dings. She steps forward and waddles as best she can straight into a slew of people. At least her issue, whatever it is, has slowed her down and my limping ass can catch up to her. Jodi follows right behind me, wearing the same curious expression.

Darcie stops and rubs her hand across her forehead. She mumbles something, but I can't make it out. When I ask her to repeat it, she leans in and whispers, "I have razor burn in places one should never have it."

"Razor burn?" My voice carries and people are starting to stare again, but I shrug it off and ignore them.

Darcie gnaws on her top lip and sighs. "After the cream incident I've been scared to try anything crazy, so I shaved."

"Ouch!" I gasp because the thought of something sharp anywhere near my vertical smile is scary as shit.

"Bollocks!" Jodi's mouth drops open as her eyes grow wide.

I feel as horrified as Jodi, but being the visual Cocksister, I need more info. "Everywhere?"

She presses her lips together in a tight line, squeezes her eyes shut, and nods her head. I brace myself because it's obvious what she's going to say is not good and when she speaks, I'm proven right. "The razor slipped and sliced one of my lady lips."

"Bloody fucking hell!" Jodi screams so loudly people have stopped staring and are now giving us more space.

That makes me cringe. Fuck using razors. "I know the thought of having a stranger near your vag makes your asshole clench, but waxing is much quicker and there's no slicing or dicing of your lady cave involved."

Jodi nods, adding, "And no muff stubble."

Then a thought hits me in the face like a stray dick. "Wait…your man is away. Why are you vagscaping?"

Beads of sweat build on her forehead. Whatever she has to say is making her nervous as a nun in a strip club. "Carter's calling me to video chat later and I needed to do some maintenance."

"You dirty birdie." A huge ass grin spreads across my face. "I like it." I elbow her side and wink.

"I knew you would." Darcie's forgetting about her embarrassment and starting to relax, which means my teasing as a diversion is working. "Can we go eat now? I'm hungry." She's ready to be done with this line of questioning, so Jodi throws her a bone.

"Of course, luv." Jodi slings her arm around Darcie's shoulder. "I'm starving to death myself."

We continue walking towards the escalators. None of us have any clue where we're going, but that's the best part of an adventure. Unless said adventure is on a huge ass ship, shit is hard to find, and you're starving. Three of us in need of nourishment means three very cranky Cocksisters.

"Do you even know where we're going?" Darcie whines like a little kid.

"Yes." *No.* We're hungry and need to eat pronto, so I glance around and point to the first place I see. "There."

Darcie's forehead creases as she reads the pink neon sign. "The Wicked Tuna?"

"Yup." I shrug. It looks promising—I think.

"I don't know about this." Her eyebrows pinch together.

Jodi smacks her on her back. "It can't be that bad, luv." Her eyes light up as she bounces up and down. "It says dinner and a show. Never been to one of those before."

"Thanks, Jo." At least she's in an adventurous mood. Then I turn my attention back to Darcie. "Maybe it's got killer seafood?"

Darcie sighs and thinks over my words for a minute. I'm used to her hesitating, so I wait it out. My hunger pangs are killing me, so I hope she makes it quick. Lucky for me, she does. "Fine. Let's do this."

Jodi wastes no time heading towards the front, leaving my limping ass to catch up. There's no hostess area, so Jodi walks right on through to find us a table. And what we find inside is amazing. There's a decent sized stage with black flooring in the center of the room. Bright pink curtains cover the rest of the stage area from view. Tables and booths with the same black and pink color scheme are strategically placed around, giving each one a front row view of the show area. Each table has a bunch of pineapples in the center that are shaped like a flower. Weird, but who am I to criticize their decor. The place is giving off a very sexy and dark vibe, thus my excitement rises. If that's the feeling I get so far then I can't wait to see what dinner has in store for us tonight.

"This place is the tits!" Jodi's mesmerized like it's her first time seeing a dick up close.

"It really is." A grin spreads across my face as I mirror her excitement.

"Wow." Darcie's still stumbling along, absorbing the scenery.

We're walking past some smaller tables towards one with six chairs. Our asses have barely hit the black vinyl seats when a topless waiter wearing a bowtie comes over to greet us. He hands us our menus and smiles. I groan as those bright blue eyes glow against his brown spiked hair. That's a look that could melt panties everywhere. Hell, mine are already about to combust. Too bad the black mask he's wearing hides half his face from view because I bet it's a sight to behold. Then I roam over the rest of the package and my mouth waters. A very firm chest leads to an even firmer six-pack then a dusting of hair draws my gaze down to the happy trail and what it leads to. Oh, hello. There's a nice size package in his pants that looks like it wants to fight its way out to greet me.

Behind me, Jodie gasps. "Fucking hell!"

And it's followed by Darcie's squeak. "Holy shit!"

The topless hunk of man meat must hear them because the corner of his mouth twitches into a half smile. "What can I get for you, ladies?"

"I'll have…" I skim the drink menu and find one that catches my attention, "the Redheaded Slut."

The slight nod of his head is the only acknowledgment I get that he's heard. Then his gaze moves to Jodi. "For you?"

Her lips twist to the side as she studies the menu. I don't blame her for taking her time. Liquor is like liquid sex and one must be cautious to find the right one to penetrate the palate. "I'll take the Leg Spreader."

"Make mine a Blue Balls on the rocks." Darcie licks her bottom lip after she orders and I know exactly what's on her mind.

Our waiter juts out his chin and then walks off to make our drinks.

I don't waste any time giving Darcie shit. She makes it too easy sometimes. "You thinking of Carter's balls?"

Darcie licks her lips as she fans herself with her menu. "Just the one he's got."

"Oh yeah." I laugh. "I forgot about that."

"What does having one nut sac look like?" Leave it to Jodi to read my mind and ask what I'm thinking.

"The skin kind of hangs like a deflated balloon." Darcie sets her menu down and cups her hands in front of her to give us a visual to go with her description.

"Really? Doesn't it get in the way of things?" I don't know why I feel the need to know this, but I do.

Darcie nods and squirms in her chair. The vinyl must not be a great feeling against her sensitive areas.

I open my mouth to ask how she's feeling when our waiter comes back with our drinks. He sets them down and then takes our dinner orders. Darcie and Jodi order while I study the menu real fast. I'm so hungry that I rattle off the first thing I see. Besides, one can't go wrong with spaghetti and meatballs. He finishes writing and heads off towards the kitchen.

"Flick my flaps and spank my arse. That bloke is fine as fuck. I call dibs on him and his knob jockey." Jodi's mouth hangs open.

"You got dibs on the last cockodile." I can't believe she's being such a cockhog. I mean she did have the last manaconda. "Dixon turned out to be a nugget-sized criminal, but still you got one hell of a ride out of it."

She shrugs, which means she's giving in and the waiter is mine. I smile in victory and take a sip of my drink. The fruity peach flavor rolls around on my tongue while I think of all the fun ways to ride our waiter.

I'm not sure how many minutes pass before I'm pulled out of my cockdreaming by the sound of my name. I twist around to find Tre and Kate approaching us, drinks in hand.

"Mind if we join you?" Tre waves, causing the silver bangle bracelets on her arm to jingle.

"Not at all." I motion for them to take the empty chairs, but my gaze is fixated on her bracelets. Anything shiny always catches my attention.

"Thanks, mate." Kate smiles as she slides into the seat next to Jodi. I take in what she's wearing and damn does she look good. Her blue bustier is so tight it looks painted on, as do her black pants.

While they're settling in, our sexy waiter brings out our dinner. He leans over the table to set the plates down, and never one to waste an opportunity, I tilt my head to the side and study his very firm backside. The aroma of spaghetti is making my mouth water, but having his fine as fuck ass bending over has me drooling. If he keeps giving me this view I may need a bucket.

"Anything else?" He licks his bottom lip as his eyes meet mine. It makes me tingle everywhere.

"I'm sure I'll be in need later." Flirting with him is coming easy and something tells me I will, too.

Tre takes the seat next to me, her purple strapless dress flowing as she does. The scent of my food hits her in the face and she groans. "That smells good."

"Want some?" I gesture down towards my plate, which has enough to feed an army.

"No thanks. That's sweet of you to ask, though." Tre props her elbows on the table and plays with the rim of her glass.

"My mom taught me to always share." Too bad it was always with my annoying ass brother, Dusty.

Tre smiles. "Your mom sounds awesome."

"She is. Just don't piss her off or she'll beat your ass to within an inch of your life with her *chancla*." I cringe at the thought of that damn shoe anywhere near me.

"I'll try to remember that." Tre laughs and takes a small sip of her drink. "Didn't expect to see the three of you here tonight."

"We're feeling adventurous and this place looked interesting." At least, Jodi and I think so. Darcie's still on the fence.

"That's one way to put it." Tre winks.

I open my mouth to ask her what she means when the lights dim and everything goes quiet.

"Show time," Kate mumbles, causing my curiosity to pique.

The humming of the microphone echoes through the speakers

before a deep voice comes through, drawing our attention to the stage. "Give a warm welcome to Mistress K and her plaything, J."

Applause and wild cat calls vibrate throughout the room as Gorilla by Bruno Mars starts to play. The pink curtain parts to uncover one hell of an interesting view. A spotlight reveals a gorgeous leggy woman dressed all in black from her Cleopatra style wig, leather dress, and choker, down to her satin gloves and thigh high fuck me boots. Even the mask she's wearing is black. Her stoic demeanor has all eyes in the room glued to her. Power and assertiveness pour off of her. This is a Cocksister who definitely owns her shit.

The crack of her whip pierces through the room with such force Darcie jumps and almost falls out of her damn chair. Then another spotlight shines on a giant black bed to the left, but it's what's on the bed that has my interest piqued. Handcuffed to the wrought iron headboard is a hunky brunette, wearing nothing but a black leather thong and a matching mask. I'm guessing the masks are a theme here.

"Just what kind of show comes with this dinner?" It's impossible to miss the uncertainty in Darcie's voice before she downs her drink.

"Umm…" To avoid answering her, I cram a forkful of noodles into my mouth and chew as slowly as possible.

"It's a—" Tre's response is cut off by the sound of material ripping.

All of our eyes cut back to the stage in time to see Mistress K standing on stage in nothing but a crotchless fishnet body suit. It even has cutouts for her girls—girls so large they could rival Darcie's. Black pasties with tassels at the end cover her nipples. She crawls on top of the bed on all fours, giving us a view of all her goodies as she climbs her way up the waiting stud.

Then she arches her back up and something silver glints against the lights, catching my attention. "Her man in the boat's wearing jewelry."

"That's bloody fucking amazing. It's like a life preserver." Jodi twists her neck to the side to gain a better view. She might as well be studying the Mona Lisa with the effort she's putting into this.

Mistress K slithers her way up the guy's body until she's standing up with her vag right above his head. She flashes us a smirk as she squats and presses her vertical smile against his mouth. He sucks and nibbles at her while she writhes against his face. The muscles of her plaything's throat are flexing as he gives her one hell of a tongue lashing. Her hips thrust against his chin until she drops her head back and lets out a scream as she has a big 'o' in front of us all. Without ever turning around, she slides off J's face, down his neck and chest, never stopping until she's right above his package.

"She's leaving her clam jam all over him," Jodi shouts so loud I'm pretty sure the entire place heard her.

A deep, guttural growl draws our attention back to Mistress K and J. She's licking her way down the same smooth chest, tasting her own clam sauce mixed with his skin. She stops halfway and stares up at him, as one hand reaches up and twists one of his nipples in the roughest titty twister I've seen since grade school.

"Ouchie." Darcie cringes and rubs against the golden silk of her dress to ease her own nipples, while Kate and Tre continue to watch like this is an everyday show.

J grunts, but doesn't make a sound otherwise. Mistress K's tongue darts out to flick his nipple a few times before leaning back on her heels. We were so focused on what her mouth was doing we should have been paying attention to her other hand. The whip cracks against his chest so fast we all jump against our seats.

Jodi gasps. "Bloody hell."

Mistress K continues licking her way down J's body, along every muscle of his six-pack, stopping at his package. A quick jerk of her head and we hear the sound of leather snapping. When she turns to the side, the leather thong is dangling between her teeth like a chew toy. She spits it onto the floor then goes back to the one-eyed monster and sucks it all the way down her throat. The guy groans and tilts his head back as she works him like a pogo stick. She gives him a few more hard sucks and then pulls away. One of her long legs kicks over until she's in a reverse cowgirl position, giving us a full frontal view of her nakedness.

"I'm thinking Wicked Tuna is not a reference to seafood." Darcie's wide eyes are staring at the stage as her words start to slur. These drinks must be strong.

"Well actually—" I open my mouth to deliver a fabulous explanation, but her shaking head stops me.

She already knows where I'm going with this. "Fishnets don't count either."

I shrug and we go back to watching the show.

Mistress K aligns the man's joystick into the right spot and slowly sinks down on him. That's the only thing she does slowly. The rest is like a wild and crazy dream. She lifts her hips up and slams down against him so hard that the sound of flesh slapping together echoes throughout the place. Her hips buck with so much force it's causing the legs of the bed to creak in protest.

"Holy shit," Darcie gasps with a fresh drink in her hand. Sometime between me watching her and the show, our waiter has brought more drinks.

"Bloody bollocks." Jodi's still excited as shit.

"Hope his dick doesn't break." I wince at the amount of force she's putting behind her thrusts. At least the bed is wrought iron and can handle her sexual acrobatics. Can't say the same for the poor cockstar taking her brutal pounding.

On one of her downward slams, a pasty falls off, revealing her nipple, and I have to do a double take. Something very distinct catches my eye, causing my jaw to drop. "I think I know her."

"Who? Mistress K?" Darcie gives me a sideways glance. She's off kilter and hanging half off her chair. I'm not sure if it's the alcohol or her razor burn incident, but I'm hoping she stays upright this time.

I nod, glancing back at the stage. "Yup."

"You sure, luv?" Jodi's face pinches together as she tries to place Mistress K.

"I'm positive. I'd know that third nipple right next to the other one anywhere." I point a finger towards the fun bag in question.

Heads dart to said nipple before they whip back towards me and start their inquisition.

"Hold on." Darcie puts her hand up. "How do you know she has an extra nipple?" Her slur is becoming worse the longer we sit here.

"I kind of, sort of, made out with her." I nudge my fork around my plate, dishing up another decent mouthful of noodles.

"Were the two of you muff mates?" Jodi's eyes light up. She's taking way too much interest in this.

I wash down my noodles with a large amount of alcohol, lick my lips and answer. "No. I never took a ride on the clam tram. I like dick too much."

"That's what strap-ons are for." Tre gives me a once over with her eyes, and I'm not sure if she's picturing her or me being fucked by the strap on. Neither one does it for me, but to each their own.

"Nothing compares to the twitch of real live dick as it's pulsing inside you." Images of Henry fill my head and while I love my vibrator, he doesn't give me everything I need.

Kate shrugs and wraps an arm over Tre's shoulders. "Works for us."

"I need more girth." And to fuck something that talks back.

"Why are we just now finding out you tried to join the muff diving team?" Darcie leans in, waiting to absorb my every word.

"Well, technically *she* did the muff diving." I tilt my head in Mistress K's direction. "I was just the landing zone. I don't see what the big deal is. It was in college, right before I dropped out. Everyone experiments in college."

"I didn't." Darcie's head tilts to the side. She's probably wondering if she should have.

"Me neither, but I'm wishing I had." Jodi's the exact opposite. I can see the wheels turning in her head at the possibilities of all the fun she missed out on.

"Anytime you want to try the jut fruit, mate, let us know." Kate blows Jodi a kiss.

"As long as there's bum fun, I just might." Jodi grins. I'm not even sure she knows what a jut fruit is, but who am I to judge?

A loud groan pulls all of our attention back towards the stage. Mistress K slams down one final time before they both lose control, groaning.

Mistress K and J stay connected, trying to steady their breathing. Silence washes over the room as everyone's eyes stay glued to them.

Then a loud burst of applause and whistling erupts from the audience. It's the damndest thing.

Mistress K leans up on her hands and gets to her feet. The bed and guy are wheeled away as she smiles and waves at the audience. Her eyes glance around the room and grow wide when they stop on me. One side of her lip lifts in a smile as she holds up a finger for me to wait for her.

It doesn't take too long after she's ushered off stage for Mistress K to show up at our table. She's ditched the black wig and has her auburn hair pulled up into a ponytail. Her body is covered in a purple silk kimono robe, and I'm pretty sure there's nothing underneath it.

"Give me a hug, twat sniffer." She wraps her arms around me in a tight embrace, the smell of sex and leather oozing out of her every pore and punching me in the face.

When we pull apart, the whole table is staring at us. It's a good thing attention doesn't bother me. "This is my friend from college, Kristyn Swallows."

"The one who took you to sushitown?" Darcie is full on drunk now. Her eyes are half open and staring wildly in Kristyn's direction.

Kristyn throws her head back and lets out a loud cackle. "One and the same." She slugs me in the shoulder. It might have been meant as a love tap, but it's much harder than a fucking tap. She's much stronger than I remember and I suddenly feel even worse for poor J. "What the hell are you doing here?"

"We were in Ireland enjoying a Badcock Tour. I saw the entry form and figured why not. We won and here we are." I twist to the side to hide the fact I'm rubbing my arm.

"What's a Badcock Tour?" Her eyes light up at the mention of those words.

"I am." Darcie shoots up a wobbly hand.

Kristyn stares at her in confusion, so I explain because Darcie is too blitzed. "It's her last name. Darcie walked in on her dirtbag ex fucking his assistant, so we helped cure her of her troubles one handsome cock at a time."

"What?" Kristyn gasps as she glances at Darcie.

"Yeah. I'm talking mid-thrust." My hands grab the table as I hump the air to give a better visual.

"That fucking cuntpickle. I'm so sorry, sweetie," Kristyn shouts and then puts her arm on Darcie's shoulder. "Please tell me you stuck a broom handle up his ass for her?"

"Damn, I should have thought of that." I slap the table so hard the silverware rattles off our plates. "I offered to shove a tampon up his dick."

"That works, too." Kristyn shrugs and rests her arm against the back of my chair.

"Thanks for the offer." Darcie presses her lips together and sighs. "I do need to use the restroom, though."

"I could use some freshening up myself." Kristyn winks and moves to lead the way.

Jodi hops out of her chair to follow them. "I'll come with as well." She moves so fast I'm pretty sure she can't wait to hound Kristyn for details on our make out sessions.

My hands fidget against the table as they go. "What's with all of these?" I motion towards the pineapples in the center of the table.

Kate grabs one and laughs like I've just told her I have a dick. "These are for when you want to swap mates."

"No shit?" I cock an eyebrow at her. She can't be serious.

Tre nods. "You carry one around and it lets whomever know that you're into it."

"What kind of cruise is this?" I've never heard of any like this or I would have taken one a long time ago.

"It's a sex themed cruise, mate." Kate's laughing so hard she can barely speak.

My head twists to the side to make sure they're not fucking with me.

Nope. They're not.

"You're not shitting me? We're on a legit Cock Cruise?"

"Not shitting you." Tre snorts and then takes in my expression. "You didn't know?"

"Nope." I shake my head. Then a light bulb goes off in my head.

"Now it makes more sense why a sex toy shop was giving away a free cruise and those guys were free balling at the pool."

Both Tre and Kate break out into hysterical laughter. Not sure why it's so funny that we were clueless to the cockfest happening on the ship.

"Are they wankered?" Jodi's voice has me twisting in my seat to see her and a stumbling Darcie slithering into their chairs.

"Something like that." I press my lips together to keep from smiling. This cruise just turned into a full-blown cockathon, and I couldn't be happier. Then I notice they're a Cocksister short. "Where's Kristyn?"

"She said she had to go take care of some work stuff." Darcie waves her hand around as she attempts to plant her ass in the chair.

The combination of her being drunk as shit and the info I just learned has me laughing. This trip really is going to be epic.

"What's so funny?" Darcie sways as she continues to fight her chair. No doubt she's seeing double at this point. She looks so carefree in her alcohol induced happy buzz that I'm not going to spoil anything. She might shit a dick, so I'll need to break this news to her gently and when she's sober enough to comprehend.

"Nothing. I'll tell you later," I whisper out of the side of my mouth to her.

After the umpteenth attempt, Darcie is finally able to plant herself all the way into her seat. The second she props her elbow on the table and rests her chin against her hand her eyes begin to close.

We need to get her out of here and in bed before she face plants onto the floor. "You Cocksisters ready to call it a night? Because I'm not giving your ass another drunken piggy back ride."

"Okay, but I want to take one of these with us in case I get hungry later." Darcie sways, but somehow still manages to swipe a pineapple off the table and cradle it in her arms like a baby. She goes as far as taking a napkin and wrapping it around the fruit.

One thing's for sure, the walk back to our room is going to be an interesting one. And I'm not even talking about the pineapple baby.

4

I'M NOT SURE HOW, BUT Jodi and I managed to make it to their room and tuck Darcie in before she passed out. Must be all the practice we've had through the years. I left her a couple of aspirin and a glass of water by the bed, and headed into my room. I'd love to say there was a little stuffed sausage action happening for me, but sadly I was too tired and went to bed alone…again.

Now, we're sitting at another restaurant trying to decide what to order for breakfast. I'm starving, so the whole menu looks good to me. I inhale to take in the aroma around me, expecting food, but instead I breathe in what can only be described as dirty ass.

"What's that smell?" My nose wrinkles.

"It's this new curl I'm trying for my hair. You like how it smells?" Jodi fluffs out her hair, causing the stench to punch me in the face once again.

Nasty odor aside, I don't have the heart to tell her I'm not seeing even one curl. "It's—"

"Interesting." Darcie saves my ass from being my usual blunt self and finishes for me. She may be hungover and look like she hasn't bathed in a month, but she's still highly alert. She's wearing a pair of dark sunglasses and resting her head on top of her menu. "I feel like death." She definitely looks like she's on its doorstep, too.

Jodi sets her menu down and pats Darcie on the back. "You were pretty arseholed last night." I hide a snort behind my menu. Her Britishisms never get old.

"Do you remember anything about last night?" I flip through the menu a few more times, still trying to decide on something.

Darcie rubs her temples. "Not much. Those drinks were pretty strong."

"They don't call it a booze cruise for nothing." My elbow taps her in the side as our waitress comes to take our order.

"Speaking of booze, when do you think it's acceptable to start drinking?" Darcie mumbles just loud enough for me to hear.

"Breakfast." And now I'm craving a drink as well.

The three of us order Screwdrivers and pancakes—the official Cocksister breakfast—and then our waitress walks off to the next group.

An older couple walks past our table, flashing Darcie an ear-to-ear grin. She smiles and waves back. Everyone has been waving at her like crazy all morning and a hint of guilt creeps its way in.

"That's the third couple to greet you since we sat down. Did you make some new friends?" Jodi teases.

"It's been like that since I left my hotel room. I guess everyone is just super friendly here. They've even invited me back to their rooms later for some games." Darcie beams and I can't keep this from her any longer. It's killing me inside.

"That's because they're swingers, Darce." There's no finesse in my confession at all and I feel a bit bad for dropping it on her like a bomb. Sometimes I'm too blunt for my own damn good. One of these days I should find my filter.

"What?" She wrinkles her nose and looks at me like I've just smacked her in the face with her mother's dildo.

"Swingers?" Jodi is wearing the same dildo slapped expression on her face.

My shoulders droop as I let out a long sigh. I wasn't planning on telling them first thing this morning, but fuck it. It's out there now, might as well give them the rest of it. "While you were in the bathroom giving Kristyn the sushi inquisition, I found out from Tre and Kate that this isn't just any old regular type of cruise. It's geared more towards a very specific market." After scaring her with my previous statement, I'm trying to word this as delicately as I can.

"Meaning?" Darcie's still not cluing in to what I'm saying.

Oh fuck me. Why can't they read between the lines? I'm just going to have to drop it on them like a bag of dicks in a nunnery. "It's a sex cruise." Silence. "So, I guess one might say we're on a Cocktastic Cocksister Cruise."

"Blow me!" Jodi claps her hands together and bounces in her seat. I knew she'd be on board with this. Or at least I think she is. It's hard to keep up with her verbiage sometimes.

At that moment our waitress comes out with our food and drinks. Judging by her wide eyes and red face, she heard Jodi loud and clear. I find this type of shit hilarious, but Darcie's not so carefree about it. At least this morning she's too focused on what I just said to notice.

Without a word, our waitress sets our food and drinks down then rushes off. Guess we scarred her for life. Oopsie.

Jodi takes the lid off her plate and digs in, cockcruise forgotten. Food and dicks make her happy every time.

I watch Darcie in an attempt to gauge her reaction. She's been known to either panic or scream in these types of situations, but this time she shocks the hell out of me. "I didn't even know that was a thing. Think they'll have some technique classes? I want to surprise Carter with some new moves. After getting drunk and passing out last night, I need to make up for the lack of phone sex when I see him next."

I open and close my mouth a few times before I answer her, but Jodi swallows her food and beats me to it. "You know I saw in a brochure they're offering yoga. Maybe it will inspire some new positions for your shagging pleasure. Not to mention limber your arse up a bit." She winks and waves her fork at Darcie.

Darcie nods her head as a smile spreads over her face. "That would be perfect."

"Um...I can't. I have this damn boot on." I gesture down to the eyesore. If my leg weren't so long, I'd slam it on the table to remind them.

"I'm sure they can modify it for you, luv." Jodi licks a drop of syrup off the corner of her mouth and smiles.

"Maybe." I despise working out. "I'll think about it." I'd rather self-serve with Henry in my room. "Today we're making port, so I want to do some sight seeing. You Cocksisters in?"

"Yes." Darcie's face lights up. I knew I could count on her to see some sights. "That would be fun."

"It sounds ace." Jodi shoots her hand up in the air, but my heart skips a beat.

"What's with the look?" Figures Darcie would notice.

"Nothing." I attempt to shake it off, but she isn't buying my bullshit today.

I sigh and give in. "It's just that 'Ace' is what the penis who shall not be named used to call me."

"Oh no. Do you want to talk about what happened?" Got to love Darcie. She's hungover as shit and still worried about her cockorexic friend.

I shake my head. "Nope. I'm good."

"I'm sorry, luv." Jodi pats my arm. "I didn't know or wouldn't have said it."

"I know." I plaster on a fake smile, but the truth is up until now I've been able to forget all about him and his amazing dick. The dick he certainly knows how to use. He works the female anatomy like no other. My thighs clench at the thought of all of the things he did with his tongue. I let out another deep sigh. Damn him and his mind-blowing dickrobatics. Oh well, he's not ruining my fun. I can give myself plenty of orgasms until I find another cockinator to wreck my cervix. I take the lid off my plate and smile down at it. This sex cruise is for sure my kind of place.

Moment gone, Darcie finally looks at her plate and notices what

Jodi's been shoveling into her mouth with pleasure for the past few minutes. She pulls her sunglasses off and tosses them onto the table then holds her fork up closer to examine the mini pancake. Her blonde eyebrows pinch together. "Are these shaped like dicks?"

"Yup. They're mini cockcakes." I grin and shove a forkful of the delicious little phallic shaped fluffy goodness in my mouth with a loud moan.

Darcie laughs and eats it up. "So, where are we porting today?"

I swallow and wipe my face before smiling. "St. Croix."

"Flick my flaps and pinch my nipples. It sounds bloody fantastic." Jodi's blue eyes light up. And yes, her voice is super loud. The whole restaurant stops and stares at our table for a few seconds and then go back to whatever it is they were doing.

Darcie's staring at Jodi with her mouth open, so I do what I do best and distract her with my wits. "Eat up, ladies. A full mouth is a happy mouth." I smile and do just that.

We finish up breakfast and head back to our rooms to prepare for the next adventure. I slip into my favorite olive colored romper and a beige sandal with a little struggle. The shorts of my romper are loose fitting and super comfy, which means no camel toe catastrophe for me. Perfect to slip over my boot too. My other shoe is still in the closet looking very sad and lonely, but I don't give it another thought as I head into their room.

To my surprise they're both dressed and ready. Darcie's wearing a cute navy sundress, while Jodi opts for a pair of khaki shorts and lemon yellow camisole. I have to say my Cocksisters are pretty damn gorgeous. I grab my phone and we head out the door.

Once we're out in the hall and heading towards the elevators, I'm distracted by the huge ass bag Darcie has hanging off her shoulder. It's some weird lime green color with an interesting pattern on it. She enters the elevator and spins around to face me, but not before she catches me staring. Her head twists down as she pulls the bag in front of her, giving me a better view of the images. "What?"

I lean in for an even closer look. "Are those hot pink dicks?" Because that's all I see.

"No." Her forehead scrunches together. "They're pink flamingos."

"If you say so, luv." Jodi snorts. I know she's seeing the same damn thing I am.

"They are." Darcie folds her arms across her chest, pushing her ginormous boobs up, and leans away from us. Red colors her cheeks. "At least the lady at the counter said they were."

Jodi and I try to hold in our laughter, but lose that battle pretty quick. Darcie ignores us until the elevator dings. She rushes out, leaving us to chase after her. Lucky for us there's a crowd of people, so she can't get too far ahead.

"Why are you taking a mini suitcase with you?" I ask when I catch up to her.

Darcie keeps walking at a brisk pace as she answers me. "I brought provisions."

"What kind of provisions?" Jodi's head cocks to the side as she ogles the bag.

Darcie stops and spins around to face us. "Some water, a towel, bug repellent, and sunblock."

"Sunblock?" Out of all of the things she grabbed, that's what surprises me. "Don't you want to get your tan on?"

Darcie sighs and scratches the side of her head. "I do, but I'm not sure how long we'll be gone and I burn easy, so I made sure to pack plenty."

"You definitely packed plenty, luv." Jodi winks at Darcie and smiles.

"You sure did, but good call. I didn't even think about that, sorry." I feel bad for not remembering Darcie doesn't have my olive complexion and will end up looking like Rudolf's dick if she isn't careful. "Any room for my phone in there?" I wave the rectangular object as a sort of peace offering.

"Sure." Darcie takes my phone and tosses it into the bag. Something tells me it might be lost now, but I was due for a new one anyways.

Dickbag issue over with, we lean against the railing on the ship's deck and wait. The breeze feels good and refreshing. After spending some time in Ireland, it's nice to be on the water for a change of scenery. Jodi and Darcie are smiling and enjoying it as much as I am.

Excitement is pouring off all three of us. One thing we love is gorgeous sights, whether it be an island or a nice hard dick.

When the ship pulls into port, it shifts forward a bit, knocking me off balance. If I had two good feet I could firmly plant on the ground, this wouldn't be an issue, but I don't, so I stumble right into Darcie. We both fall face first with a loud thump.

I roll off her to my side and hope we didn't break anything. "Shit. Sorry, Darce. You okay?"

Darcie's laid out flat on her stomach like a deflated blow up doll. She rolls over with a soft groan and flops onto her back. Both Jodi and I gasp.

"What is that?" I point to the white mess all over the front crotch area of her dress.

"Oh no!" Darcie wipes at it, but all she ends up doing is making a bigger mess. "The sunblock exploded when I landed on it."

"It doesn't look too bad." My teeth dig into my bottom lip to keep her from noticing I'm blowing smoke up her ass.

Darcie's eyes narrow into tiny slits. "Doesn't look too bad? It looks like I have man sauce all over me." She's right. It looks like she took a bath in someone's nut butter. She shakes the excess off her hands, sending white shit flying everywhere, and climbs to her feet.

"Just hold the bag in front of you until it dries and you'll be fine." I adjust the dickbag so the side that's covered in what resembles pole milk is against her dress. "All better."

"No one will even notice the trouser gravy, luv." Jodi nods her head and smiles.

Darcie sags and lets out a long breath. "I hope you're right." She's still embarrassed and it's killing me.

Jodi and I stare at each other in an unspoken conversation. Time for us to take one for the team. I hold out my hand. "Give me the sunblock."

Darcie cocks an eyebrow at me. "Why?"

"Just give it." My hand motions for it again.

"Fine." She pulls it out of her bag and it's covered in white stuff.

I rub my hands against the lotion on the outside and it ends up looking like I'm jacking off a bottle of sunblock in the middle of a crowded ship. People are walking past us and some smile, while others do a double take at my hand job action. I ignore them and focus on what I'm doing. Once I've gotten enough, I toss the bottle over to Jodi and she does the same thing.

Darcie's blue eyes are glued to us in what can only be described as a mixture of horror and fascination. Once Jodi is done lubing her hands up, we both wipe the sunblock on the front of our shorts, giving us the same man yogurt stain as her.

Darcie's lips break out into a smile as she laughs. "I love you girls."

"We'd never leave you hanging like a limp willy, luv." Jodi brushes her hands off and grins.

"Cocksisters always have each others' backs." I wink as we start to follow the herd of people off the ship. Only a few of them are obviously staring at our schlong juice coated crotches. Jodi and I are good with it. We did this for our Cocksister, Darcie, and their opinions don't matter to us.

The second we're on the dock, my jaw drops. Pictures don't do this place justice. Everything is beautiful. Teal water washes right up to the shore of the white sandy beaches, while the bright greenery of the hills and homes acts as the perfect backdrop. My stomach flutters. Definitely scenery porn.

"This place is the fucking tits!" Jodi shouts, mirroring my own orgasm from the view.

"You Cocksisters ready to have some fun?" My lips spread into a wide grin. "I know I am."

"We hitting a bar?" Darcie snorts.

I wrap my arm around her shoulder and bend down to her height. "Booze is always on the top of my list, but first let's check out this rainforest tour they have before I'm too fucked up to remember it."

"I'm good, as long as I get to shag a few blokes later. Don't want my flaps getting musty." Jodi's honesty is always a welcomed addition to any conversation.

"Sounds like a plan to me, too." Darcie glances around and points behind me. "There's a cab over there."

As we stroll towards the cab, only a few of the townsfolk are staring at our crotches. I guess the shit doesn't dry clear like I was hoping. Oopsie.

We slip into the cab and the driver does a double take at our clothes in his review mirror, but otherwise he doesn't let on he's noticed. I tell him where we're going and a slight nod of his head is the only clue I get that he's heard me.

The ride isn't too long, but it's on nothing but dirt roads. It's a good thing none of us get carsick, but poor Darcie has to hold her tits in place or else they'll smack her in the face. Sometimes I'm glad I'm president of the itty bitty titty committee.

The cab drops us off in front of a fenced in area where people are entering and we're smacked in the face with a sweet flowery smell. It's fresh and clean, like laundry detergent.

We take a good look around and die. If we thought we were awestruck before then this place is on a whole new level. The trees are so tall we can't really see much, but the little plants and flowers we can spot through the fence are gorgeous.

"Wow! These trees are huge." Darcie's jaw drops open. If she's not careful she might catch a mouthful of bugs.

Speaking of, a couple of insects are flying around way too close to me. The last thing I need on this trip is to be bitten. "Can I borrow some of your bug spray, Darce?"

"Sure thing." She reaches in her bag and hands it to me.

While I'm spraying myself, Darcie and I both watch Jodi. Her head is whipping back and forth to take everything in so fast I'm afraid she's going to end up with dicklash. "This place is the mutt's nuts!"

I laugh and hand the spray back to Darcie. Half the time I don't know what Jodi's saying, but I just go along with it. "You're right about that."

We follow the dirt trail inside and the view just keeps getting better and better. Some of the biggest trees I have ever seen swallow us up into heavy shade the further in we go. Vines hang down from the tops of the trees as we hear the cries of birds and other animals. Lush green shrubs and bushes line the path the entire way. It's like we've walked onto a different planet, and I love it.

The trail is winding with lots of dips and curves, but to my surprise my booted foot manages just fine. If I keep up a slow, steady pace and stay alert, I shouldn't have any issues.

We walk for a bit before I have my first insect encounter. I bend forward at the waist and escape it. I'd like to say it's the last insect issue I have, but sadly it is not. No sooner than I'm free, another two are flying around me. This is getting on my last nerve. "I don't think your bug spray worked, Darce. I'm being eaten alive."

"I haven't had any trouble." Jodi glances around and she's right, her area is insect free.

"Maybe there's natural repellent in your curl cream?" Or it could be they don't want anywhere near that nasty ass smell.

"I think you might need to reapply." Darcie sets her bag down and squats to rummage through it for the bug spray. It only takes her a few seconds to find it. When she reads the can, her lips purse together. "Fuck me in the ass with a donkey!"

"What?" This doesn't sound good for me at all.

"It's not bug spray. I must have grabbed the wrong one. They were right next to each other, so it was an honest mistake." She keeps rambling and it's a dead giveaway she's nervous about something.

"Bugger!" Jodi's eyes grow so wide they look like they're going to pop out of her head.

"Then what did I spray all over me?" My eyebrows shoot up to my forehead as I dread her answer.

"My honey scented body spray." Darcie's teeth dig into her top lip as she waits for my reaction.

"Shit." I could freak out, but there's really nothing else I can say. These fuckers are going to eat me alive now.

"Pecker up, luv. At least you'll smell fresh." Jodi pats my shoulder and continues along the trail.

I follow her a few more feet when one of the biggest fucking wasps I've ever seen flies right past my head. He's so big he sounds like a helicopter buzzing in my ear. Shivers rush over me. No insect should be bigger than my finger…ever! Hell, it might even be bigger than some dicks I've seen—and that's just wrong.

"What the hell is that?" Darcie jumps and runs out of its way.

"Bollocks!" Jodi screams and follows her.

I attempt to rush after them, but my boot slows me down. I'm limping like a spastic dick trying to catch up to them. Buzzing next to my hair has me ducking my head so fast I get dizzy. This damn wasp won't leave me alone. "Go away! Shoo." My hands swat at it, but the fucker isn't listening.

"I don't think it's smart to antagonize it." Darcie pants as she watches me from a much safer distance.

"I want to burn its ass to a crisp." Next time I'm bringing a blowtorch with me. Screw bug spray. I'm stumbling along faster to try and out hobble it when I trip over a tree root, landing on my knees, ass up. This is usually one of my favorite positions, but not right at this moment. There's not even a second to brace for what happens next.

Sharp shooting pain in a place I've never experienced, a place no woman should ever experience it, engulfs me. "That little fucker just stung me on one of my muff flaps."

"Bloody hell!" The horror in Jodi's tone doesn't go unnoticed.

Darcie rushes over and bends down at my side. "Are you okay?"

"No," I manage to squeak out after a few minutes of holding my breath. "My lady lips are on fire." It takes me a minute or five, but I'm eventually able to get up off the ground and to my feet. The second I'm standing upright, I feel woozy. This can't be good.

"You birds may want to move because he's coming back," Jodi shouts.

Darcie wraps my arm around her shoulder and helps me limp out of the line of attack. A funny feeling washes over my body with each step. I tug at the collar of my dress. It's tighter, cutting into my skin like it's sucking the oxygen from my body.

Darcie stares at me like I've just spit a mouthful of jizz all over her. "Umm…are you allergic to them?"

"Not that I know of, why?" My legs squeeze together in an attempt to contain the itching wildfire happening in my downstairs region. I haven't itched this badly since the first time I shaved it.

"I'm thinking you might be, because you're starting to swell up like a balloon." Darcie's face looses all its color.

I let her words sink in. Then I feel everything all at once. My throat constricts. It's becoming difficult to breathe. I smack at my chest as I gasp for air.

Darcie freaks out, grabs me from behind, and squeezes my abs in a weird version of the Heimlich maneuver. With each thrust of her hips, I'm jerked forward. If I could speak I'd tell her it looks more like she's fucking me from behind than anything else. I slap at her arms and she finally stops.

Jodi's holds up her hands. "Don't panic. I'll call for help." She whips out her phone, presses a button and holds it up to her ear. Lack of oxygen is getting to me. My vision narrows as she comes in and out of focus. Just before I black out, I hear Jodi shout into her phone, "Help! We have a flap emergency."

5

A BLINDING LIGHT HITS ME the second I open my eyes. It's so bright they squeeze right back shut. *Ouch!* Blinking a few times, my vision finally adjusts and I can focus without squinting. White ceiling tiles with a few water stains swallow my vision. My head tilts down and I cringe. The scratchy white linens and awful gown reveal what I feared. I'm in the ship's infirmary and stuck in a hospital bed...again. Then I'm punched in the face with a familiar foul odor. One that damn near made me lose my breakfast earlier—dirty ass.

I twist to my side and find the cause of said stench. Jodi and Darcie are sitting next to my bed, eyes closed, heads back and looking like they've had one hell of an all nighter. This hits me with a sudden sense of déjà vu, like when Darcie shot me in the foot in Ireland. Before I can think better of it, a groan escapes me, and their eyes pop open.

"You awake, luv?" Concern is evident in Jodi's tone, which scares the shit out of me. She's never worried unless there's a serious problem.

"No." I whine. "Why am I always the one who ends up in a damn hospital bed?" My throat feels like sandpaper, but the throbbing pain radiating from my lady lips is taking precedence over everything else. "And why does my vag feel like I have ten day old crotch rot?"

"A case of bad luck, I'm afraid." Jodi sighs and softly pats my thigh.

Darcie, on the other hand, doesn't feel the need to be gentle with me at all. She jumps out of her chair and storms towards me like a madwoman on a wild dickhunt.

"You scared the shit out of us," she shouts from the end of the bed, so loud I'm waiting for security to come escort her out of my room. Her hand slaps against my booted foot, causing her to scream out again, and she's lucky that I'm in too much pain downstairs for it to even register. She, on the other hand, isn't so lucky. "Ouch. Mother fucker!" Her face pinches tight, as she shakes out her hand. That had to hurt like hell, but I can't focus on anything except the raging inferno of torture happening in my lower region.

"And downstairs?" It takes all my strength to croak those two words out.

Darcie plops back down in the chair with a loud flop and sends me a look that could shrivel dicks everywhere. Clearly, I'm not getting off the hook for scaring her just yet. "Apparently you're allergic to wasps. Why didn't you tell us?"

"I didn't know. Up until now I've never been stung." Of all the rotten fucking luck, it has to come out while I'm on vacation.

"Not to worry. The good news is they were able to save your flaps." Jodi beams, like she's just told me she's found the golden dick.

Well, I guess that's something. "Awesome."

At that moment, the doctor comes in and stops on the side of my bed. She's a petite brunette who's swimming in her white coat. Her head barely even makes it over the rails of the bed. The smile she has plastered on her face should be comforting, but in truth it makes my asshole cringe. "You're awake."

I nod and clear my throat. "How long was I out for?"

"Not too long." The doctor's facial expression never changes as she talks. The only time I've seen this happen is after Darcie's mom gets one of her many botox injections. "You did give your friends quite the scare. Thankfully, they're quick thinkers. We were able to give you a shot of epinephrine before things could become life-threatening."

"Thank you, Dr—" I wait for her to fill me in on what the hell to call her because I'm thinking 'plastic nugget' wouldn't be appropriate.

"I'm Dr. Julie Hummer. You can just call me Dr. Hummer." Of course that's her last name.

I fight the urge to laugh my ass off in front of her, and focus on the bag of pills she's handing me. After all, I'm not an asshole and she did save my life. I'll just laugh about it when I'm alone later.

"We already administered some steroids to help with the swelling, but I want you to take these for the next couple of days to be safe." She shakes the bag to emphasize her point and I take it from her for fear she'll hit me with it if I don't.

"Thanks." I clutch the sack against my chest like it's an actual ball sack.

She nods and keeps talking. "Inside is also an epipen in case this happens to you again. Other than that you're free to go, but to be safe I would like you wheeled up to your room. I can have a nurse take you?"

I open my mouth to agree when Jodi bursts forward like a wild dick and takes hold of the wheelchair. "Nope, I've got her arse."

Dr. Hummer nods again. "I hope you enjoy the rest of your cruise." She backs away, allowing Jodi room to push the wheelchair to my bed.

I watch her for a minute to gauge how serious she is and wait for her to pop out an "I'm just kidding", but she doesn't. Damn it to hell!

My body twists to the side to climb off the bed and into my new ride, when my inner thighs brush against my vertical smile. Pain shoots through me like a motherfucker. I suck in a deep breath and plop my ass into the chair with a slight wince. Of course it doesn't go unnoticed.

"You okay?" Darcie rushes up to me, like the mother hen I knew she'd be.

"I'm fine. I just feel like I have elephantiasis of the vag." My throat is still a tad sore, so I also sound like I've been stabbed in the tonsils with one too many dicks.

"I don't think that's a thing." Darcie shakes her head at me. Maybe not the vag part, but the dicks is a big hells yeah.

I lean against the back of my new wheels and let her comment go as Jodi turns the wheelchair. She forgets to account for my foot rests, though, which means my good foot ends up slamming into the wall with a loud *thud* and I groan. "Bollocks. Sorry, luv. This is a bit bigger than I'm used to but I can work this like a willy. Don't you worry." She winks as her face breaks out into a huge grin.

My eyes squeeze shut and air whips me in the face as I'm wheeled off at a fast pace. The ride to my room isn't as bad as I was expecting. Jodi only bangs me into a couple more walls and runs over a few people along the way. That's a win in my book.

Once we're back inside my room, Jodi wheels me off into a corner and sets the brakes.

"You want to shower before we go eat?" Darcie watches me like she's expecting a freak out to happen at any moment. Little does she know I'm too tired to care. Today has sucked ass and zapped me of all my energy.

"Sure." I toss my bag of meds on top of the bed and head into the bathroom before she can say another word.

Minutes, and I'm not sure how many mishaps later, I'm finally showered and ready. Let's just say nothing about showering with one good leg and a swollen vag is easy. I feel like I deserve a medal for being able to accomplish it.

Darcie and Jodi are already waiting in my room with simple summer dresses on. Darcie's is a butter yellow, while Jodi's is black. I'm feeling braver than normal because I've slipped into a white summer dress myself. My stomach chooses this opportunity to growl so loudly it echoes. I place my hand against it in an attempt to muffle the damn noise. "I guess it's been a bit since I last ate."

"Yes! Same here. I could eat a horse between two bread vans. Let's go." Jodi hops towards the door like a bunny on crack.

Darcie and I stare at her for a minute, letting her words sink in. Yeah, I don't get that one. Then Darcie turns her attention back to me. "Dr. Hummer recommended this great buffet place. You up to going?"

She eyes me and I know she's checking me over to make sure I don't need a damn wheelchair again. Little does she know while they showered, I had Eric come up and take it away.

"Sure."

I grab my pills from the bag off the bed and debate on shoving them in my bra when Darcie says, "Here. I'll keep them in my purse for you. Oh, and I still have your phone in here from earlier."

"Thanks, Darce." I hand the pills over and watch her shove them inside her dickbag. It seems to be her favorite accessory this trip. *Note to self, burn the bag later.*

With that, we're out the door and on our way. When we step off the elevator into the restaurant area, I'm hit with an instant foodgasm. Whatever they're cooking smells so damn good.

We walk a few steps when I see a store that has my mouth watering even more. "We are so going in there." I point to the bakery and the window full of chocolate dicks on display.

Darcie reads the name out loud. "The Erection Confection."

"Oh! Count me in, luv. I love a good sweet willy that melts in your mouth." Jodi bounces up and down like a little kid. I knew she'd be game and I'm holding her to that later.

We continue walking along until we come to a horde of people. Darcie and Jodi step into the line and join the crowd, while it takes my exhausted ass a minute to realize this is where we're eating. Once I clue in, I follow their lead and stand in line, too. This must be a popular place because it's super crowded. My head tilts up to read the bright blue lettering and a grin spreads across my face.

"The Hungry Beaver?" My gaze darts towards Darcie.

"Dr. Hummer swears by their meat buffet." She scratches her temple and shakes her head.

I'm intrigued by the name alone. "At least we know it's all-you-can-eat."

"Looking forward to stuffing my face with a good sausage." Jodi snorts as she stares straight ahead. I giggle and also share her opinion. Stuffing one's face with meat of any kind is always a good time.

The line moves at a decent pace, so we're able to pay and head straight to the buffet in no time. Just like the name states, there are lots of angry stuffed beavers placed around the room. It reminds me of my parents' restaurant. The only differences are that it is decorated with lots of wood and beavers, while my parents' Mexican restaurant is full of Roy Rogers memorabilia.

All three of us move right for the salad bar. One can never go wrong with a kick ass salad. I'm tong deep in lettuce when a female voice next to us snickers. We turn our heads to see an older woman with a huge blonde beehive, bright blue eyeshadow, dog dick red lips, and a fake smile.

"You eat like a rabbit." There's no missing the rudeness in her tone. Some people are just assholes for no reason, but judging by the way this one is staring at Darcie's tits, I'm pretty sure hers stems from jealousy.

Darcie's too polite to say anything and Jodi's too busy playing with the cucumbers to notice; however, this Cocksister is not. Years of dealing with this have left me little patience. I lean in so close I can feel her hot breath blowing against my cheek. The stench of rotten fish hits me, and it takes all my concentration to remember what I'm going to say, but I do. "She fucks like one, too."

Darcie drops her tongs and gasps. I guess she wasn't expecting me to say anything. Oopsie. I'm used to her reactions, so I ignore the commotion and keep my attention on beehive lady.

The woman blinks in shock, but once my words register, she gives Darcie another once over and this time with an entirely different intention. Her tongue licks along her bottom lip and she looks like she's ready to devour Darcie whole. "Really?"

Well, that backfired. Time for another type of intervention. I wrap my arm around Darcie and pull her up against me. "Sorry, I don't share my bitch."

Darcie goes as stiff as a dick in a gynecologist's office. I haven't pretended to be her girlfriend since high school when she was being stalked by Asher Michaels—well, she was until the school talent show.

The woman backs up and throws her hands up. "Not to worry. I have my own BAE." It doesn't stop her from giving Darcie one last glance before she walks off. Darcie and I both cock our heads to the side and stare at her retreating backside.

"What the hell does B-A-E stand for?" Darcie whispers.

"Um...Balls Are Empty?" I have no fucking clue, but I think my guess is perfect.

"Maybe. Or it could be Bitches Are Everywhere?" Darcie laughs, as she puts another helping of lettuce on her plate. She's really over doing it with the veggies.

Jodi snickers, still loading up on cucumbers. "No. It's pronounced 'bay' and means Before Anyone Else. Like a willy you're shagging on the regular." She sets the salad tongs and her plate down and then she starts humping air to give us a proper demonstration.

"How the hell do you know that?" I stare at her dumbfounded—not because of the air humping; that happens all the time. It's the fact she knows something I don't. Not many things go over my head, but this one sure did.

"With Lit Lickers Promotions, I have to know this social media stuff or I look like a bloody idiot. Plus, I overheard some young blokes talking about it the last time I was in America." Jodi shoves a piece of cucumber in her mouth and crunches down on it so hard I almost feel sorry for any dick that's been near her mouth.

"I like my version better." I shrug and hobble off towards the meat section with them trailing behind me.

There are so many options I'm drooling. It's like a smorgasbord of heaven that has my mouth watering. Then again, any meat makes me drool. I lean over to grab a nice sized piece of steak when my underwear shifts and it's like a lightning bolt explodes against my clit. Alarm bells go off in warning, but being the smart person I am, I ignore them and concentrate on the food in front of me.

"Now that's some tasty looking meat." Jodi flicks her tongue out and licks her lips like she's about to devour a twelve inch cock for the first time.

Darcie laughs and grabs a small piece of grilled chicken. Suspicion creeps in because she's never taken such little food like that before.

I nod and open my mouth to ask Darcie about her food choices or lack thereof, but the tingling happening downstairs starts up again. My legs shift to ease some of the sensation and I regret the decision the second I do. Shivers rock through my body as a loud groan escapes from deep within my throat. I clench my plate in my right hand as I lean over and prop my left hand against the side of the counter to keep me from falling over. My fingernails dig into the wood so hard it creaks.

"Those shrimp look sooo—" Another moan leaves me before I can finish my sentence. My toes curl as my whole body goes tight. I have no idea what the hell is wrong with me. Even the slightest friction of my shorts has my vag ready to explode at any moment. Lack of dick has to be the cause of this. I need to get penetrated like yesterday.

"You okay?" Darcie cocks her head to the side and stares at me like I have jizz on my lip.

Beads of sweat are now trickling down my forehead as my body burns from the inside out. "Yup. I'm good. Great even." My voice comes out high pitched in between every panting breath I take. I sound like I've just had an all night cockathon. I'm hoping she doesn't notice and buys my answer. I really should have been more worried about my crazy Brit instead.

"Bollocks! You sound like your flaps have just combusted," Jodi damn near shouts in the middle of the restaurant.

I'm sure everyone is staring, but I don't give a fuck at the current moment. Blood is pumping in my ears and the only thing I know is I need to sit my ass in a seat to stop me from getting in real trouble. "I'll meet you guys at the table." I don't wait for an answer before I'm spinning around and heading towards a table. Every step is complete torture. My body hunches over as I fight to keep my plate from hitting the floor. I'm sure I look like I have to a take a massive shit, but I don't care. Nothing matters until my ass is able to plop down in a chair and wait for whatever this is to go away. The second the cold vinyl hits my legs, I sigh in relief. I'm assuming it's like putting ice on one's balls and stopping things dead.

Not long after, Jodi and Darcie take their seats next to me. I ask

Darcie for my pills and take one before I forget. A shiver runs through me as I swallow them down. It has the most disgusting after taste, like rotten dick.

Jodi grabs a fork and digs right into her food. Darcie, on the other hand, takes her time and pecks at her plate like a damn bird.

I'm having my own issues right now, but I can tell something is off with her and I'm getting to the bottom of it. "Where's the rest of your food, Darce?" My chin dips down towards her plate.

"I'm trying to be good. We're not twenty-five anymore. I can't eat like I used to. " She waves a piece of lettuce around as she speaks.

"Is Carter saying shit?" My temper flares at the thought of him saying anything remotely close to that to her. "I will cut off his balls— well the one he's got— and roast it for you if he is."

"That's sweet of you, but no. It's me." Darcie sighs and hangs her head. "I found a gray hair."

Jodi leans over the table until she's nose to nose with Darcie. "Cheer up, luv. It's when it starts snowing in the basement you should worry." She means to whisper this, she really does, but it comes out at full volume.

Laughter erupts from the table behind us. It's obvious they heard every word of our conversation, but I shrug it off and focus on Darcie. She's my main concern.

"Fuck me in the ass with a fork." Blood creeps into Darcie's face as embarrassment floods her. She needs a distraction and lucky for her I'm all about that.

"There has to be more to it. I can't believe one strand of gray has you eating bird food." My hand waves towards her sad plate. Just that little bit of movement has me squirming in my seat and I do my best to act natural. The damn urges are back full force. Not good.

"When we put our bikinis on the other day, I found some cellulite on my thighs. I'm not going to age like a desirable block of cheese. I'm going to be the old moldy one nobody wants to eat." Darcie's so into her speech she isn't realizing the extent of her volume and I'm not going to be the one to tell her.

I cross my legs to keep my focus on her, and what a big mistake that is—one I undo as fast as I can. When the urge lessens, I continue on with my train of thought. "First off, everyone has cellulite. Second, it's a stupid word. I prefer body dimples."

Jodi shoves another cucumber in her mouth and nods her head. "She's right, luv. You're perfect the way you are. Anyone who says different can suck on our lady balls."

"Exactly." My fingers curl around the side of my chair as I try to keep my mind on our conversation. It's not working. Things are even worse. "I think I'm gonna head back to my room." I jump out of my chair and attempt to make a clean getaway, but my damn boot causes me to trip over my own feet. My knee hits the underside of the table, knocking all of our drinks over. "Shit, sorry."

Darcie stops mid-chew and stares down at the mess I've just made. "It's fine."

"You feeling okay?" Jodi narrows her eyes and watches me with rapt curiosity.

I wipe away the bead of sweat that's dripping down my temple. "Uh-huh. I just need to lie down." Every sound I make comes out high pitched once again, like I've been snorting helium.

"Okay. We're probably going to head off and do a spray tan, since my sunblock didn't quite work and I don't want to get fried to a crisp later on." Darcie wipes at the water that's dripping into a puddle on the floor. Even that small movement is getting me worked up.

I'm going to combust on the spot if I don't get my ass out of here. "Sounds good. See you later." I wave my arm behind me, as I storm off towards my room. I'm out of time and can't stay here any longer. The way things are feeling, I may have a snail trail running down my legs if I don't hurry up.

No sooner than I get back to my room do I slam my door shut and reach for the most important thing to me right now—Henry. My blood is pumping all the way down to my clit. The slightest movement has me groaning with need. It takes everything I have to rip off my underwear. They get caught on my boot and I leave them there. The friction is too much to handle, so fuck it. My dress is also staying on because I'm not chancing any more issues.

I plop my body on the bed, hike up the bottom of my dress and spread my legs. The second the cold air hits me, it's like a fire ignites all over my body. "Oh God." This keeps up I'm going to be a minuteman.

The sound of Henry vibrating isn't helping to decrease my situation. I'd use my personal playlist to give me a rhythm to work with, but my phone is still in Darcie's damn dickbag. I turn on the radio next to my bed for some musical stimulation and cross my fingers for a worthy lady jam. What I get is Achy Breaky Heart by Billy Ray Cyrus. This shit is not going to work. Country is not for this girl. Pressure builds from deep within me, causing my finger to fall off the knob and back down south for some support. The slight slip causes the station to change and this time I'm serenaded with Whitney Houston's version of I Will Always Love You. It'll have to do because I need release ASAP.

I lie back and focus on the mission at hand. My eyes close, as I get lost in the song, working Henry as hard and deep as I can. "Sing it, Whitney."

My strokes are steady and fast as I force Henry in and out, rubbing against my clit every time. Each thrust sends me closer to the edge, but I just can't quite get my body to fall. I need some spank bank inspiration.

Blue eyes, a cleft chin and gorgeous brown hair lead the way into one hell of a fantasy. Henry Cavill sets my loins on fire. A few strokes in, I feel the familiar build up I need to get rid of this sexual tension that's suffocating me. Too bad that's when another set of dark blue eyes and features similar to Cavill's invade my mind. Leave it to Logan to take over my thoughts and make me wetter. It's all he's done since I met him. Damn man.

On it's own accord, my hand responds to the vision of Logan. It pumps Henry at warp speed with each image of that man and what his tongue can do. The friction causes warmth to pool in my belly. My hips thrust up and grind against him for more. Clenching my thighs, I work him faster against me while the fingers of my other hand rub my clit. An intense ache builds up until I'm past the point of no return.

Whitney hits her high note at the same time I hit one of my own. Of course, I sound more like a dying bird and nowhere near as graceful. The orgasm consuming me is well worth sounding like a thousand dying birds, though. An explosion of sensation courses through me as I squirt all over the place and find my way into Orgasmville. I'll be washing my bedding later—much, much later.

I expect things to subside and to feel satisfied, but I'm not. It's only getting worse. Even the way the sheets are scratching against my skin is sending me into orgasm number two.

A cramp forms in my wrist as I grind my teeth and keep working Henry through it. This is why sex is supposed to be a team sport, not a solo act. I do my best to ignore the pain and focus on the pleasure. I can't stop. I need more. Multiple orgasms are a necessity at this point. I may die from self-serve overload, but it's a price I'm prepared to pay. I just hope my poor vag can keep up with my demands.

I'm working Henry as far and deep as he can go, in hopes of another orgasm rocking through me, when there's a knock on my door. My whole body tenses up at the sudden noise. I rip Henry out of his favorite watering hole as fast as I can, which is a bad idea. I'm so wet the fucker slips and ends up flying into the one remaining lamp on the side of my bed. The lamp shatters to the floor making a loud crashing sound.

"Lisa, are you okay?" Darcie's muffled voice shouts through my door.

"I'm fine." I'm panting so hard I'm sure they can hear it in my voice. "Just give me a second." I roll off the bed onto the floor in search of Henry as my hand pushes against the radio, sending it into the wall. The force is so hard the radio breaks and I'm left in awkward silence, trying to get my shit together. "I'm coming!" At least I was.

After a few more seconds of hunting, I find him on the floor looking sad and lifeless. My finger flips the switch, waiting for the vibrations, which always bring a smile to face, but nothing happens. "Henry? No!" It's like a part of me has just died inside. I clutch him to my chest and shout so loud it sounds like I'm being murdered.

That's when my door bursts open. Darcie and Jodi take one look at me on my knees, cradling a blue dildo, and scream back at me.

I take in their bright orange appearance and let out another loud ass one myself. "Why do you look like a couple of oompa loompas?"

"Why are you on the floor?" Darcie shouts back. We both stare at each other, letting our minds come to terms with what we're seeing, which takes a while and a lot of blinking.

"Um…sleeping mishap." I hide Henry behind my back and stand to my feet, careful to avoid direct eye contact. I'm not ashamed of what I did. It's just I'm still in need and can't stand to have this conversation right now.

She studies me for a second and moves on to my question. "It's all this one's fault." Darcie points an angry orange finger at Jodi.

"Oh bollocks! How was I supposed to know the spray tan would do this?" Jodi gestures towards her and Darcie. "I made sure the bird behind the counter knew we wanted to look like a Cheeto."

"Cheeto?" Darcie's face freezes. "I told you to ask for the cheetah. The animal, not the damn chips. And they're actually called 'Cheetos' with an 's'."

"Flick my flaps and buy me a corndog. My bad, luv." Jodi smacks herself on the forehead. "I thought it was strange you wanted to look like a crisp."

"Maybe you can wash it off?" I attempt to be the voice of reason, which is something new for me. That never happens.

Darcie shakes her head. "Nope. If I scrub it I'll end up looking like I have a bad case of leprosy. I have to wait for this crap to wear off." She takes another glance at my disheveled appearance. Then her eyes glance down at my feet and her eyebrows pull together. "Is that your underwear?"

My head twists to look at my booted foot. Damn it! I knew I forgot something. My foot slides back in a poor attempt at hiding it at the same time I toss Henry on the bed.

Jodi's blue eyes light up as soon as she puts the pieces together. "You naughty bird. Were you self-serving?"

"Um…yes." I laugh and shake it off. My legs feel like jelly and I'm not ready to discuss my solo afternoon delight, so I change the subject. "What are we doing tomorrow?"

"Yoga!" Darcie claps her hands and grins. My insides shrivel up and die. Unless I'm sweating from riding some serious dick, I don't exercise. Kill me now.

6

After the sad disposal/burial of Henry and another hour spent on calming my 'Cheetos' sisters, I was able to attempt some sleep last night. It didn't come, though. Everything that touched my skin turned me on. I was ready to dry hump a table for some fucking relief. Nothing helped ease the need. I feel like an unused dick this morning. It's the only reason Darcie is able to enter my room and wake my ass up; usually it's the other way around and I have to say this isn't pleasant.

A giant smack echoes around my room, at the same time a sharp stinging pain hits my left ass cheek. "Cocksister wake up call!"

"Why are you up so damn early, Darce?" In my head I'm gagging her with Henry for some peace and quiet.

"Because we're on a time schedule. Yoga starts in an hour." She nudges the side of my mattress, making the whole bed bounce. A small part of me is starting to regret doing this to her in the mornings because I know she's paying my ass back.

My head lifts to see her wearing a pair of burgundy yoga pants, a grey tank top, and her blonde hair is pulled back in a neat ballerina bun. I'm impressed her Cheetos tinted skin coordinates with her wardrobe choices. She looks ready to conquer the day. I, however, am not. "You go and I'll stay here." I tug the blankets over my head and enjoy the darkness it brings, but it only lasts a second before Darcie's pulling them back down.

"Nope. I did a tour of the Jameson Distillery after flashing a stranger my tits for you, so you are going to get up and do this for me." Her hand comes down and cracks against my right ass cheek this time. Now my entire ass is stinging and I didn't even get laid.

"Fine. I'm up." I roll out of bed and head towards the bathroom. On the way, I stop to lick the side of Darcie's face and I'm a bit disappointed she doesn't taste like Cheetos.

"Gross!" She yells and tries to get me back, but her short legs are no match for my long ones—even with my boot.

I slam the bathroom door before she can get me back, and do my morning business. Once I'm finished, I head back out towards my dresser to grab some clothes.

Darcie's sitting on the edge of the bed watching my every move. She's like the damn yoga police. I do my best to ignore her and continue getting ready for this hour of torture.

The first pair of black yoga pants my fingers grab work for me. They're my tighter pair, so I whip off my underwear and throw them on the floor. I slide my boot off and sit in a red chair to pull the pants up my legs. Then I move on to a sports bra and navy tank top I found.

"Are you going commando?" Darcie watches me from the bed like I have a dick sprouting out of my ass.

It doesn't take me long to finish dressing and then I'm standing with my annoying boot back on. "You see all of this?" I reach back and smack my own ass. It's still tender from Darcie's love taps earlier, but I fight through the need to wince because I have a damn point to make. "Yoga pants can barely contain it. How can it accommodate my *chonies* too?"

She thinks on what I've said for a second and then nods her head. "I guess you're right. There's a reason I have to double strap the girls." She adjusts her boobs from inside the two sports bras she's wearing. Even underneath all that, she is packing some serious lady lumps.

Jodi struts into my room wearing a hooker red pair of yoga pants and a black tank top that says 'Cocksister' in matching red lettering across the chest, with her hair thrown up in a messy knot. Her skin isn't as orange as Darcie's, but it's still noticeable. She's carrying two cups of coffee, and a brochure is tucked under her armpit. She looks more like she's ready to go clubbing than to do yoga. And, to be honest, I'd much rather do that with her instead. "Bollocks! We need to hurry. I read the time wrong. Yoga starts in thirty minutes."

Darcie takes one of the steaming styrofoam cups from her hand and starts sipping it. I take the other one, but before I can even get a sip, Jodi's nudging me out the door. The movement of fabric against my bare bits causes sensation to erupt downstairs, which has me pausing and second guessing the no underwear idea. I don't get long to wonder because the motion of Jodi's tug causes the lip of my boot to catch on an uneven space on the carpet. My body wobbles, causing my coffee to fly out of my hand and on to the floor in the process.

"No!" I can't believe this has happened. This morning is not off to a good start at all.

"It's okay, luv. We'll ask room service to clean it up." Jodi pats my arm in comfort, but I haven't had any coffee yet. My brain isn't functional and rational thoughts aren't happening.

"It's not okay. First I don't get any morning dick and now my morning fuel is turning into a big shit stain on my carpet. I need coffee, stat, or I may murder someone." And I'm not even joking.

"Here. Take mine." Darcie takes one last big sip and then hands me her cup.

"Thanks, Darce. I love your face."

"Don't mention it." As we step out the door, she swings the straps of her dickbag around her shoulders and I fight the urge to cringe. I guess I'm going to have to play nice with that bag until I can dispose of it properly.

My mouth opens ready to unleash a smartass comment, but I think better of it. She did just give me her coffee. I press the cup to my lips and suck back a huge gulp. The second it hits my tongue, I cringe and spit the coffee out. I don't realize Darcie is still close to me, and it's now all over the front of her tank top. "Oopsie."

Darcie's standing frozen in shock. When she snaps out of it, she takes some napkins and starts wiping at the coffee on her shirt.

"I'm so sorry, Darce." I feel like such an asshole, but I will never swallow something that foul—ever.

"It's fine." She tilts her head to the side and focuses on wiping up the coffee mess. There's quite a bit, so one napkin isn't going to doing it.

"I got you, luv." Jodi takes a napkin from her and helps, mostly focusing on Darcie's chest area.

"Why does this taste like ass?" I wrinkle my nose and hold the abomination out for her to take back.

"It's decaf." Darcie sighs and takes the cup with her free hand while Jodi continues to wipe at her boobs. "I'm good, Jo. The girls are dry."

Jodi stops wiping and darts her head towards Darcie with her mouth hanging open. "Why the bloody hell are you drinking decaf?"

"I'm trying to cut back on my caffeine and drink more water. It's good to hydrate your skin." Darcie dabs at the few stray spots of coffee splattered on her neck.

This is blasphemy. "Caffeine is a nectar of the Gods. Drinking decaf is like having sex without an orgasm. There's no point."

"Yes! It's like wearing knickers when your loose flaps hang out." Jodi nods her head so hard the blonde knot on top of her head bobbles back and forth.

Darcie's eyes crinkle as she thinks on what Jodi's just said. I just roll with it, giving a supportive shrug and head tilt. "You guys are right." She grabs Jodi's dirty napkin and tosses them both back inside her bag. I make a mental note not to ever use one from her. "It does taste like ass."

"Of course we are, luv." Jodi grins as we continue down the hallway.

Once we exit the elevator and turn down the walkway, the smell of chocolate has my nipples perking up. "After yoga, we are going to get some chocolate."

"I thought you wanted dick?" Darcie has another attempt at adjusting the strap of her dickbag into a more comfortable position higher up on her shoulder, but it keeps falling back down.

"Chocolate and sex make the world go 'round. Since I haven't been able to enjoy a dick, there's nothing better than having a chocolate one in the mean time. Am I right?" I reach over and help Darcie with the damn strap because it's killing me to watch. The weight of the bag catches me by surprise. It's even heavier than last time. She must have all kinds of shit in there today.

"We must. I want a chocolate willy." Jodi claps her hands and bounces up and down like she's about to dive head first into a pit of balls.

When we reach the corridor, we hear music and strange animal sounds coming from one of the open doorways. We walk close enough to peek inside and it's not what any of us expected to see this early in the morning.

"What do we have here?" My lips spread into a wide grin. This room looks *interesting*. There are men on all fours biting down on leather bridles, wearing leather thongs. Nothing else. The women are dressed like S&M cowgirls in black leather bikinis, holding matching riding crops.

"Is that a horse tail coming out of his butt plug?" Darcie cocks her head to the side to gain a better view.

Jodi has the brochure open in her hands as her gaze flicks between that and the sight before us. "It's the pony play room." No sooner than the words are out of her mouth do we hear a few of the men neigh like a bunch of wild horses.

"The what?" Darcie's face contorts and I can't tell if she's shocked or interested. The gleam in her eye has me leaning towards interested.

What Jodi's saying makes perfect sense and clicks in my brain. "Fascinating."

"Yoga is in the next one." Jodi moves down to the next doorway and we follow, but not before I give the pony show one last glance. I must gaze a little too long because the next thing I know, Darcie's tugging me away by the back of my shirt.

"Can't blame a girl for looking." There's no stopping the shit-eating grin that appears on my face. I love this cruise!

"True, but I don't want to miss this class." She walks towards Jodi with a slight bounce in her step and stops at the open doorway.

When we walk into the room, we come to a dead halt. A few people stop and stare at us as we make our way further in the room. Their eyebrows shoot up to their foreheads as their gazes linger in our direction. It takes me a minute to realize they're staring at the orange disco balls next to me.

I ignore the stares and go back to checking out our surroundings. The space itself isn't much to take in. It's a traditional big white room with floor to ceiling mirrors. There are even a few mounted up on the actual ceiling.

Then we survey the rest of the room. There are bodies everywhere. I never thought there would be this many people interested in yoga, but seeing what I see now, I know why.

"Why aren't some of them wearing any clothes?" Darcie's jaw drops open so wide I'm surprised it's not popping out of its socket.

"Bloody amazing! You can see everyone's dangly bits." Jodi is smiling and not even attempting to hide the fact she's staring at the naked ones and their 'bits'.

I must admit I'm intrigued for this workout now. "You've been holding out on us, Darce. If we knew clothing was optional, we'd have come with you to this a long time ago."

"I didn't know they offered this either." Darcie's head tilts to the side as she studies one of the naked women stretching in the far back corner. The woman is bending in half into a bridge position, giving the entire room a preview of her goods. It's impressive as hell and going on my bucket list of things to try.

"That's the tits! I want to do that. It's like she can lick her own flaps." Jodi shouts so loudly it echoes against the walls. Everyone in the room stops what they're doing and stares at us.

Darcie blushes, and I laugh and pat Jodi on the back. "Same here, Cocksister. Can you imagine the possibilities of being able to do that during a cockride?"

"Loads." A devilish grin spreads across Jodi's face as her mind spins with ideas.

"I guess we should grab a spot before it gets too crowded." Darcie heads off to the right corner and sets her bag down. She grabs enough mats and bottles of water out of it for all three of us. Jodi and I both snag them and watch her reach back inside the bag for more stuff. This time she pulls out a towel for each of us too.

"What the hell do you have in there today?" It's like a magical dick-bag. I wonder what she'll pull out next?

"Stuff." She shrugs and sets out her mat. "I didn't think either of you would know what to bring, so I packed for all of us."

"Thanks, luv." Jodi places her mat down next to Darcie and plops down into a seated position.

"Yeah, thanks. It's a good thing one of us is always thinking ahead." I take my mat and do the same on Darcie's other side. The movement causes my clit to rub just right against the seam of my pants. That's normal, but when one isn't wearing any underwear and they're super sensitive from too much self-serving, it's an automatic orgasm inducer. A shiver runs through me and it's clear this shit is not going to get better on it's own. I'm debating on running out the door and vetoing this yoga shit. That's when a female voice I'm assuming belongs to the instructor shouts for everyone to take their places. Any plans of escape are officially lost to me now.

When I lift my head to focus on the instructor, my jaw drops. This is another unexpected surprise. Mistress K, aka Kristyn, is standing on the platform in nothing but her birthday suit, her rocking body on display—third nipple included—for all to see.

"Welcome everyone. Who's ready to get limber?" she yells across the room and it's hard not to react to her enthusiasm. Applause and cheers echo right back. I'm not even ashamed to admit Jodi and I are screaming the loudest. "Let's have a seat on our mats and begin." She takes a seat and sits Indian style with her hands in a prayer position.

Everyone quiets down and mimics her position. Jodi and Darcie have no trouble following, while I am not so lucky. Not only are my legs longer, but the boot around my foot makes it impossible to bend properly. After a couple of failed attempts, I give up and just bend my free leg. Lucky for me, we don't stay in this position long before we're moving on to a different one.

That's pretty much how the entire class goes, with the added bonus of a bunch of heavy breathing. It sounds like we're all balls deep in orgasms. This doesn't help the situation in my downstairs region at all. Sweat is dripping off my body and I'm not sure if it's from the positions or the raging inferno of hormones racing through me. I'm about to lose my mind when Kristyn calls out, "Plow Pose."

My attention shoots to Darcie for a clue on what the hell that even is. She lies back and swings her legs over her head until her toes touch the mat. Jodi does the same, with ease. Because of my boot and the fact my legs are longer, I have to use more momentum to get me in the right position. I end up getting stuck halfway and my legs are free dangling in the air. As my legs struggle to hit the floor, the friction of my yoga pants hits my magic bean just right. A small groan escapes me and the guy next to me takes it as a cry for help. I guess it is, but not the kind he's thinking.

"Let me give you a hand. First time can be tricky." Warm hands grab my legs and pull me the rest of the way. The force of the movement causes my clit to throb with need. I bite down on my bottom lip to keep from moaning again and giving him the idea it's him doing this to me.

Once my legs are in the right spot, I watch as he lies down and gets back into Plow Pose. Folding himself in half puts his junk right in front of his face. This wouldn't be too weird, but I'm thinking the fact he isn't wearing any clothes is. This takes my mind off of my current predicament for a brief moment.

"His willy is in his face!" Jodi's so excited she forgets to whisper. I knew she would notice and mirror my thoughts. This causes Jodi and I to snicker like children the rest of the time. I love my filthy Brit. Darcie does her best to ignore us, but I do catch her lips twitching. My head is stuck between my legs, but I see we've managed to gain a few dirty looks from the other people. Oopsie.

I'm not sure how long we stay in the Plow Pose before Kristyn's voice cuts through our giggles. "Now, let's lie down into Happy Baby." She eases back down, pulls her knees into her chest, and grabs the bottom of her feet.

We lie back and mirror her movement. Well, I get one leg in the right position. Our breathing is slow and steady as we relax our bodies into the stretch. This is not a good position for me. The pants have ridden up giving me an extreme camel toe. With every deep inhale I take, the thin material stretches, amplifying my urge downstairs. I'm fighting not to make a sound because the room is so quiet you could hear a dick drop.

On a deep exhale, Darcie lets one rip right beside me. "Oh no," she groans.

"It's okay, luv. Everyone's backdoors creak." Jodi does her best to make Darcie feel better, but I'm not sure telling everyone it was her is working.

I want to offer up some words of wisdom or change the subject, but I'm too busy fighting my own issue at the moment. My heart is racing as my fingernails dig into the sides of my legs. Every limb on my body is trembling as sweat trickles down the side of my face. Whether it's from the yoga pose we're doing or the sensation hitting me downstairs, I have no fucking clue. All I know is that I'm seconds away from orgasming in a room full of strangers.

The build up is forming. I can feel it pool deep within my belly. I attempt to take shallow breaths in an effort to ease the feeling, but it doesn't lesson the sensation at all. If anything it makes it worse. There's just no stopping it. I'm going to come from having a fucking camel toe.

I can hear people laughing at Darcie, but I'm lost in a fog of my own at the moment and nothing else is registering. Everything sounds like I'm in a tunnel. I hear sounds and see colors, but it's like I'm floating outside my body. Another small exhale leaves me and that's like the spark on a tip of dynamite for me. Tremors rock through me as I convulse and my hips thrust up of their own accord, riding the wave of release that's short-circuiting every nerve ending I have. A loud groan escapes from deep inside my throat as all the tension leaves my body and I don't even care who hears me.

Having an orgasm in the middle of a yoga class at the same time Darcie lets one go isn't our best circumstances, but shit happens and I don't think my heart rate has ever been so high. I lose track of time and what we're doing. Everything falls to the back burner as I become one with the floor with a smile on my face.

As soon as Kristyn says, "Namaste and enjoy your day," Darcie jumps to her feet and hauls ass out of the room in the opposite direction. If I could move, I would follow her lead, but my body is still enjoying the after effects of my orgasm. My head tilts towards the front of the room in time to see Kristyn stand and glance around the room. She's wearing a satisfied smile on her face like she was just thoroughly fucked, too. At that moment, a bald shiny head, aka Eric, peeks in the doorway and gestures for her to follow him. She gives a slight nod of the head and addresses the class.

"It seems someone is in need of Mistress K's services. Don't forget to come and see me at tonight's show." She winks and disappears out the door.

Once I can peel myself off the floor, Jodi and I grab our stuff and head out to check on Darcie. My body feels like jelly the entire way back to our rooms.

Back inside Jodi's room, we find the light on in the bathroom. I limp over and give the door a light knock. "You okay, Darce?"

The toilet flushes and I hear the water run a few seconds before she opens the door. She's cradling her stomach and slumping against the doorjamb. "Sorry. I only have this reaction to—" Her eyes dart to Jodi. "What type of creamer did you put in my coffee?"

"Some reduced fat goat's milk. Not that nasty cow stuff." Jodi plops down on her bed and bounces against it while she talks to Darcie.

"Fuck me in the ass with a goat!" Darcie rubs her temples. "You do know there's still lactose in goat's milk right?"

Jodi stops mid-bounce and stares at Darcie like she just told her she can never have dick again. "Really? Bugger. I didn't know that."

Darcie stares at Jodi a beat and nods her head. Situation settled, she turns her attention to me. "And what is going on with you?"

"I have no idea. Everything is on sensory overload." I gesture down towards my crotch. "Anything touches my magic bean and I explode. Ever since I was stung by the damn wasp, things have been intense. It's like I'm in need of some serious D.O.D. at all times."

"D-O-D?" Darcie's eyebrows crease together.

"Dick On Demand. Everything turns me on. I can't even rub my legs together without coming all over myself. I'm like a man with two dicks—over stimulated as fuck." I wave my hands around like a wild banshee.

Darcie studies me for a minute and then rushes to my room. Jodi and I follow her with a curious expression. She has my bottle of meds in her hand, reading the label, when she hears us approach and looks up.

"What?" I'm not liking the look she's giving me.

"It's a side effect from your steroids."

"Flick my flaps and buy me a cheesecake! Can I have some?" Jodi takes the bottle from Darcie and heads back into her room.

I turn my attention back to Darcie and do my best to contain my frustration, but it's boiling over. "Ugh! Well, I still need dick." My voice is sharp and loud. I'm pretty sure they can hear me in the next room, but I don't care. Getting laid has never been as dire as it is right now.

"Then let's go out tonight and fix that."

"Yeah?" My whole face lights up at her words. It's like Christmas, but with dicks—Dickmas.

Darcie presses her lips together in a big smile. "You took care of me when I had that whole shit happen with Richard. I've got your back, too. Cocksisters before misters. Tonight, let's get you dressed up and dicked up. I'm going to shower because I smell like a wet dog."

"Abso-fucking-lutely!" There's no hiding my excitement. I grin back at Darcie as she bounces back into her room.

"Check out the meatloaf he's packing!" Jodi shouts over the music, in between sucking back sips of her third drink. I'm thinking the combination of peach schnapps and vodka is going to hit her hard and fast in a bit.

"You think he stuffs his seam beast?" Darcie hiccups and laughs as her body shakes. I just hope her boobs stay inside her strapless dress. She's had one too many, but drunk Darcie is always entertaining. I'm just not telling her that gold clashes against her orange skin. At least Jodi went with a blue summer dress that compliments it. I hope that spray tan fades soon.

My head tilts to the side as I study the package of the cock candy in question. After our yoga escapade, we were wiped out and slept all afternoon. Now, we're back at the Wicked Tuna for some drinks and cockgazing. We arrived late, so we missed Mistress K's performance and I'm not sure if Darcie is upset about this or not. Judging by the gleam in her eye from staring at the guy's junk for the past few minutes, I'm sure she's good. The only thing I know is that I'm getting laid tonight and I am not doing all the damn work myself. I even came prepared for some action in my favorite form hugging black dress.

"Does it matter?" I lean back against my chair, but never take my eyes off the guy's ninja claw. "As long as the cockmeat sandwich makes my mouth water and satisfies my hunger, I'm good with whatever he's packing."

Darcie opens her mouth to say something when one of the two waiters that have been tending to our table comes by to check on us. Judging by the dusting of dark facial hair and deep blue eyes that are peeking out from underneath his mask, it's the mute one. The black mask covers the entire top half of his face, giving off a mysterious vibe. Add in the fact that he can't speak and I'm done for. I do love me a strong silent type. He gestures towards our glasses and the three of us are not so far gone that we don't know what he's asking.

"I need another Screaming Orgasm," Darcie shouts over the music, loudly enough to draw attention from passersby. A few of the women eye her up and down, but she's too focused on getting her next drink to notice.

Our waiter nods and smiles. The dark brown stubble around his chin moves, drawing me right in. Most of the time I prefer a clean-shaven face, but with a mouth like his I'll make an exception. He's cockoliscious and I want to lick him from head to toe.

"Another Tight Snatch for me, luv." Jodi licks her lips together and leans back in her chair.

I glance down at my half empty glass. One more drink won't hurt me either. "Pop My Cherry, please."

The corners of his eyes crease and his lips twitch as he fights the urge to laugh. Can't say I blame him. Coming up with names is part of the reason I love creating my own drinks.

Orders taken, he turns and heads towards the bar. I watch his ass the entire way. It's firm and I want a nibble. "He's definitely going on my fucket list."

Darcie's face scrunches together. "Fucket list?" She continues to slurp on her drink and stare at me. The glass is empty, but she's too drunk to realize this.

"It's like a bucket list, but with dicks." I lean in closer until it doesn't appear she's staring at two of me anymore.

"Yes. It's a list of all the willies you want to ride before you die." Jodi bobs her head along to the beat of the music as she plays with the straw of her drink.

"I've never had a fucket list." Darcie rests her head against her hand, squishing her cheek against her face while her eyelids begin to droop. She's getting more fucked up by the minute.

"Not to worry. You get to be balls deep in Carter cock anytime you want." I reach over and pat her on the back.

Her eyes pry back open. "That's true," she sighs. "I miss his cock." At that moment the same mute waiter comes back and drops off our drinks. Judging by the expression on his face, he's heard every word. Oopsie.

Once he's gone, Jodi decides it's time to give some helpful insight. She smacks her hand down on the table so hard we jump. "You need a BUC!"

Darcie shakes her head, as her eyebrows pinch together. "Gross. No way. I am not fucking a deer. Beastiality is not my thing." She sticks out her tongue and cringes.

Jodi and I look at each other and lose it. We laugh so hard we have tears and our sides hurt. "You crack me up, luv. Not a buck. A BUC. B-U-C." Jodi widens her mouth to accentuate each letter.

When Darcie's face remains blank, I take it upon myself to enlighten her further. "It stands for Back Up Cock, Darce." My cheeks hurt from laughing. It could be the alcohol, but I haven't laughed this hard in awhile.

"Oh." Darcie's lips purse together in an 'o' shape before she takes a small sip of her drink. "I'm more of a one cock at a time kind of girl. Besides, I could never find another man to give me the amount of orgasms that he does."

I prop an elbow on the table and lean against my hand. There's no stopping the sigh that escapes me. She's one lucky Cocksister. "I miss good sex that leaves you breathless like you've just climbed the shit out of Mount Everest."

"Me too. Can you imagine all of the poor birds who go their whole lives without gushing like a geyser." Jodi shakes her head, looking like someone just ate her last cucumber.

My head nods so hard I feel the strain in my neck, but this is tragic stuff. "It should be considered a state of emergency. Sex without orgasms is like riding a bike without a seat. Dangerous and should never be attempted." I raise my glass in their direction and do a spur of the moment toast. "To all our Cocksisters who are being let down by their misters." We're so buzzed it takes us a few attempts but eventually we manage to clank our glasses together.

Hours later, we're still going strong. Another round of drinks has come and gone and my bladder is at maximum occupancy. "I'm going to use the little girls room. I'll be right back." Mustering all of the drunken coordination I can, I slip to my feet and head off towards the restroom.

There isn't a long line, so I'm able to do my business and head back towards my table in a decent amount of time. I'm halfway towards the table when I feel a slight tug on my arm. My head whips up at the same time I make a fist, ready to kick someone's ass out. To my surprise and excitement, it's our hot as fuck mute waiter. "Oh, it's you."

His dark blue eyes hold mine as his lips spread into an orgasm inducing smile. It's enough to sober my ass right up. That mask makes him look dangerous and forbidden. He tilts his head to an open door behind him, letting me know exactly what he has in mind. Being the woman I am, I must indulge in all of it—ASAP.

My tongue licks along my bottom lip as I glance around to see if anyone is watching us. Most are busy doing their own thing. I swing my gaze over to my Cocksisters. They're busy tossing back more alcohol, having their own conversation. Something tells me I won't be missed by either of them any time soon. I turn my attention back to him and nod my head. Once I give him the go ahead, he doesn't waste a second yanking me inside the doorway.

There's no time to take in much of the room except all of the cleaning supplies and that it is small as shit inside. I'm thankful that the lighting sucks and I can't make out much else or I may be having second thoughts.

Mystery man spins me around, bringing my focus to him. He slams me up against the wall so hard the shelf next to us rattles. I don't have time to catch my breath before he's wrapping my legs around his waist and grinding his erection against me. He may be mute, but that doesn't stop him from getting his point across. With body language like this, who needs words at all? My hands brace against his shoulders for support. The roughness of his pants against my silk thong has me shivering. I'm ready to combust and he hasn't even touched me yet.

He grabs my wrists with one hand and pins my arms against the wall above my head. His other hand travels down south. A quick tug and my thong is ripped off. Where they go after that, I don't know and I don't care. The only thing that matters is that I'm finally going to get my cockride on. This is what I've been missing. Been craving. No woman should ever have to go without a decent dick for so long.

His blue eyes glow against the darkness of his mask and I can't look away. It's like I'm lost at sea, but in this case drowning is totally worth it.

I gasp as one of his fingers slides inside me, slow and deep. My gaze never leaves his as he continues a few more skilled strokes, rubbing my clit with the heel of his hand. He plays me like I'm a finely tuned instrument and he's the master conductor.

Pressure builds and my body can't hold out anymore. "I need to be fucked." There will be no foreplay. This is going to be quick and dirty, just the way I need it.

A smile spreads across his face as he tugs his zipper down. His hips tilt back and then he's slamming them forward, burying himself balls deep inside me. He gives me a second to get accustomed to the welcome invasion and then he's jack hammering into me like a madman.

Each thrust is wild and demanding. I'm getting wall burn from the friction and I'll wear that shit with pride, but it isn't enough. I still need more.

"Harder." My heels dig into his ass, adding more pressure. I'm wound tight and ready to explode. I just need a few more deep, hard thrusts.

Music pounds through the door, matching our wild rhythm. My heart feels like it's going to burst out of my chest from orgasmic bliss, and what a way to die.

A few more hard slams, and my back bows off the wall. I'm coming so hard I feel the sudden rush of warmth all the way down to the tips of my toes. My thighs clench tighter against him at the same time my insides squeeze the life out of his dick. I relax into the wall, enjoying the feel of him twitching inside me. We stay connected, staring at each other until our breathing returns to normal, his hands gently stroking my thighs the entire time. The way he's caressing me almost feels like we're lovers instead of a random hook up. It makes my heart ache for Logan. He must see the rush of emotions on my face because just as quickly as this started, he's fixed his clothes and shot out the door, leaving me without a backwards glance.

I shake off the feelings Logan always manages to stir as best I can and attempt to move. My body is limp and sated, making movement a struggle. When I think I can manage, I step towards the door. It's dark and hard to see where I'm stepping, so I tiptoe on my good foot, but it does nothing for my boot. I end up stepping on something slippery and my feet go out from under me. My arms flail as I reach for anything to grab onto, but there isn't dick in here. I'm going down and not in the way I prefer. On my way towards the floor, I hit the side of the yellow mop bucket. It tips over, causing the dirty water to spill all over me. If that isn't bad enough, whatever I slipped on flies up and lands smack dab in the center of my forehead, making a wet splatting sound as it does.

It takes a beat or two of lying there before I'm able to breathe again. I lift my arm and pull the shit off my forehead. Laughter rolls through me. It's the damn condom.

Wait…we didn't use a condom.

7

D<small>REAMS OF THE MASKED STUD</small> slamming into me play on repeat in my mind all night long. Needless to say, I've gotten the best night's rest ever. A thorough dicking helps any girl sleep like a drunk frat boy. Darcie and Jodi choke on their cockcakes as I fill them in on my adventurous night over breakfast. There was no time to fill them in last night. We passed out as soon as we hit our beds.

"Someone had a wild night," Darcie teases in between bites of food.

"I was just happy to get laid. The after effects of those damn steroids are finally out of my system. The other plus is my lady lips are fully functional again." I fidget with the napkin that's resting in my lap.

"Bloody hell! You had sex with a strange bloke and didn't make him wear a cock sock?" Jodi claps her orange hands together like a proud parent. She's on her third Screwdriver and I'm pretty sure she's feeling a nice buzz.

"I'm thinking mute may be the way to go with cockrides. It's all about the please me and leave me type for this girl from now on." My shoulders shrug and I attempt to play it cool, but inside I'm a mess. I still can't believe I forgot to make him cap it before I let him tap it.

That's never happened to me. I blame my lack of common sense on those damn steroids. I'm so glad I gave them to Jodi

Darcie leans her elbows against the table—the orange hue of her skin a bright contrast to the white tablecloth—and twists her lips to the side as she studies me. "Does this mystery ride mean you're over Logan?"

I take a moment to think over her words. Am I over him? Not at all, but she doesn't need to know that. My lips spread into a plastic smile. I'm about to do something that will have me sent to Cocksister Hell—lie to my friends. I pride myself on having no filter and speaking my mind, but admitting that one dick can make me so weak at the knees is something I'm not ready to do. It's best to stay in denial and forge ahead. "Logan who?" Before Darcie can say more, I shove a forkful of pancake into my mouth.

Jodi slaps me on the back. "Good for you, luv. There are plenty of men in the sea. You'll find the right seamen for you when you're ready." Jodi holds up her Screwdriver in a silent toast, and drinks.

"Don't you mean 'seaman'?" Darcie's eyes narrow into small slits.

"Nope. The more the better." Jodi winks and tosses back another huge gulp of Screwdriver. It doesn't escape my attention her words are missing their usual enthusiasm. I'm going have to ask her about it later.

I hold up my glass and do the same toasting motion, but my lips stay glued shut. The cockcake I was chewing on is going down my throat like sandpaper. I'm not a complete liar. I'll be over Logan soon. At least I fucking better be. I'm Lisa the cockslayer. I can't be hung up on a guy I only spent a handful of times with—even if they were some of the best orgasms of my life.

Darcie changes the subject and I could kiss her. "Where are we making port today?"

My current pre-dick-ament forgotten, I focus all my excitement on today's agenda. "Barbados. I signed us up for a tour of the Erection Confection Candy making factory. We won't even have to flash our tits to get in this time." I can't stop the huge smile that plasters across my face. I've been dying to go since I found out it was one of the stops on this cruise. Candy and cocks are two of my favorite things.

"Sounds fun. I'm sorry we couldn't make it to their shop yesterday. After the yoga incident, it was a while until I could leave my room." Darcie buries her face against her orange hands. Something tells me she won't be forgetting what happened anytime soon.

"No worries, Darcie. Shit happens." I wave off her apology. Neither of us was in the right frame of mind to admire chocolate dicks yesterday.

"Literally." Jodi snorts and swallows down the rest of her Screwdriver while our waitress brings her another one.

"You might want to slow down on those. I'm not sure if there's a bathroom on this tour." Darcie is always the voice of reason and common sense out of the three of us. Sometimes I wonder what shit Jodi and I would be in without her there to keep us straight.

"This is my last one. I promise." Jodi keeps her word and sticks to water the rest of breakfast.

Once we polish off our food, we dress and make port. The second we step off the ship there's a pep in my step. It could be from the amazing cock ride I had last night, or it could be from the fact I'm finally going to enjoy the taste of chocolate dicks melting in my mouth.

From the second we step inside the factory into the small holding room, our senses are on sugar overload. Even through the solid metal door the goodness seeps out.

The group we're with is a bit larger than I'm used to, but as long as we have fun, I could care less. It's a melting pot of individuals. I'm more surprised by the amount of males, but no judgment here. We clearly share the love of dicks in our mouth and that makes them my tribe. Jodi and Darcie both give me orange thumbs up, coming to the same conclusion.

All conversation ceases at the sound of a deep voice coming from the platform in the front of the room. "Welcome to Erection Confection, where the candy is always hard and makes your taste buds moist. My name is John Thomas." He's a nugget-sized, elderly African-American man, bald and wearing a pair of the thickest coke bottles I've ever seen. It's amazing he can see anything at all.

Jodi snickers next to me. "Bloody hell, who named that poor sod?"

Darcie and I share a blank look. Either Jodi's still drunk from breakfast or we're missing something. My eyebrows narrow as I turn my attention over to Jodi. "We're not following you, Jo?"

"His name is also known as a blokes knob back home." Jodi thinks she whispers out of the side of her mouth—she really does—but that's not at all the case. Indoor voice is not in her vocabulary and she's too excited to be quiet.

The room goes silent at her words. People in front twist around and give us a once-over. Judging by the constipated glares, they don't appreciate the commentary or they're awestruck by Darcie and Jodi's glowing orange skin. Oopsie. Our bad.

I forget about them and take in more of John's appearance. Things are starting to make even more sense about his name. He has one of the most wrinkled foreheads I've ever seen. There's so much excess skin hanging around that it resembles saggy foreskin. "He's even got forehead skin." The words tumble out of my mouth before I can even process what I'm saying.

"Is that a thing?" Jodi's face perks up at the new phrase. Excitement radiates off of her and I bet my left tit she's picturing herself stroking his forehead skin.

"Apparently so. I wonder if they can castrate one's forehead." I'm putting way more thought into this than necessary, but I can't help it. It's the way I'm wired.

"That's called a facelift." Darcie presses her lips together as she fights the urge to laugh.

The metal doors part and John Thomas leads us into a hallway. There are two doors: one for males and one for females.

"In order to fully enjoy your backstage experience and to protect the quality of our product, we require each visitor to wear a set of scrubs." He sweeps his hands out towards the doors. "Through there you'll find everything you need. Please come back out here when you're ready and we'll resume our tour."

Single file, we do as we're instructed. Inside the room there are sets of white scrubs, a matching hat and blue gloves for each of us. We toss the scrubs on over our clothes, while the hat takes some work. With long hair it's a pain in the ass process. After fucking with it for a few minutes, I'm finally successful. When I glance over at Darcie and Jodi, it's an interesting view. Darcie's still trying to pull up her scrubs, while Jodi is a different story entirely.

When I grab my gloves, I find I have an extra pair. "Look who got extra gloves." I stuff them in the pocket of my jeans because who knows when I'll need them.

"What are you going to do with latex gloves?" Darcie frowns. She's thinking way too hard on this.

"I don't know, but a game of doctor is going on my fucket list." My lips curl into a wide smile.

"Same here." It's like Jodi and I are from the same planet. She always knows what crazy shit I'm thinking.

Darcie's eyes narrow as the two of us focus on Jodi. She blows up one of her gloves until it resembles a decent sized ball sack and holds it in front of her crotch. "Look at that! I have four willies."

"You look more like a mutant smurf." I take a finger and stroke each one of the 'willies'. "They're a bit smaller than Henry, but I think they'd get the job done just fine."

"I can't take either of you anywhere." Darcie shakes her head at us, but breaks out laughing at the same time. "Speaking of Henry, when are you getting a new one?"

"I don't know." Up until now I haven't given Henry much thought. I'm sure my nameless cock from last night has lots to do with that. Still, I'm going to need something to supplement the real thing incase of another dry spell. "Vibrators are like pets."

"Irreplaceable?" Darcie cocks her head to the side, no doubt trying to understand where I'm going with this. Truth be told, I don't even know it until the shit's out of my mouth.

"In need of lots of love and continuous stroking." I wriggle my eyebrows and flash her a cheesy smile.

"That was my other guess." Darcie nods her head and slips the white hat on. She flares out her arms and strikes a pose. "How do I look?"

I tilt my head to the side and give her a thorough once over. "Like a walking sperm."

"Ditto, twat face." She slaps my shoulder and laughs.

"I'm a walking jizz factory." Jodi bends into a deep squat and twerks her ass back and forth. The other women rush past her like she's a flaming dick that's going to kill them in their sleep, and out the door. Darcie and I enjoy the show that is Jo a bit longer before we nudge her out into the hall.

We're still laughing when we join our group and hear a familiar voice. "Christ! Who let you in?" Kate body checks Jodi and smiles. She and Tre are wearing the same white ensemble as the three of us.

"You birds fancy chocolate dicks, too?" Jodi's blonde head darts back and forth between the two of them

"Those are just about the only dicks ever making it past these lips." Tre points to her mouth and smacks her lips together at the same time to emphasize her point.

Our snickering is cut short when one of the guys in front of us hands me a small box with a slit across the top. "What's in here?"

"Face masks." He rolls his eyes as he places the mask over his face. I take one out, pass the box around and do the same. The smell of musty mothballs hits me and I fight the urge to gag.

"Are you ready for the best mouthgasm of your lives?" John Thomas laughs so hard at his own joke his forehead skin jiggles from side to side.

Darcie rolls up onto her toes and cranes her neck to gain a better view. "I hear him, but I can't see a damn thing."

"The doors are opening. Get ready for some Cocksister fun." It really pays to be the tallest one sometimes.

John Thomas leads us down the hall to a wall of windows that show a mini video on the history of the factory and how delicate the process of picking the perfect cocoa beans for their chocolate is. This I can appreciate. It's the same with myself spending endless hours with my alcohol concoctions. My damn boot echoes against the linoleum with each step I take, but I do my best to ignore it. This will not bring me down today.

Things are moving along great. I'm learning so much on the involved process of turning these little things into the tasty treats we love. The chocolatey goodness is basically the sperm of the cocoa bean. And this girl enjoys swallowing both types of jizz.

Half way through the tour, we're watching them mold their hard penis candies when Jodi begins bouncing on her feet. The mask is blocking half of her face, but her eyes are beginning to water. "Everything okay, Jo?"

"No. I need to visit the loo." She crosses her feet and clenches her thighs while she grabs herself. It's an adult version of the pee pee dance.

"I told you to ease up on those Screwdrivers." Darcie glances around for our group, but they've already disappeared around the corner. Even Tre and Kate, who were hanging back with us, are gone. "Can you hold it until the tour is over?"

"Not bloody likely." Jodi sucks in a deep breath, causing the mask to suction against her face, and bends over. Her skin is beginning to turn more green than orange. "I need to piss like a racehorse."

I put my hands up to stop her from taking off and running around like her pants are on fire. "Don't worry. We'll find you a bathroom."

"At this rate I might have to make my own water closet in the nearest corner." She's clenching her fists and bouncing around like a dangling dick.

"Not to worry. I got you." I nudge her and Darcie to follow me along the corridor. I'm not sure where the hell we're going, but there has to be a bathroom around here somewhere. We stay on the path and follow the direction we think our group went in, but keep coming up empty. There have been several dead ends that have us all twisted around. Every time we come to a set of doors and I think we're good, it turns out to be a damn storage closet. It feels like we've been walking forever. Not sure how we'll find our way back out of here, but right now the only thing that matters is finding Jodi a bathroom. Judging by the loud groans behind me, we're running out of time before there's a yellow puddle of piss for us to follow.

"Deep breaths. In. Out." Darcie helps her walk as she rubs her back and coaches her to take each step. Each breath they take has them making a Darth Vader sound beneath the masks.

I feel for Jodi. There's nothing worse than having a full bladder and nowhere to go. "What's with the Lamaze breathing? She's not in labor, Darce." My attention stays straight ahead, hoping our luck changes soon.

"Bloody fucking feels like it." Jodi groans so loud I'm afraid we're going to get caught sneaking around.

"Where the hell are the fucking bathrooms?" The stress is starting to get to Darcie. She wipes at her forehead and pats Jodi on the back.

My head whips around, hoping like hell this is it because I'm running out of places to look, and we're in luck. "Found it!"

Jodi barrels past me, barges through the door, plops down and does her business. Darcie and I lean against the wall and wait outside. Another Cocksister crisis averted. Minutes later she comes out wearing the biggest smile.

"All good now?" Darcie pushes herself off the wall and waits for Jodi's answer.

"Never better." Jodi blows out a sigh as her whole body sags, and pats her belly a couple of times.

Darcie glances down at her bare hands. "What happened to your gloves?"

"I may have leaked on them, so I had to throw them in the trash bin." Jodi throws her hands up in the air, demonstrating her reasoning.

"Not to worry. I still have that extra pair." I pull the waistband of my scrubs down and dig inside the back pocket of my jeans. "Here you go."

"Thanks, luv." Jodi takes them and slips her hands inside.

"Now, lets go find our group." I clap my hands together and start walking. Where to, I have no clue, but I'm sure it will lead to somewhere.

"Do you know where you're going?" Darcie asks.

"No clue, but I'm taking us back the way we came. What could go wrong?" I shrug my shoulders and keep walking. Maybe I'm too stubborn for my own good, but I just know I'm heading in the right direction. I can feel it.

We continue walking around another series of winding halls and nothing is looking familiar at all. This is not good. I should say something, but I don't want to worry Darcie unless it's necessary. Instead, I push on and keep us heading in what I assume is the right direction. I don't even see any candy making machines anymore.

"I don't think we're in dicktopia anymore." Darcie's voice invades my head, mirroring my thoughts.

"Maybe we're in the boiler room?" At least I hope that's where we are.

"Do candy factories even have those?" Leave it to Jodi to be the voice of reason right now.

I'm about to panic when I finally see a couple of guys in expensive suits standing in front of a door. They look like they're straight out of a mafia movie, which is a little odd, but who am I to judge? Both have their hair slicked back with enough grease to lube an entire village of dicks. One is about my height and the other one is slightly shorter. I sag my shoulders and walk in their direction. Help has finally arrived.

The shorter guy in the suit takes one look at us and his whole body stiffens. "Hey!" It's clear by the look on his face we're in deep shit and not supposed to be in here. Then he lunges towards us.

"Oh shit!" I push Darcie and Jodi back the way we came and move as fast as my gimp ass can. "That's not the way. Go back!" I spin on my good foot and hobble back the way we came.

Jodi stops so fast her shoes slide against the linoleum and go out from under her. Darcie and I hook our arms around hers and drag her back up to her feet before she can hit the ground. The sudden rush of adrenaline has given us a serious muscle boost. We haul ass back in the opposite direction, well at least I think we are. My handicap hasn't slowed us down too badly. By some miracle, I'm keeping up with their short asses just fine.

When it becomes painful to breathe, we stop and suck in all the oxygen we can. I glance back and Mr. Angry Suit Guy is nowhere to be found.

"I think we lost him." My body's hinged at the waist as I try to stop myself from hyperventilating. I'm not cut out for running like this. My mask moves back and forth with each breath I take. "That was close."

"Who the bloody hell was that bloke? He looked cheesed off." Jodi sounds just as winded as I am. If her mask weren't blocking most of her face I would know for sure.

"No idea, but let's not hang around and wait for him to find us." Darcie is the only one who sounds like she could go for another five mile run and it almost makes me wish I worked out as religiously as she does—almost.

Our legs only make it two steps when a woman's stern voice stops us. "Where are you three going? You're late. Evening shift started an hour ago."

We spin around to face the wrath of a woman twice our age. Every line is visible on her face and she looks like she's been starving herself for years. The hollows of her cheeks are sunken in like a couple of craters, while the loose skin around her neck resembles a vagina.

"Lunch break?" All this excitement has my brain scrambled and I can't think of anything else but that lame ass excuse.

Her face pinches tighter as the vagina that is her neck spasms with each swallow. It takes everything in me not make a comment and I'm damn proud that I manage not to. Adulting win for this girl.

"Lunch isn't for another couple of hours. Follow me." She takes us through yet another door and into a room with a ton of machines and moving parts. "Your station's over there. You need to collect and sort the sweet from the sour candy coated penises." I'd like to say the three of us don't snicker like teenage boys at their first sight of boobs, but I'd be lying my ass off. With that, she leaves us to our own devices, which is never a good thing.

Our station is a decent sized counter with a small conveyer belt that runs down the back end of it. All I see are buttons and knobs I have no clue how to work. "How the hell do you start this thing?"

"Just push a button. It's bound to make something work." Darcie ogles the equipment with equal fascination. When it comes to the electrical stuff she's as lost as I am.

"You push that little lever and Bob's your uncle." Jodi reaches over and slaps a button. I brace myself, waiting for something to go wrong. To my surprise, it doesn't. Candy starts to come out slow and steady. Between the three of us it's not so bad. If my bar idea fails maybe I have a shot as a candy girl.

"Bloody amazing! I want one of these for home." Jodi's eyes are like giant saucers. I nod my head because she's right. It would be kick ass to have one of these for home.

Then Jodi hits another button and the machine moves faster. Shit starts whipping down the conveyer belt one after the other, so fast that my eyes can barely keep up. It's like a rogue treadmill that's spitting out bags of dicks at warp speed. This can't end well.

"What did you do, Jo?" I can't keep up this quick pace for much longer.

"I just helped it along a little. It was going too slow." She shrugs. Too slow my ass!

Darcie and I scramble to grab the candy before we miss one, but it's damn near impossible. I begin grabbing them by the handfuls and dropping them in piles on the counter in front of me. Sweat beads down my neck, but we catch up and perfect a rhythm.

Commotion near the front catches my attention and my stomach drops. Mr. Angry Suit has found us. "Shit! It's been fun, but I think it's time to go." My heart pounds as another burst of adrenaline shoots through me. Darcie and Jodi look towards the door and spit out a strong line of F-bombs.

We start to move, but Jodi stops. She grabs a handful of candy dicks and moves to shove them in her pockets, but her scrubs are in the way.

"What are you doing?" Judging by the tone in Darcie's voice and the look on her face, Jodi may want to reconsider.

"I'm grabbing some dicks for later, luv. You never know when you'll need a good willy in your mouth." She has a point, but I think she may be going a bit overboard with the amount of free willies she's taking. Candy coated willies are poking out in between her fingers.

"That's stealing." Darcie waves a finger at her.

"No, it's wages earned for all of this." Jodi gestures to the massive piles of candy we've done a half ass job sorting.

"Fine. You can take one handful. Put the rest back." Darcie's stern tone brooks no argument. Only these two would bicker over stealing dicks. Jodi listens and sets back down the excess. The rest go in her bra.

"Can you guys argue about this later?" Sometimes it's like dealing with a couple of toddlers. "We need to get the hell out of here."

That shuts them up. The three of us peel away from the machine, towards the back of the room to a dark corner, and find an emergency exit. We slip through the crack and welcome the sight of the sun and fresh air. The second we take off the outfit and masks they gave us, I feel much lighter. We stuff them in a trashcan next to the door and catch our breath. From past experience we know stopping now isn't smart, so we keep moving until our asses are back on the ship and safe in my room.

"Flick my flaps and fist my muff, that was a hoot." Jodi plops down on my bed next to Darcie and reaches into her bra, pulling out the bags of candy she stole.

"The guy guarding the door was insane. It's just a candy recipe, not a sex toy."

"Maybe they're protective of their secret recipe, luv?" Jodi eyes the candy on the bed. Just like that our short attention span is diverted and we're all focused on the tiny dicks. "These wee willies look scrummy." She rips open the package and bites down on one. Her muffled crunching gives me more time to wrap my head around what happened.

Darcie holds out her hand towards Jodi. "Willy for a friend?"

"Of course." Jodi hands her a couple and then passes some to me. I toss a candy-coated dick in my mouth and chomp down on it.

"This was an experience I won't forget anytime soon." I'm excited to see what fun we find when we hit the beachside bar tonight.

8

SAND SQUISHES BETWEEN THE EXPOSED toes of my one flip-flop while getting stuck and causing irritation in the boot on my other foot. The brochure said it was a casual bar, so the three of us dressed simply: skirts, tank tops, and flip-flops. No Southern California girl goes anywhere without a decent pair of flip-flops. Or in my current case, a single flip-flop.

We stand at the entrance enjoying our view. I wasn't sure what to expect with an island bar on a beach, but this place is better than anything I could have imagined.

Massive piles of dried palm leaves rest on top of bamboo sticks as a roof. Tiki torches and some white string lights are wrapped around the bar area. Multi-colored lanterns hang from the ceiling as additional lighting, setting a romantic mood. The bar is a decent size and made completely out of bamboo sticks. Swings attached to the roof align the entire bar and are something my drunk ass will be enjoying later. Dozens of small circular bamboo tables are spread out along the sides of what I assume is their dance floor. Off in the corner is something that grabs my attention and has me ready to pounce.

"Is that a giant mechanical dick?" Darcie points to the cause of my excitement.

"Hells yeah, it is. Now that's a cockness monster, Darce." I clap my hands together and admire the brass colored masterpiece. The amount of detail has this Cocksister appreciating every mouthwatering inch. A roadmap of veins travels down to a perfect mushroom tip. There's even a pink horse saddle on top of the balls with a pair of stirrups. "I'll be riding the shit out of it later, too." It's better than climbing on top of a bull any day.

"This place is the dog's tits!" Jodi's head whips around the bar wearing a smile like she's just been smacked in the face with a thousand dicks and she couldn't be happier about it. Having the night sky and ocean as a backdrop only adds to the awesomeness of this view.

"It's like Cocktoberfest." I grin and find us a table that's an equal distance from the dance floor, the bar, and the bathroom. Location is everything when one is out with her girls.

A topless waiter comes and takes our drink orders before moving on to the next table. He's cute, but nothing compared to the masked hunk who pounded the shit out of me last night. My body clenches at the thought of a repeat performance.

"What's with your look?" Darcie is too perceptive for her own good sometimes.

I relax my face muscles and give her my best blank expression. "What look?"

"The one that says you're still dickmatized by the bloke who shagged your muff last night." Leave it to Jodi to call me out on my shit.

"Fine. Maybe a part of me is hoping I run back into him on the ship. Is there something wrong with me?" I chew on the inside of my lip and feel like such a horny bitch right now.

"Not at all." Darcie shakes her head.

"Nothing wrong with enjoying a good go around with some hot community cock." Jodi's voice carries, earning some odd looks from other patrons and of course, it's also the exact moment our waiter appears with our drinks. Oopsie.

"My only problem is that once wasn't enough. This Cocksister needs more. It's like the older I get the more penetration I need. I'm so horny I'd fuck a doorknob. I think I may have blue balls." I rest my elbows on the table and cradle my glass.

Darcie scrunches up her nose. "I don't think women can actually get blue balls."

"Then what would the female equivalent be? Blue waffle?" I take a long sip of my drink and let my words marinate inside her head. With the amount of drinking we've been doing on this trip so far, it's a must.

Jodi bobs her head back and forth between the two of us like we've just grown dicks for noses. "What is a blue waffle? Some weird type of American breakfast food?"

"Not exactly." Color flushes Darcie's face. Her orange spray tan is starting to fade, so her cheeks turn dog dick red.

My lips twitch, but I force my smile down. "I'll show you later, Jo." This answer seems enough for her because we move along to another topic.

We spend the next hour and several rounds of drinks discussing our lives and their lack of dick. It's nice being able to just drink and hang out with your girls. Jodi's attention keeps diverting towards a blond guy at the front of the bar. Blonds aren't my type, but this one is worth jumping on the cocktrain express for.

"See something you like, Jo?" I pride myself on being a Cocksister Cupid of sorts, and if she's interested I'll do my damndest to help her out.

"Maybe." A long sigh escapes her and I'm not liking the body language. The self-confident, cock slaying Jodi is missing. This is deeply concerning.

"What's with the sigh?" Darcie didn't miss the body language either.

"I think Ryder broke my muff. He was the whole package—trailer parks and red solo cups." She hangs her head. "I've found a few knobs that looked fun, but nothing happened. It's like every bloke I see makes my minge cringe."

"Aw, Jo. Don't say that. I'm sure your—" Darcie waves her hand in the vicinity of Jodi's crotch, "—muff is just fine."

"You're right." She sucks in a deep breath and puts on a plastic smile. "It's not like we had a chance. I mean, I'll be going back to England after this and he lives in the states."

It's not at all like her and we can't have that. It's time for some Lisa love. "You can bang any guy here. You are beautiful, Cocksister. Remember that. Stick your chesticles out and go grab any hunk by the dick." I wave a finger in front of her face; I'm just not sure it's the right one because I'm beginning to see at least three of her.

"Only if he consents," Darcie, ever the voice of reason throws out.

"I guess that would be good, too." I shrug.

"You're both so bloody right. A bloke would be lucky to munch on this." Jodi leans back and gestures at the crotch of her skirt. Her words are slurring as badly as my brain. That's a dead giveaway that the bartender knows their shit and we are indeed getting drunk off our asses.

"That's right. And you're not alone. Darcie wishes she was balls deep in some Carter cock right now." I tilt my glass in Darcie's direction.

"I really do." She nods her head so hard I'm surprised she doesn't develop and bad case of whiplash. "I need a dickover."

I raise my glass in the air and give one of my off the fly toasts. "Here's to a dicktastic night!"

Darcie and Jodi hold up their glasses and do the same. I toss back the rest of my drink and slam the empty glass on the table. Tonight is going to be an adventure. I can feel it.

Hands brace the table from behind and there's a sudden rush of warmth at my back that wasn't there before. My head tilts back, making contact with a hard chest, followed by a familiar phallic-shaped mole. "Dance with me, Coxy." Justin's brown eyes darken as his gaze travels down my body, and I do the same. I may not be into him, but a girl will always look. He's replaced his leather thong with tight leather pants and a white button up shirt that he's left undone. He looks like a Princess Bride extra—weird mustache and all.

Jodi nudges my arm, spilling a bit of her drink on my lap and cutting into my package check. "Take your own advice and throw him a bone, luv. He looks like a lost puppy."

I must be more fucked up than I thought because I actually listen to her advice. My hand slips into his and I let him lead me to the dance floor. I sway and almost trip a few times along the way, but he catches me and keeps me upright.

Couples are grinding against each other to some island beat, but the music switches as soon as we enter the dance floor to *Despacito*—the Justin Bieber version. The timing is too perfect for this to be a coincidence. I cock my head back and arch an eyebrow up at him. "What did you do?"

His lips twitch, causing the curled ends of his mustache to wiggle. He tugs on my hand and pulls me up against his chest. "I figured this song was a perfect fit. Like us." Dark eyes bear down on me, and Jodi was right. He wants a trip to pound town. I better set this shit straight before he gets any other ideas.

"One dance, Justin, and that's it." I hold up a finger—at least I think it's one—and try my hardest to sound stern. Either I'm drunker than I thought or my blue balls is fucking up my brain because I sound like a panting wimp and Justin is unaffected by it.

"Whatever you say, Coxy." His nose grazes the side of my cheek causing the little hairs of his mustache to tickle my skin. His hands squeeze my hips in a firm grip and maneuver them back and forth, as we dance like we're the only two people in the room.

Together we move as one to the slow, steady rhythm. One thing I can say about Justin is he makes up for his lack of skills in the bedroom with his awesome dance moves. My hips shimmy around until my back is to him. Justin wastes no time in taking advantage of this position. He yanks me back against his groin and I can feel his hard dick between my ass cheeks.

Alcohol is the only reason I can think of for why I haven't put a stop to this yet. I've been on this ride once before and know how it ends. I'm not doing it again.

The more I move, the more the room starts to spin and go out of focus. My head begins to feel heavy as it falls against his chest. The mixture of humidity and all these bodies moving is causing some serious sweat to drip down my neck.

Justin fists my hair and arches my neck further back until my mouth is exposed to him. "You look beautiful tonight, Coxy." He bends down and brushes his lips against mine. The kiss is slow and sweet, but the fine hairs of his mustache are making my nose itch like a motherfucker. Not at all what I was expecting. Perhaps Justin has learned some new moves since high school. He kisses his way down my cheek towards the side of my face. Then his tongue thrusts inside my ear. This is meant to be sexy, but it's not. It makes me cringe and come out of my lust-filled fog. And he was doing so well…

I use the tempo change as an excuse to twist out of his grip and face him. That's a much safer distance. No more wet willies from this position. Justin isn't having it and nudges closer against me once more. There's no room between us at all now. The warmth of his breath brushes against the side of my face and I realize I need to do something quick or I'll be subjected to another tongue lashing in my ear. I raise my arms over my head and get lost in the music until the last note fades.

"I need some water." *And to wipe the spit out of my ear.*

When we make it back to the table Darcie and Jodi have switched out their liquor for water. Darcie takes one look at my sweaty face and nudges a glass towards me. I give her a nod of thanks and down the entire glass. Justin takes the vacant chair next to me and gives me a wide grin.

We make some small talk and keep the conversation light. I'm not a total asshole. I won't kick him straight to the curb after a dance.

"So, how did you end up working on a cruise ship?" I take another sip of water and let the cool liquid run down the back of my throat.

"I was working on Ball Street when one of the cruise directors came up to me after a show and offered me a lot of money to do what I had been every night, but this way I get paid to work while I travel and see different places—places most people would kill to see." Justin leans his elbows against the table, causing the open collar of his shirt to shift and expose a good amount of chest hair.

I open and close my mouth a few times, but there's really nothing for me to offer on this subject. Justin seems unfazed by this and continues talking for several minutes about anything and everything. Halfway through our conversation, he holds up a finger and motions towards a guy in a dimly lit corner of the bar. The guy comes forward and bends down next to his ear as the two converse. The music is too loud for me to hear what they're saying, so I distract myself with trying to make out the new guy's appearance. He's not bad looking, but the lighting isn't the best for me to get a good look. He pulls a bag out from inside his dinner jacket and tosses it on the table in front of Justin. Without another word, he spins on his heel and heads back the way he came, but not before I catch a quick glimpse of what looks like a crescent shaped scar on the side of his neck.

Justin grabs the bag, bringing my attention back to him. The corners of his mouth twist up into a wide grin. "I know how much you love chocolate and I managed to snag some of these from the candy factory for you." He holds the bag of chocolate dicks out to me and I die.

The fact that he remembered my love of chocolate makes my belly flutter— or it could be the alcohol. "That's so sweet. Thank you so much." I kiss his cheek and waste no time in popping a dick in my mouth. A full mouth means he can't attempt to kiss me again. Darcie and Jodi both help themselves to the mountain of chocolaty goodness as well. After another glass of water, we switch back to alcohol. Chocolate just goes better with liquor.

I'm not sure how many chocolates I consume in between rounds of drinks, but my whole body feels like I'm floating on a cloud of dicktastic proportions. I lift my hand to grab another one when I glance down. "Oh shit! I have seven fingers. Why is my skin purple?"

"Because you're a giant bloody eggplant." Jodi laughs so hard she falls out of her chair.

"A talking eggplant." Darcie snorts and leans forward. Her hands come to my mouth and she makes my lips move like I'm a damn puppet. "Suck my eggplant." Her voice comes out much deeper, like she's somehow grown a dick in the last few minutes. I do my best to stare at her face, but she's got two heads and I'm not sure which one I should be looking at. Justin snorts, but I ignore him because this situation takes precedence.

I open my mouth to tell them where they—all of them—can shove their eggplant when she comes back into focus. "Why do you have scales?" My hand comes up and strokes her skin. "You're so green and pretty, like a gecko." I rest my head on her shoulder and sigh.

Jodi climbs back up to her chair and braces against the table. Her face is covered in sweat as she shakes the material of her tank top back and forth like a fan. "Bollocks! It's hotter than sweaty balls in here. I need some water." She grabs the pitcher of water off the table and downs it all in one go. Water drips down her face, but she doesn't give a fuck. She swallows like the champ she is. Then she starts spitting it out in a slow stream. "I'm a spitter."

I throw a napkin at her face. "You look more like a drippy dick than anything."

Darcie screams. "Everyone is staring at us!" She begins to hyperventilate. "Why are they looking over here?"

"Bollocks! They know I stole the candy. We have to get out of here." Jodi stands up so fast our empty glasses knock over.

"We need to hide." I slip underneath the table and hold onto the leg for balance. "Quick! Get under here. They won't find us." My hands wrap around their wrists and pull them down with me. The three of us huddle against each other as our heads whip back and forth.

Justin bends at the waist and smirks down at me. "What are you doing, Coxy?"

"Sh. We're hiding. We can't let them find us." I press my finger against my lips in an attempt to silence them.

"We're too pretty for prison," Darcie shouts from behind me. "I don't want to end up someone's bitch."

The corner of Justin's mouth twitches. "No one is coming to get you, any of you."

"You sure?" My fingers tighten against the table leg and I try to ignore the fact his mustache has come alive and is inching across his face like a damn caterpillar.

He studies me for a few beats before he nods his head. Relief floods through me at his words, but I still don't move. It takes a few more minutes of coaxing before he's finally able to get all three of us out from underneath the table and back in our seats.

"That was a bloody close one." Jodi blows a puff of air out of her mouth as she plops back in her chair.

Then a buzzing noise in the corner catches our attention and all is forgotten. It sounds like a maximum strength vibrator. Our heads whip around and we almost die of excitement. One of the bar employees has started messing with the mechanical dick. All previous thoughts are lost the second I see that big cock in motion. I hop out of my seat and strut towards the bronze perfection, with Darcie and Jodi hot on my heels. We only have to grab onto a few tables for support along the way.

Justin strolls behind us, wearing an impish grin the entire way. We stop and admire the bronze masterpiece, my hands gliding along every seam and ripple. This thing is fucking amazing. It's cocktastic perfection at its finest.

"Hop on, Coxy," Justin whispers against my ear.

I waste no time sliding on and putting my feet in the stirrups. "Dick me up, Scotty!" At my command, Justin jerks his chin and the employee hits the button. My hips buck and roll with the motion. It's one hell of a feeling. People are screaming and cheering me on. It's the ride of my life. Still smiling, I hop down and slap the employee on the shoulder. "Thanks." He toys with the ends of his mustache and winks at me.

Jodi bounces up and down. "Let me have a go at that huge willy!" Her mouth is damn near drooling, but I'm more distracted by the antennas growing out of her head. What the fuck? I close my eyes and shake my head. When I open them they're no longer there. I must be losing my mind.

Jodi rubs her hands together before she does a running sprint and jumps onto the dick with the precision of a professional gymnast. Who knew our dirty Brit had such slick moves? Darcie and I clap our hands as we cheer her on. She sits upright, one hand on the pink saddle and one in the air like a professional bull rider. The second it's in motion

Jodi's all business.

"My turn." Darcie swallows the last of her chocolate, wipes her hands on her skirt and climbs onto the giant dick. I'd say it was graceful, but nothing about this is. She does an awkward jump and lands with her body bent forward, facing the back. Her skirt is up over her ass, giving the entire room quite a view.

"You're facing the wrong way, Darce." I motion with my hands for her to turn around even though it does no good. My skin is so numb my limbs feel like dead weight.

"The balls are supposed to be behind you, luv." Jodi swipes at the sweat on her forehead and wipes it on her skirt.

Darcie waves us off. "I've got this." Then she grabs on to the balls with both hands, like they're handles, and holds tight.

Jodi laughs and encourages her to stay put. "Just keep a firm grip on the knackers and ride that fucker hard." She clenches both of her hands out in front of her for emphasis.

Darcie licks her lips and takes Jodi's advice. She focuses off in the distance, but snorts. "It's weird to feel two balls again."

The three of us lose it laughing. That's when Justin nods to the employee and he turns it on once again. The dick does a slow wave, slowly picking up speed. This gives Darcie a newfound confidence. She releases her hold on the ballsacks and sits upright with her hands over her head, her ginormous tits bouncing with each motion. "I got this."

"You go, Cocksister!" I watch with pride as Darcie rides the shit out of it while sipping on my drink. This has turned into one hell of a night. My face hurts from smiling so much.

The longer she rides, the more confident Darcie gets. Pretty soon she's waving her arms over her head like she's on a rollercoaster. Her body rolls with each wave of motion and things are going great, until it turns. That causes her center of balance to shift, sending her flying face first onto the mat.

"Cocksister down!" Jodi yells so loud the music stops and the entire bar watches us.

"Are you okay?" I roll Darcie over and help her up.

She sits there a minute, grabs her head, and gives it a big shake.

Then she's bouncing against the floor in excitement. "Did you see me take that bull by the balls?"

"It was more like a dick by the balls, but yup. You nailed it, Cocksister." I yank her up to her feet and throw my arm around her shoulder.

"That was bloody fantastic." Jodi comes up on her other side.

Darcie starts fanning herself. "It's so hot in here." Sweat is pouring off of her.

"Let's go get some air." The three of us walk out towards the beach. We make it a few feet when my flip-flop catches a clump in the sand and the three of us fall on our asses.

"I'm making a sand angel," Jodi shouts as she moves her arms and legs.

"You're going to have sand in every crack tomorrow." Darcie laughs so hard she comes down with a mad case of the hiccups.

I lie there and listen, but don't move otherwise. Every limb on my body feels like weighted cement. My eyelids grow heavy and a nap feels like the best idea ever. I plop my body in the sand and shut my eyes. I'll just rest for a second. That's what I tell myself, but the last thing I remember is Justin whispering something in my ear before everything goes black.

9

LIGHT CREEPS INTO THE ROOM like an unwanted dick. It's so bright I yank the covers over my face to block it out. The movement causes my head to start pounding and I feel like I've been hit by a damn semi. My lips smack together, but the inside of my mouth is so dry my tongue sticks to the roof of it. I have one hell of a hangover, which is weird because I hydrated with coconut water in between drinks and I only had four at most—a small amount for me.

What the hell happened last night?

My mind tries to conjure up images of what happened, but it's all a fuzzy blur. Flashes of us riding a giant cock fill my head and then my brain shifts on to another one. Justin and I grinding against each other like a pair of horny teenagers. Then I vaguely remember him having a drink with us and feeding us a shit load of chocolate dicks before everything went blank.

Darcie and Jodi have to know what happened last night. I throw the covers back and hop out of bed, ready to haul ass inside their room when I freeze. It takes my head a minute to focus and catch up to the rest of me. Sudden movements are not a good idea right now. Then cool air hits my body causing me to look down, and I about shit myself. "Where the fuck are my clothes?"

My eyes skate across the floor and find them thrown off in the corner. At the same time, I take in bits of the room and frown. There are brown accents where there should be bright hooker red. Something isn't adding up. I glance down at a picture frame next to the bed and my stomach drops. There's a picture of Justin—pre-porn star mustache—with his sister Eden at their parents lake house.

"Fucking shit!" Sleeping with Justin and ending up in his room buck ass naked was not part of my plans—ever! I scramble to get my clothes on as fast as I can, which isn't easy given my current state. Getting out of here before he comes back is the only thing running through my head and forcing me to work though the fog. Once I'm dressed and step towards the door, my boot steps onto something squishy. I look down and a tingling suspicion washes through me.

When I pick up the baggy of what looks like black sludge with chocolate stuck all over it, my blood boils. Growing up in LA one recognizes mushroom goo when they see it. Everything clicks into place for me at that moment as I storm out of the room. "He drugged me with chocolate dicks. What a motherfucker." I slam his door shut so hard I hear a loud thump followed by glass shattering. A sense of pride washes through me. "Take that, asshole!"

With that parting line, I get the hell out of there. I need to shower Justin's stench off of me and find my Cocksisters ASAP. After a series of wrong turns, I finally make it inside my room and what I find only fuels my anger. Shit is tossed around everywhere. Pillows are ripped to shreds and their stuffing litters the floor. Someone has ransacked my room.

I barge through the connecting doorway to check on Jodi and Darcie. Their room looks just as fucked up as mine. Rage is consuming me. I know Justin is responsible for this. It's bad enough he took advantage of me, but to fuck with my friends, too? That's where I draw the line. "He's a fucking dickhole!"

My outburst scares the shit out of Darcie and Jodi, who were out cold until then. They jolt upright from their bed at the sound of my voice, wearing matching confused expressions.

"What the bloody hell happened last night? I feel like I've just sucked a bloke's dirty knob. And why is there sand in my bum?" Jodi's hair is sticking up all over the place like a rat's nest. Black smudges of mascara and eyeliner cover the tops of her cheeks. The red lipstick she was wearing last night is smudged across the side of her face. She always was one wild sleeper.

Darcie rubs at her temples. "I don't even remember how we got back to our room, but I know we didn't trash it like this." She doesn't look as torn up as Jodi, which means she didn't eat as many chocolate dicks as we did. "And why is my head pounding?"

I wave the plastic bag around. "He drugged us." Maybe I should have eased them into this conversation, but I'm too pissed to be subtle.

Darcie's blonde eyebrows pinch together. "Who?"

"Justin! The chocolate dicks he gave us were laced with mushroom goo." Shouting isn't the best way to keep calm or help my raging headache, but I've lost all sense of logic at the moment. I spit out the rest in one long breath, but when I get to the part where I woke up naked in his bed they both explode.

"That arsehole! I'm going to feed him his own willy." Jodi's face is getting redder by the second and I don't blame her.

"Wait until I find him. I'm going to shove a whole box of tampons up his dick!" Darcie demonstrates with her hands exactly how she plans on doing that.

"I'll be right behind you with more." I pace back and forth imagining all of the ways I'd like to castrate him.

"Do you think he slept with you while you were drugged?" Darcie's forehead wrinkles.

"I don't know." I swallow down the lump in my throat and hope things didn't go that far. "My shit's not even sore, but he's always had the world's smallest dick. So, that could be why." My inner voice says no, but until I hear it from him there's no way to be sure.

"This doesn't make sense. Why would he drug us? And do what he did to you?" Darcie waves her hands around like an animated blow up doll.

I stop mid-thought and stare at her. "Excellent question." A wicked grin spreads across my face as I picture the pain I will be inflicting on him. "Let's go ask him."

Minutes later, the three of us are showered, dressed, and ready to confront the little weasel dick. We anticipate giving a beating, so we're dressed for battle—hair in messy knots, shorts, comfy t-shirts, and running shoes. Or in my case, *a* running shoe. I'd prefer a steel-toed boot to crush his nuts with, but I don't own any. Nonetheless, we're prepared to fuck him up. Darcie even managed to bring her dickbag along and I'm sure she squeezed a first-aid kit inside it somewhere.

We wander around the damn ship for what seems like an hour and there's still no sign of him. It turns out Justin is harder to find than we were expecting. I'm about to lose hope we'll find him when finally I catch a glimpse of him going through one of the doors to the engine room.

I nudge Jodi and Darcie with my elbows. "He went through there."

"You sure?" Darcie asks.

"Unless someone else has a dick shaped mole on the side of their face, I'm positive."

"Let's go blow his arse. He made a total cock-up by screwing with us." Jodi smacks her hands together. Her temper has gotten worse the longer she's had to stew on what happened to us, which makes her Britishisms even more colorful. Darcie and I stare at her for a second and then nod our heads. Whatever she just said, she's right. He's messed with the wrong girls.

"I couldn't agree with you more, Jo. You mess with one Cocksister, you mess with all of us. Cocksisters before misters, motherfuckers." I'm feeling inspired to tattoo this little reminder on Justin's tiny cock.

"That's right. Chicks before dicks." Darcie nods. She's becoming as worked up as Jodi and myself over this whole situation.

We walk through the door ready to confront him and raise some hell, but we stop when we hear multiple voices—very angry, very loud voices. Two of them are male, but the other is a female and sounds familiar. My ears strain to catch what they're saying, but we aren't close enough.

I tilt my head for Jodi and Darcie to follow me. We inch closer towards the voices to gain a better feel for what's going on because as soon as they're done, Justin is ours. The more we close the distance the better we can hear the conversation and it doesn't sound good.

"You fucked us. More than half of the last shipment is missing." A thud is followed by a loud grunt.

"I didn't touch the shit, I swear." The guy is panting and sounds like he's about to piss his pants.

My head creeps around the corner and I'm not sure what to make of what I'm seeing. Justin is standing in front of a guy who's on his knees. A closer inspection has me almost shitting myself. I'd know that bald head anywhere.

"How much did you steal from us before you ratted us out to the Feds, Eric?" the female voice demands, and when I see who it is I have to do a double take because this cannot be happening right now. Sadly, it is. Kristyn is standing in front of Eric, wearing one of her all black leather dominatrix outfits and thigh high boots. She looks like a sexed up Cruella Deville.

"None. And I didn't give them anything they could use against you. It was all bullshit." Eric fists the edge of her bustier and pleads up at her. "Mistress K, you have to believe me?"

She flashes him a wicked grin before pressing the tip of her boot against his shoulder and shoving him back. "Did I say you could touch me?" She juts her chin forward in a silent signal and Justin starts moving.

He clenches a fist and slams it into Eric's stomach a couple of times. I flinch with every hit. Eric's grunts of pain echo through the room and lucky for us it's loud enough to cancel out Darcie's gasps of shock. I'm just not sure how long we can push our luck. I tilt my head in a silent plea for her to keep quiet, but Jodi beats me to it and wraps a hand over her mouth.

"Enough, Justin." Kristyn squats down in front of Eric. "Remember now?"

"Please?" Eric's head hangs in front of him as he begs.

Kristyn gets to her feet and sighs. "I suppose you've had enough."

Eric's body relaxes at her words. "Thank you, Mistress K. You won't regret it."

"I never regret anything." Kristyn lifts the corner of her mouth in a half smile and turns her head towards Justin. "Do it."

"With pleasure." Justin grins as he cocks the gun and pulls the trigger. Eric's body jerks with the motion and falls back into a limp pile. All three of us jump at the sound of gunfire causing Darcie's bag to knock against the metal railing. The clanking sound it makes has my heart ready to explode out of my chest.

"What was that?" Kristyn looks our way and we suction ourselves against the massive engines, hoping they hide us from view. She stares our way for what seems like an eternity and I swear I feel my pulse in my throat.

"I didn't hear anything." Justin grunts and fiddles with the tips of his mustache.

"Must be the damn rats again. Get rid of this." She nudges Eric's lifeless body with the tip of her boot. "Our next shipment arrives tomorrow night. While everyone makes port, we'll unload it inside the factory."

"What about the girls? We searched their rooms and couldn't find any trace of bugs or cameras in them. I don't think they're being watched." Justin sounds put out by this and I want to strangle him. "And whatever shit he did steal isn't in their rooms either." He kicks at Eric's lifeless body.

"Take care of them." Footsteps head in our direction and stop. "Just make sure it looks like an accident, Justin. We can't afford to have their Fed boyfriends all up in our shit."

"But—" Justin begins, but Kristyn cuts him off.

"But nothing. We didn't go through all the trouble of setting them up to win this damn cruise to have shit fall apart." Kristyn puts her hands on her hips and glares at Justin. "They were our way in to find out how much the Feds know, and since they haven't shown up yet, it means they don't know dick. The girls are no longer useful, so get rid of them." Her words hit me hard and I grip the metal railing to keep myself from charging in there to bitch slap her and give us away.

He stares at her, unmoving for what seems like an eternity, but once he nods his head our fate is sealed. We need to get the fuck out of here ASAP.

Jodi opens her mouth to scream, but this time Darcie's reflexes are quicker. She returns the favor and slaps a hand over her mouth to muffle any sound. I motion with my head for us to slink back the way we came. Darcie and Jodi nod and follow my lead. Each step seems to take an eternity.

My boot catches on a small piece of metal sticking out between the railing and the engine, causing me to trip. I lose my balance and fall forward, but Jodi is able to catch me before I go down. A silent sigh of relief escapes me. That was a close one. We continue on our way out and all seems good as we near the door. Then Darcie sneezes, causing her dickbag to smack against the railing, and it all goes to shit. The metal ping echoes like a bomb went off in the small space.

"Hey!" Justin has his gun out and is sprinting towards us with Kristyn right behind him.

"We've been made! Run!" I grab some loose engine parts I find and chuck them in their direction. They nail my targets. Justin and Kristyn are knocked on their asses.

Darcie grabs my hand and yanks me behind her. She's running so fast I can barely keep up, but I'm not stopping. The footsteps pounding behind us remind me of what's at stake if I do. We run down a set of stairs in the opposite direction from where we came and it forks off into two different halls.

"Which way?" Jodi's blonde head whips back and forth, waiting for directions.

"Go right." I'm talking out of my ass, but at this point what do we have to lose? Darcie leads the way, still pulling me along. We run through the doorway only to wind up at another dead end. I guess that wasn't the correct way. Oopsie. The three of us backtrack to the other hall and rush inside. This time there isn't a dead end, but it's worse—much worse. There's a long ass flight of stairs that leads down.

"I'm so fucked. There's no way I can do all those stairs." Panic bubbles up inside me and starts to take over my common sense.

"Not to worry. I've got this." Jodi bends down in front of me and slaps her back. "Climb on, luv."

"You can't be serious? I'm like twice your size." There is no way this will work. She's out of her damn mind.

"You have a better option, we're all ears?" Darcie throws her hands up in a hurrying gesture as she glances behind us to make sure we're still in the clear.

My gaze swings from her to Jodi. Sweat covers their faces as they pant and wait for me to get my shit together. I clench my eyes shut. "You drop me and I'm going to shove a cucumber up your ass."

"Been there done that, luv." Jodi winks and holds her hands out for me.

I hop on to Jodi's back and hold on like my life depends on it. "You good?"

"Perfect." She hitches me up a little higher and begins our decent down the stairs. To my surprise, my legs don't dangle on the ground. Perhaps this isn't so bad after all. We make it all the way to the second to last step when I'm proven wrong. My leg hits the center pole, which is solid metal. Pain shoots up my leg. It hurts like a motherfucker. I seriously want to cry right now.

"My leg, Jo." It takes everything in me to get those words out. I can't wait for my foot to heal and get rid of this damn boot.

"Bugger. My bad." Jodi nudges me up a bit higher and we continue on our way. When we get to the bottom of the stairs, she sets me down. My body rejoices, happy to be on solid ground once more.

There's a door a few feet in front of us and we waste no time running towards it. I'm moving on adrenaline right now, and pain—if any from earlier—isn't registering at the moment. As we reach the metal door, the one at the top of the stairs opens and a familiar voice taunts us.

"Where you going, Coxy?" Justin's voice is cold and detached, nothing like the smooth playful one he had last night. I glance up to see him standing at the top of the stairs aiming his gun at us like some cheesy villain, and I want to rip that fugly mustache off his face.

"You drugged me!" My earlier anger resurfaces, but I tamp it down and slide in front of Darcie to block his view of her and what she's doing. I need to keep him distracted to give her enough time to open the door. If he realizes what she's doing behind me we're all dead. Keeping calm and forcing all of his attention on me is my only option. Images of waking up naked in his bed hit me and it sets my temper over the edge once again. "Did you fuck me while I was unconscious?"

"Jesus, calm the fuck down. I might be willing to put a bullet in your head, but I'd only ever fuck you conscious. I like my women to be more active in bed." He's so focused on my accusations he hasn't noticed Darcie turning the handle on the door.

"We didn't bone?" Relief courses through me. Not at reliving the awfulness of losing my V card to him, but at the fact I never had sex with him last night.

"You didn't shag the bloke." Jodi slaps my shoulder and nudges closer, blocking Darcie even further from his view.

"No. You got hot, ripped your clothes off, and did a strip tease in my room. Never could handle mixing your liquor with drugs, could you? It's just too bad you won't get the chance to ride my dick now." He flashes me a deviant grin as he cocks back the trigger of his gun. "Goodbye, Coxy. It was fun while it lasted." The gun goes off and I stand there waiting for the pain of the bullet to tear through me, but it never does.

Darcie pulls Jodi and I backwards and shuts the door just in time for the bullet to ricochet off of the thick metal. I rest my head against the door for a second. My ass almost got shot—again.

"Open this door right fucking now!" Justin slams his body weight against the door, but it's thick metal and not budging.

"Eat a dick, Justin!" It makes me feel a bit better to insult him until he starts firing bullets at the door.

"Bloody fucking hell!" Jodi jumps away like it's on fire.

"One way or another, I'm coming in, Coxy." More slamming as the door rattles.

"I'm shaking. You could barely get it in the first place." Taunting a lunatic is not the smartest thing I've ever done, but who can blame me? The asshole has it coming.

"We need to get out of here." Darcie pulls me away from the door and leads me into the room, and the sounds of Justin slamming against it fade into background noise.

"Where are we?" I don't like this at all. There's nothing in here. It's like a tiny storage space.

"This must be where they store their water sports stuff." Darcie flips on the light switch, revealing two jet-skis connected to what looks like the front of a speedboat that has a platform big enough for a person to lie on.

Jodi's face lights up like she's found the golden dick. "Bite your arm off. I can't wait to see what this twat can do." She straddles one of the jet skis and starts playing with buttons while Darcie does the same to the other one.

"Stop playing with that and help me figure out how we're getting out of here?" A soft buzzing noise startles me. "What the hell was that?"

"Our way out." Darcie smiles and juts her chin at the front of the boat. Sunlight is creeping in as the wall in front of us opens up into a ramp.

"We need the keys, Jo." Every time it looks like our escape is near there's a damn obstacle thrown in our way.

"Who needs one of those? I've got hot wiring skills thanks to Ryder." Jodi messes with some wires, slips the lanyard in and pushes a button. Low and behold, the engine purrs to life. Darcie mimics her movements and her jet ski starts as well. I've never been happier to be proven wrong.

Then the jet-ski boat jerks forward and starts to glide down the ramp in slow motion. "Oh fuck! Don't leave without my ass."

"Get on, Lisa." Darcie waves me over to climb on behind her. My stomach sinks. There isn't enough room for my long ass legs.

"I won't fit back there. I'm too tall." Defeat is attempting to settle its way in, but I'm trying my damndest not to let it win today. "Let me drive."

"Budge up so she can fit." Jodi motions with her hands to Darcie.

"No time to switch places." Darcie shakes her head as the boat slips further down the ramp. Things are going from bad to worse.

"Stop waffling about and get in the front and lie down then. We got this, Cocksister." The look on Jodi's face does little to set me at ease, but we're out of options.

As the front of the boat touches the water, I'm still debating on my options. Time is running out and I need to decide fast. Sadly, there's no other choice. I suck it up, hobble over, and plop my ass on the platform in the front just before it hits the water. "If I fall in, you better save my ass."

"No worries, luv. Got that covered, too." Jodi tosses me a life jacket. I slip it on and gaze ahead. The second my ass is situated, the door slams open from behind us.

"Ready or not here I come." Justin sounds like a drowning hyena as he laughs.

I glance over my shoulder to see Kristyn is not far behind him. "Been there, done that," I yell back.

His response is lost as the boat slips into the water. Jodi and Darcie rev the engines, jetting us forward and away from Justin's crazy ass. The boat bounces against the waves, knocking me around. It's a good thing I don't get seasick or I'd have tossed my cookies at least twice already.

Water splashes up, catching me in the face. The taste of salt fills my mouth, making me gag. I shake it off and stare straight ahead as best I can.

Jodi and Darcie are so focused as they steer the boat. It's like they're one person. Amazing. We might get out of this clusterfuck after all.

A speedboat barrels right past us and I realize I've spoken too soon. Being pulled by the boat is a man on water skis. His eyes are as big as saucers when he sees us heading straight for him.

I open my mouth to scream, but end up with a mouthful of seawater instead. Jodi and Darcie swerve out of his way just in time to avoid a crash, but the wake of the waves is too much. He loses his balance and face plants into the water.

"Bollocks. I'm sorry. Here, have a bag of willies!" Jodi throws a pack of candy-coated dicks at him. I'm not even sure where she's keeping them, but right now I'm too busy hanging on for dear life to ask. Then I glance over my shoulder and realize we're about to be screwed and not in the way I like.

"You're going the wrong way. The docks are back there." I point over my left shoulder.

"Fuck me in the ass with a pencil! There's no time to turn around. What do we do?" Darcie voices my thoughts out loud.

"We run this cunt straight ahead." Jodi cranks the handles and we pick up speed. Darcie doesn't even hesitate as she follows her lead.

Fucking hell. They're going to run the boat right up to shore. This can't end well. "Look out. There are people in the water." I start yelling and waving my hands around like a crazy person at the swimmers to get them out of our way. Having a front row seat to the shit show of their driving is giving me an ulcer.

The second the front of the boat hits dry land, it flips, sending the ass end up and us flying forward onto the beach. The lanyards on Darcie and Jodi's wrists are yanked out of the jet-skis, stalling the engines. All the air is knocked out of us as we land flat on our backs. Darcie's dickbag lands right between her legs with a muted thump not long after.

Everything is quiet around us as we take a minute to process what the hell just happened. The three of us lie in the sand like limp dicks and catch our breaths. This is not how I expected my day to go at all when I woke up in Justin's room.

I cough up a mouthful of sand and gasp for air. "This is why I drive."

"Holy shit! That was close." Darcie's heavy breath blows against my ear.

Then Jodi grunts. "Flick my flaps and pinch my nipples. That was one big cock-up."

The three of us lie there wondering what the hell we just got ourselves into. This day did not turn out as planned at all.

10

Darcie sits up and begins brushing the sand off of her dickbag while Jodi and I still lie there, trying to catch our breaths. Talk about a fucking workout. I said it once and I'll say it again: if chases are going to be a regular occurrence on our girls trips, we may need to start going to the damn gym with Darcie on the regular.

A horn blares through the air, cutting into our short reprieve. Darcie stops what she's doing and glances over her shoulder. Her whole body tenses the second she does. "Guys, we have a serious problem."

"I'm coming for you, Coxy!" Justin's voice causes the tiny hairs on the back of my neck to stand on end.

Why can't we get away from this asshole?

I bolt upright in a sad attempt at standing up, but fall right back down on my ass. The soft sand makes traction difficult and there's no way I can do this on my own. "A little help here, please? I've fallen and I can't get up." Darcie and Jodi each grab an arm and with no effort at all have me up on my feet. "Thanks."

"Don't mention it, but we might want to get moving." Darcie tosses the strap of her dickbag over her shoulder and starts heading off towards the resort that's a short distance ahead of us.

I glance over my shoulder and about shit myself at what I see. Justin has docked his boat and made his way down the docks, heading straight for us with a gun in his hand. *Why was he never this determined to give me orgasms in high school?* "Run!"

Jodi and Darcie waste no time hauling ass towards the crowd of people while I do my best to keep up with them and ignore the pound of sand seeping inside my boot. It takes everything in me not to stop and shake it out, but the thought of uncertain death has a way of motivating a girl.

Bullets whiz past us and into the sand next to our feet, causing us to jump and pick up the pace even more. People next to us scream and start running all over the place in search of a safe place to hide. We, however, do the opposite. Bodies crash into us and knock us all over the place like a damn game of ping-pong. It's complete chaos.

"That crazy cuntsicle is trying to kill us." Jodi decides right then and there is the perfect place to give him a piece of her mind, but Darcie and I know better. We grab her wrists and yank her ass forward. Timing was never her strong suit.

"Not a good idea right now, Jo." No matter how much I agree with her need to tell him off, we need to keep moving.

We force our way through another throng of shouting people and somehow wind up on the edge of a golf course. I guess when on a beautiful island, people wear funny pants and whack some tiny ass balls. Who knew?

Jodi stops to catch her breath while my head darts back and forth, struggling to come up with a decent plan on the fly. Not a damn thing is coming to me, though, and I want to scream. Things don't look too promising for us at all. There are no trees to hide in—not that my ass could climb them anyways—or buildings to run into. Wherever we go we'll be exposed and he'll have a clear shot at us.

"Bloody hell! This is exhausting. I might need to lay off the crisps after this." Jodi bends over and pants like a chain smoker.

"Where to now?" Darcie glances around, taking in our new surroundings as fast as the current circumstances allow.

"There!" I point to the first thing I see, which happens to be a golf cart parked a few feet away from a group of tourists. Tourists who happen to be wearing the most awful pants I've ever seen in my life, and coming from me, that's saying something. It looks like a rainbow threw up all over them. They'd match Darcie's dickbag perfectly, though.

We take off running once again, and I do my best to ignore the cramp that wants to form in my foot. I'm having to overcompensate so much for my boot that this shit is hell on my sore leg. Lucky for us, when we approach the group we're able to blend in unnoticed. Everyone is so focused on the game they wouldn't even know if a woman streaked right in front of them, which works in our favor because it gives my bum leg a bit of a reprieve.

After a short breather, we traipse through the grass and shuffle as quietly as possible towards the cart. I glance back to make sure we're in the clear because I have a sneaking suspicion this was too easy, and I'm right. Justin is hot on our heels. This bastard just won't quit! "Pick up the pace," I whisper out the side of my mouth as we move faster.

When we reach the golf cart, Darcie goes to sit in the driver's seat but I stop her with a vigorous shake of my head. "I don't think so. After swallowing half the ocean, it's my turn to drive."

"But your foot—" she starts to argue, but I cut her off.

"Will be just fine." No way am I letting her drive after the jet-ski fiasco.

She stares at me a beat wanting to press the issue, but then she catches a glimpse of Justin over my shoulder and slides in to the passenger side without further complaint. I plop my ass down in the driver's seat, taking a brief moment to enjoy the fact that I'm the one driving, and floor it.

"Bollocks! Wait for me." Jodi does a running jump and dives into the back seat just as I pull away. Shouts from the group of golfers barely register behind us as we get the hell out of there.

Tearing off down the golf course, we drive right through the middle of several more games. We do our best to ignore the strings of profanities shouted our way, or the raised fists, as we make it further down the field of green.

"Relax and enjoy a bag of willies!" Bags of dicks magically appear in Jodi's hands as she tosses them out along the way. It's like she's the princess in a parade of dicks. I'm really going to have to ask her where the hell she's keeping them when this is over.

My attention is divided between what Jodi is doing and the path in front of me, which is why I don't see the damn hill until it's too late. We hit it so hard we catch some serious air before slamming back down. The force of our landing has Darcie and I knocking heads. I ignore the brief flash of pain and fight to keep my grip on the steering wheel. My arms tense as I use some serious muscle to keep from falling out of the damn cart, but my foot isn't as stable and slips off the pedal.

We start to slow down, which sends us all into a panic. Then Darcie becomes the bearer of even better news. "Fucking shit! He stole a golf cart, too. He's going to catch us."

"Not if I can help it." I slam my foot back down on the pedal and off we go. This cart has a bit more get up and go than any I've been on before, but as long as it gets us out of here that's all that matters. The motor whines as it climbs back up the hill, taking us further towards safety. I'm not sure how much more this thing can handle, but I just hope it lasts until we're safe. I glance around for another escape route and quickly find it. It's not the best option, but right now it's our only one. I swerve to the left and head towards a clearing of trees at the other end of the golf course, next to the parking lot, which means we're driving through more games and dodging a lot of balls.

A flurry of white sails past our heads the further in we go. I'm so focused that I don't even know what's happened until I hear the thump.

"Ouch!" Darcie groans and clutches her forehead.

"Please tell me you aren't shot, Darce?" My eyes dart between her and the green in front of me.

"Bollocks, no. She just took a ball to the face," Jodi offers up from the back.

"You okay?" At our speed, that had to hurt just as bad as taking a bullet.

"Yeah. I'm fine." Darcie shakes her head and focuses her attention straight ahead of us.

"You sure?" She looks fine, but I'm not convinced. The last thing I need is for her to lose consciousness and fall out of the damn cart. Running over one of my best friends would certainly put a dampener on things.

"Because it was a hard hit, luv." Jodi voices my thoughts.

"I'm good. Don't worry about me. Just get us out of here." She brushes off our concern and goes back to freaking out about my driving instead.

Crisis averted, I go back to what I'm doing, but in typical Cocksister fashion, things don't stay quiet for long.

"Where's the bloody music coming from?" Jodi leans forward in the space between Darcie and I, and cocks her head to the side.

I tilt my ear to listen better and realize where it's coming from. "Your dickbag is ringing, Darce."

Darcie bends over and pulls it out. "Hello?" She listens for a beat before holding the phone out to me. Judging by the look on her face I'm not going to like who's on the other end. "It's Dusty."

I knew it. "Tell him I'll call him back." My eyes never stray from the path in front of me as I answer her. I'm going to strangle my brother. There's no time to take a damn phone call when our lives are on the line.

She puts the phone back to her ear and does as I asked, but turns back to me. "He says it's important."

"Put him on speaker." I sigh and roll my eyes. My brother is such a pain in the ass sometimes.

"Lisa!" His voice booms through the phone. He sounds as annoyed as I am right now and it's so not a good time for any family drama.

"What do you need, Dusty?" My grip tightens against the wheel as I maneuver us through a few more golfers. They shout at us, but my brother's voice drowns them out.

"Ma is pissed and worried you haven't called to check in, *Hermana*."

He sounds like my father the way he's scolding me, which is annoying as hell.

"Now isn't a good time to talk to her." The last thing I need to do right now is speak to my mother and freak her the fuck out.

A loud ping drowns out Dusty's response. Bullets are penetrating right through the golf cart. Darcie and Jodi scream as I glance over my shoulder to see Justin with one hand on the steering wheel and the other aiming his gun in our direction. The motherfucker is shooting at us out in the open. I scoot down in my seat, but keep the pedal to the floor.

"Are those gun shots?" Dusty's voice booms through the phone.

"Um…" I struggle to come up with a believable answer. The last thing I want to do is worry my family. "Fuck! Gotta go, Dusty. Tell Ma I'll call her back." We hit another dip and my phone is knocked out of Darcie's hand. It lands under the golf cart's tires with a loud crunch.

"My bad." Darcie hunches in her seat, gnawing on her bottom lip.

"Don't stress, Darce. We get out of this alive you can get me a new one. We'll just add it to the list along with a new Henry." I shrug it off and turn my attention back to driving. Losing my phone is the least of our worries at the moment.

We finally come to the end of what must be the longest golf course in history, and jump the curb. The landing is so hard Jodi almost falls off the back into the parking lot behind us. Darcie grabs her arm and pulls her back in.

"Thanks, Cocksister!" Jodi buckles her seatbelt and grips the oh-shit bars tighter.

"We'll lose him through that clump of foliage." My chin tilts to our right as I turn the wheel. It's starting to pull a little funny, which isn't a good sign.

"Don't freak out, but I think one of the tires is flat." I manage to keep my voice calm as I explain as best I can what's happening and how fucked we might be. Just not in so many words.

"Fuck me in the ass with a nickel!" Darcie screams and puts her hands over her face as we head into a cluster of trees and plants. "What are we going to do? If the tire goes flat we're screwed."

"Relax, Darce. I've got this shit." Confidence oozes out of me, but inside I'm dying and hoping I don't crash into a tree and kill us.

Giant green leaves whip back and slap us in the face the faster we move through them. Darcie opens her mouth to scream again when one smacks her right in the mouth. She whacks it away and starts hacking. "I think I just swallowed a bug." The way she's coughing has me worried she might throw up.

"A little extra protein never hurt, luv." Jodi does her best to comfort Darcie while I keep driving.

I'm almost positive we've lost Justin because I haven't heard his shouts in a while, and the gunfire has ceased, but I'm not taking a chance at stopping until we've made sure to put enough distance between us. We move through another few miles of foliage when I hear a sound that has me ready to shit myself.

"Is that running water?" Leave it to Jodi to notice and confirm my worst fear.

"It is." Turns out it's a lot closer than we think. I barely get the words out before we're right in front of it. All at once everything goes quiet as the cart goes over the side of the cliff, sailing in the air.

"Oh fuck!" I scream the entire way down the twenty-foot drop as butterflies do flips in my stomach. It's worse than any roller coaster I've ever been on.

Darcie and I are thrown a few feet away from where the cart lands. Splashing drowns out our cries as we hit the ice-cold water ass first. Somehow, I manage to avoid swallowing a mouthful on the way down. I don't waste time shooting up to the surface, gasping for air as I wipe water out of my eyes. It's a good thing I skipped makeup in preparation for Justin's ass kicking or I'd look like a rabid raccoon at the moment. When I glance around for the girls, I find Darcie's dickbag bobbing up and down against the water like a floating dick.

A wave knocks me under again and this time I do choke on a mouthful of water. I shake it off and move my arms back and forth to keep from drowning. I glance around to make sure we're all okay, but only find Darcie floating next to me. Her ginormous tits are acting as a makeshift floaty. Another glance around reveals Jodi is still nowhere to be seen. When I finally find her, she's still sitting on the back of the golf cart. That's odd. Then the cart begins to submerge further into the water. Things keep going from bad to worse. "Jo, you need to get off of there. Right now."

Jodi's arms move and then her face pales. "Bloody hell! My fucking belt is stuck." She's in full on panic mode. "Get me out of here. I'm too young to die. I haven't even had my red solo cup party or lived out my trailer park dreams yet." Her hands slap against the water as her anger takes over at the thought.

Darcie swims over towards her with me right behind. "Hang on. I got you." She gives me a telling look and I nod my head before she dives under the water.

I keep myself afloat, trying to ignore the aching cold that's filling my limbs or that I just got my bad leg wet, and do my best to calm Jodi down. The water is creeping higher and is now to her shoulders. The last thing I want to do is alarm her because she could wind up sinking faster if she struggles. "You'll be okay, Jo. Remember, no Cocksister left behind. Ever."

"You're right, but I can't swim." Panic crosses her features as she notices the water rising up to the bottom of her neck.

"Lucky for you, both Darcie and I know how. You'll be just fine." I keep her attention focused on me and ease her fears as best I can. I'm not sure she's buying it, but she still nods her head.

Then Darcie bursts through the water like an angry dick and wipes at her face. Her ginormous titties are bobbing up and down in the water like a pair of buoys. "Come on." She grabs Jodi's arm and takes on her weight. Together they float away with her boobs keeping them afloat, just in time, too. The cart submerges the rest of the way in the water the second they're free. Jodi escapes without a scratch. Saved by the boobies.

Angry shouting from behind us catches my attention and I spin around to find Justin standing at the edge of the cliff, yelling obscenities at us as he waves his gun around. The three of us raise our hands and give him a one-finger salute before we swim to the shore. We outsmarted him and he can suck on our lady balls.

Jodi doggy paddles alongside Darcie, as we let the current of the water carry us down stream. Halfway, a blur of lime green and pink catches my eye. Darcie's dickbag is floating right past me. As much as I hate it, I know she loves the damn thing, so I grab the nearest strap and pull it in against me. Whatever she has in here is making it act as a fabulous floatation device.

When we reach the shore, we drag ourselves out along the sand and crawl the rest of the distance until we're a good few feet away from the water. The three of us plop down on our backs and let the weight of our bodies sink into the soft sand.

Every limb on my body is sore and achy. My lungs are on fire as I gasp for all the air I can drag in. All this cardio and adrenaline overload have done all three of us in. I don't know about them, but I'm ready for a weeklong nap. Something tells me it won't be happening anytime soon.

We're lost in a rainforest and need to find our way out. And we will, just as soon as I can move. Things could be worse, though. We could be dead. For now, we'll just take solace in the fact Darcie survived a ball to the face and lived to tell the tale.

11

The sun beats down on my face, warming me up from the inside out. For a brief moment I'm in a cloud of denial. There's no asshole ex trying to kill us. It's just me, my girls, and a relaxing day at a spa. Then Darcie speaks, bringing reality crashing back down on my fantasy like the dirty whore she is.

"We should probably get going and cover as much ground as we can before it's too dark to see." Darcie's always the voice of reason.

"Yeah, we should." I roll over onto my stomach and push up onto my knees. Dirt is caked onto my soaked clothes and exposed skin. It's like I've spent a day at the beach, complete with sand in my cracks. I lift myself up, but water has soaked into my boot making it feel like there's a damn boulder attached to my leg. I'm so tired I don't even care that I got my wound wet. Darcie and Jodi see me struggle and come over to help me up. One swift pull and I'm up on my feet. "Thanks."

"Anytime, luv." Jodi pats me on the back causing water to seep out of my clothes and trickle down my legs. It's so warm and feels like I've just pissed myself. Jodi stares down at the small stream flowing down my body. "Whoops. Sorry about that." She wipes her hands on her legs.

"This way." Darcie interrupts our conversation and waves us over to follow her along what I assume is some trail she sees. How she sees this is a mystery. All I can see is the same shit in every direction—green, dense, and full of creepy crawlers.

I cringe, but bury that worry down, way down deep. Someplace so far I won't even think about it until much later. The only way out of here is through this rainforest, so I have to strap on my big girl panties and forge ahead.

Jodi and I follow Darcie, taking in every new sound. And let me just say that there are lots. It's amazing the shit you hear out here if you listen close enough.

We walk a ways before Darcie starts to fidget and walk like a drunk duck. The strangled moan she lets out is all I can take.

"Something wrong, Darce?"

"Nope. I'm good." Her voice comes out much higher than normal and I know she's full of crap.

"Doesn't sound like it, luv." Jodi voices my exact thoughts.

When she ignores us and keeps walking, Jodi and I stop in our tracks. We can wait her out all night long until she's ready to answer. After a bit, she realizes we aren't following her anymore and spins around to face us.

"We're not buying it, so spill." I put my hands on my hips and tap my booted foot.

"I have to pee! Okay?" Darcie blurts out in one rushed breath.

"Oh." That wasn't what I was expecting her to say, but the power of suggestion is strong because now I have the overwhelming urge to go as well. "Same here." I do a quick assessment of our surroundings and come to a very sucky realization—one I know she's not going to like at all. And I don't blame her. Times like these I wish we had dicks. "There's a bunch of trees and stuff to squat behind over there." I point my finger off towards the only low clearing of foliage I can find.

Her eyes squeeze shut as she comes to the same sad conclusion. "Great."

"Loo time." Jodi claps her hands together. She isn't as upset about this as we are. If anything, she looks excited about the idea.

We climb over the fallen tree branches and pick a spot to do our business. Choices are slim, but we each manage to find an area with a bit of privacy.

"This sucks." Darcie sets down her dickbag and sets off to find a spot she can safely squat in.

I shake off some of the excess mud that has now turned to dirt on my shorts and unzip them. It takes me a few tries, but eventually I'm able to peel down my damp shorts, which is a workout in itself, before bending over. On the way down, a sharp pain explodes on my right butt cheek. My body snaps upright as I freak the hell out. "What the fuck just poked me in the ass?" I twist around, ready to kill whatever it is that stabbed me. My only thought is that it better not be another damn wasp because I don't want to go through any of that shit again.

"Everything alright over there?" Darcie's voice floats over from the trees.

"I'm good. Just a dead branch poking me in the ass." I rub away the pain, which is still lingering. Man, it stings like a bitch.

"Bollocks! Could be worse, though. It could have gotten you right in your puckered starfish," Jodi shouts from off to the side. Shit, she's right. That was a close call. A few more inches and I'd be crying a whole different tune. This just offers further proof I am not a nature girl. There's a reason I don't have sex outdoors. Camping in RVs is as close to roughing it as I like to get.

Once my heart rate comes back down, I bend over and try again. This proves rather difficult. Squatting out in the open isn't the most comfortable thing in the world. Not to mention my quads are shaky as hell from all the damn walking we've been doing and my boot is water logged, which is making me unstable. I'm not sure how much more my bad leg can take before it gives out on me.

My hand braces against the tree for support to keep it from doing just that and things seem to be fine so far. I just hope I don't piss on myself in the process. Things start flowing and I guess going outdoors isn't too bad. That feeling doesn't last too long. Mid-flow, my concentration is broken by Darcie's screams.

"It touched me!" Darcie hobbles off with her shorts and underwear still slung around her ankles. She has so much momentum she tumbles forward, landing face first, her bare ass up in the air and her goods exposed for all to see. Then something slithers down her back, across the crack of her ass cheeks.

"Don't move, Darce!" In a matter of seconds, my pants are up and I'm next to her, examining the creepy crawler. "What the hell is that?" It's the biggest worm I've ever seen.

Darcie remains still, but tilts her head to the side. "I don't know and I don't care. Just get it off of me." She looks calm, but I can sense the storm of panic brewing on the inside.

"Not to worry, luv. I've got you." Jodi rushes forward with a big ass branch in her hand. She raises her arms above her head, ready to strike.

Once I realize what her intentions are, I jump in front of her with my hands extended. "Hold on there, Cocksister. Let me get it off of Darcie before you go smacking the shit out of it and breaking her ass in the process." She nods and waits. My gaze skates across the ground for something to nudge it off of Darcie's backside with because there's no way in hell I'm touching it with my bare hands, but I come up empty. So, I do the next best thing. I use my boot and kick the fucker as far as I can, which sadly isn't very far at all. It lands maybe about a foot off to the side.

"Thanks." Darcie pushes up to her feet and does up her shorts before we go over to inspect it. "Is it a worm?" Her hands go to her stomach as her face pales. I'm worried her breakfast might be coming back up.

"On fucking steroids." I cringe and continue to stare at it. "Gag me with a dick! It's so ugly."

"It looks like a rat with two arseholes," Jodi pipes up from next to me. Then without warning, she slams the branch down against the ground, over and over again. "Die, you bloody bastard."

Darcie and I jump back a foot at the unexpected action from our crazy friend. I'm thinking the elements here are beginning to take their toll on Jodi's sanity. After a couple of minutes of watching her go at it, Darcie grabs the end of the branch. "Jo, it's gone. I think it burrowed underneath the leaves or went underground."

Jodi blows a stray strand of hair out of her mouth. "Bugger."

"At least we know it's gone and won't be coming back." A sigh escapes me. This day just keeps getting more interesting by the minute.

After we take a moment to collect ourselves from the creepy crawler, the three of us get back on our way. We're tired, but we're must keep going. Taking too many breaks will only slow us down and we need to cover as much ground as we can before it gets too dark to see.

The more we walk, the dryer my clothes get, which is a miracle. The moisture in the air is so thick I'm a sweating mess and my hair is a dark frizzy bush. Humidity is such an evil whore.

It isn't much longer before the exhaustion becomes unbearable. There's also a dull ache starting in my leg. I stop walking because it's all becoming too much to handle. My body slumps against the nearest tree like a limp dick. "I can't go on anymore."

"Same here." Jodi bends down and grabs her side. "I have a cramp. How much further do you plan on going, luv?"

"Not too much." Darcie hasn't even broken a sweat; meanwhile Jodi and I are dying, hanging on for dear life. Damn her and her fitness regimen.

A strange growling sound cuts through my internal whining and everything else falls to the back burner. "Where is that noise coming from?"

"My stomach," Jodi groans. "We missed lunch and I'm bloody starving."

Darcie holds her hand up. "No problem. I've got something." She bends down and pulls out a bottle of water and protein bar for each of us from her bag of tricks.

"Thanks, luv. I'm so hungry I could eat a horse between two bread vans." Jodi grabs the bar and goes to town on it, devouring the whole thing in one go.

I take small bites of my bar, pretending to savor the chalk like texture. It's super hard and chewy. Plus, it tastes like dirty dick, but it's better than nothing at all. "What the hell else do you have in there?" I spread open the flaps of Darcie's bag and peer inside. I'm still amazed it can hold so much stuff. It's like the MacGyver of dickbags.

"Not much. Blankets, a flashlight, and a magazine. You know, the essentials. Well, the magazine might be ruined from the fall in the river, but the rest are still good." She shrugs and chomps down on her bar. "These are good, right?"

My jaw hurts from chewing on the bar, but I force it down my throat anyways. It feels like a chunk of dirt is scratching my insides. I wash the taste away with a huge gulp of water before answering her. "Sure."

Darcie tilts her head to the side and studies the area. "It's getting darker. I guess we should stop here for the night. It'll give us time to collect leaves and make up a bed."

"I'm on board with that idea." Sleep has never sounded as good as it does right at this moment.

"Me too." Jodi yawns in between the last bites of her bar.

We spend the next hour grabbing giant palm leaves and spreading them out on the forest floor like a blanket. It's not much, but it will have to do. A barrier between the ground and us is a must out here.

"You think we have enough? The last thing I want is to wake up with some creepy crawly all up in my cockpot." I've read some crazy shit about the types of insects on a jungle floor and it has my imagination in overdrive.

"Cockpot?" Darcie stops adjusting her leaf and gives me a sideways glance. "Vaginas are cockpots?"

"Yup. The slower we marinate the meat, the juicier we get." My hand gestures down between my legs to emphasize the point.

"Oh." Her lips purse together in thought, then she shakes her head in amusement and goes back to what she was doing.

By some stroke of luck, we manage to finish our bed right before night falls and everything is covered in a blanket of blackness. It's just too bad I'm on the other side of them and can't see shit. My eyes strain to make out shapes, anything at all, but it's too difficult.

"I feel like a blind man fucking." I reach my arms out in front of me, searching for my friends.

"Lost?" Darcie asks from somewhere.

"No. All hands." I keep stumbling along, hoping I'm headed in the right direction. Suddenly, a light to the face blinds me. "My eyes!"

"Whoops, sorry." Darcie whips the flashlight to the side, covering me in darkness once again.

"It's fine." I blink away the spots and move towards the light. Darcie keeps it aimed on the ground in front of me until make it to where she and Jodi are standing. Once I reach them, we lie down on the makeshift bed and get as comfortable as the leaves will allow. The second we stretch out, I realize our mistake. My feet are dangling off the edge and onto the ground. In our exhaustion, we miscalculated the length of the damn bed. Being tall really sucks sometimes. I scrunch up my legs as best I can to keep any part of me from touching the ground. It's one hell of a struggle, but somehow I manage.

Darcie keeps the flashlight nestled between her and myself, so we can have some visibility throughout the night. It makes our situation less stressful and offers a bit of comfort—even if it's all bullshit.

Jodi sighs into my ear on my other side. "You think we'll make it out of here alive?"

"Of course we will. There are too many cocks for us to conquer." I put as much bravado as I can into my words. The last thing we need out here is to feel defeated. I'm talking out of my ass so well I even manage to convince myself that everything will be fine.

"You sure you don't want a permanent one? I really thought you and Logan hit it off." Disappointment laces Darcie's voice, and I'm not sure if it's with Logan, me, or the both of us.

"Nope. That ship has sailed." Or at least it will once we get out of here. "Why do you ask?"

"No reason. I'm just curious. That's all." Darcie turns over, pulling some of the blanket with her.

"What about you, Jo?" Darcie asks.

"I'm good with free willy for now." Jodi yawns and sinks her head deeper against my shoulder.

Darcie and I laugh at her answer as we lie there. Humor is good. It keeps a person from going insane. Things are starting to look up for us.

Then the rain starts. It's no light sprinkle either. It's a full on downpour. Water pelts down on us like rocks. We scream and scramble up to our feet, seeking shelter of any kind.

A nearby tree is the closest thing that has leaves big enough to act as a canopy, but water still drips through. It's like sitting under a leaking roof. Darcie holds the dickbag over our heads and it helps to absorb some of the wetness.

"What do we do now?" Darcie looks to me for an answer, flashlight clutched against her chest.

"We'll have to sleep here. Everywhere else is too open and we'll get pelted by rain all night long." This whole situation is making me want to hunt Justin down, rip off his balls, and feed them to him.

"Goodnight then." Jodi couldn't care less about this new predicament. She curls her head on my shoulder and passes out. At least one of us has no trouble sleeping out here. And sleep like the dead she does. Darcie and I, on the other hand, struggle to get into a comfortable position.

We fidget for what seems like hours, huddled up together underneath the tree for warmth, with the flashlight acting as one giant nightlight. Wild sounds of the jungle mixed with rain, and Jodi's snoring in my ear, serve as the only background noise. Being stranded out here is scary as hell, but thanks to Darcie, we have the essentials. Her dickbag has saved the day and we are able to drift off without getting completely soaked.

12

Pain explodes along the side of my neck, and shoots down my back straight to my ass. Last night was a long and uncomfortable one. Between the rough bark of the tree digging into my back and Darcie's dickbag falling off our heads and onto the floor sometime during the night, I didn't get much sleep. Not to mention my body is sore as fuck. Everything inside me aches. I'm too damn old to sleep sitting up like this. I attempt to move my head into an upright position, but I wind up with a nose full of hair instead. My chin tilts down as I pry my eyes open to find a mound of blonde hair staring back at me.

My shoulder shrugs a few times until Jodi's head falls off. It lands back against the tree trunk with a loud thump. I'd be worried about how hard it hit, but she never even stirs. A string of drool hanging out the side of her mouth catches my attention and my hand goes right to my neck. Sure enough, there's what feels like a nice size puddle on my shoulder. I'm not positive it's all saliva, though. The humidity has me drenched in sweat, so it could be a mixture of both.

I decide to not think about that and focus on my surroundings instead. Dense fog covers the forest, making it hard to see a damn thing. Birds chirp from amongst the treetops, but I don't hear anything else and it's a little unsettling—like the calm before the storm. Not at all what I'm used to. As peaceful as it is, we need to get a move on and find our way out of here. The last thing I want is for Justin to catch up to us.

Darcie isn't a morning person, but hopefully the fact that we're out here will make it easier to wake her. "Darce?" A light shake of her shoulder does nothing. She's still out cold. I have to jerk her harder a few more times until she finally stirs.

Darcie yawns and sits up. "I had a nightmare we were trapped in a rainforest and you had bugs in your cockpot." She rubs the sleep from her eyes and glances around at the same time her shoulders sag. "Shit. I guess it wasn't a nightmare."

"Unfortunately not. Well, except for the bugs inside my cockpot. Luckily, that did not happen." A shiver runs through me at the thought of anything creepy crawly slithering inside there and my legs firmly squeeze shut. "We should get an early start today."

"You're right." Darcie stands and stretches her arms over her head, letting out another loud yawn. "How's your leg?"

I glance down at my booted foot. "It's better. I am going to need to take this off," I gesture towards the leg in question, "and let it air out all night, so it'll prevent an infection from setting in."

"That's a good idea." Darcie nods and then tilts her head in Jodi's direction. "What are we going to do about her? She's out cold."

"I'll wake sleeping beauty. You go ahead and grab our shit." I wave off her concern.

Darcie nods her head and starts packing up the stuff that fell out of her dickbag. A part of me wants to watch her to appease my own curiosity about what's actually inside there, but the other part of me thinks some things are better left unknown. On that note, I reach down and shake Jodi's shoulder.

"Five more bloody minutes." She groans, but doesn't move an inch. Time to resort to drastic measures. I stick my finger up her nose and wiggle it, which does the trick. She bolts upright, smacking at her face. "Those fucking wankers are in my nose."

My lips twitch as I take in her appearance. Her hair is a rat's nest in the back and there are leaves tangled in between blonde strands. A hot mess doesn't even come close to describing how she looks right now. "It's just me, Jo."

"Phew." She sags against the tree. "I thought I had another bad case of crabs."

Darcie stops what she's doing and stares at her like she's grown a third tit. She opens her mouth to ask more, but this will take up too much time and even though it kills me not to pry into what I'm sure is one hell of a story out of Jodi, I intervene.

"Almost finished there, Darce?"

Darcie shakes her head and brings her attention back to what she was doing before Jodi dropped the crabs bomb. Her hand smacks the flashlight a few times, but nothing happens. She sighs and plops it back inside her dickbag. "The flashlight is dead. If we don't find our way out of here by tonight we'll be screwed."

On that note, we get up and do our morning business—without creepy crawlers getting anywhere near our shit this time—before we begin another fun-filled day of hiking. We spend most of the morning stumbling through foliage without any issues. Today is starting off much different than yesterday.

Too bad the positive vibe doesn't last long.

A tree branch snaps behind us followed by a loud groan and I freeze where I stand. "Please tell me that was your stomach, Jo?"

"No, luv. It wasn't me." Jodi halts beside me.

"Shit. I was afraid you'd say that." Dread fills me as my imagination runs wild. Out here, there are so many things it could be and none of them are good.

Darcie also comes to a stop as the rustling of leaves catches our attention. "Think if we ignore it it'll go away."

"It's highly unlikely. Whatever it is it sounds huge." I wipe the bead of sweat off my forehead and try not to panic. It will only make things worse.

Then the bushes move again. I twist around into a basic karate stance, ready to kill whatever it is. I don't know dick about karate other than what I learned from watching The Karate Kid, but this is all I can come up with on the spur of the moment.

"Whatever's coming for us is one big motherfucker." Darcie's breaths become faster with each word she speaks.

"Maybe it's a bear?" I shrug and can't decide if I'm hoping to be proven right or wrong.

"Bears don't live in the rainforest." Darcie's voice cuts through my thoughts.

"Then what the bloody hell is it?" Jodi's breathing becomes erratic as her body starts to shake.

"I don't know and I really don't want to find out." I bend down to pick up one of the broken tree branches from the forest floor and hold it out in front of me like a bat. I've never played baseball in my life, but I'm planning on hitting a home run on whatever crazy ass thing appears. An unexpected ounce of courage strikes me at the thought, and I feel like we could take this creature on without a problem. Time to encourage the other two to get on board as well. "We got this, Cocksisters. Stick your chesticles out and show this fucker who's boss."

Both Darcie and Jodi stare at me a beat like I've lost my shit, and I probably have, but it's all I've got right now so I'm going with it. It must be enough because Darcie and Jodi stand next to me, a little bit taller than before, wearing the same *don't fuck with me* expression and ready to fight back. We might be insane, but at least we'll go down swinging.

Each second that passes feels like an eternity as we listen to every sound and wait for it to appear. After what seems like decades, even though I'm sure it's only seconds, it finally does. Everything happens so fast after that I don't even wait to see what it is because my survival instincts kick in. I'm not sure the thing has balls, but it's worth a shot. I take my tree branch and slam it right into its crotch. It goes down with a loud grunt, which sounds an awful lot like a man. I lift my arm ready to strike it again when a familiar voice stops me—one that has my body stiffening. It also has my vagina spasming in excitement, the treacherous bitch that she is.

"Good to see you, too, Ace."

I blink a few times in hopes my imagination is playing tricks on me. Nope, it's real. He's here in front of me, in the flesh, and I just smacked him in the nuts—hard. "Logan?"

He doesn't stop cupping his balls as he nods his head up at me. "Yeah, Ace. It's me."

"Bollocks. You mashed his bangers." Jodi stares down at Logan and cringes like it was her nuts I smashed.

"Oopsie." I drop the tree branch and bend down to help him to his feet. "You all right?"

He grunts, sucks in a gust of air, and stands all the way up. "You've got one hell of an aim. My nuts feel like they're lodged in my throat."

Logan's words are lost on me as I take in him in from head to toe. His light brown hair is a bit longer since I last saw him and his cleft chin is covered in a light dusting of hair. I will say the muff scruff looks good on him. My eyes keep going and take in the rest. A grey t-shirt hugs his perfectly chiseled upper body and shows off my favorite part of him—his biceps. Jeans hugging muscular legs give way to one hell of a fine, firm ass. There's just something about a guy with bulging biceps that turns my panties to mush. It doesn't help to cool the raging inferno of lust swarming through me when I know what he looks like without any clothes on. My tongue itches to lick every inch. Oopsie. I'm getting completely sidetracked. I shake myself out of my dickfog and come back to reality.

"How did you find us out here?" I have to remind myself not to stare at the huge mooseknuckle in his pants as I talk.

"We installed tracking systems on all of your phones back in Ireland." He steps back a foot, giving me room to digest what he's just said. Wise choice.

"You did what?" Someone better give me the strength not to smack him in the nuts again.

Darcie's face turns beet red. "Wait until I see Carter. I'm going to crush his last remaining testicle with my bare hands." She makes a fist and shakes it in the air to emphasize her point. Logan's smart enough not to touch the subject, but he does look rather pale at the thought. Considering I might have just smashed his, I can't say I blame him.

"Didn't our mobiles die after we fell into the water?" Jodi doesn't appear to be as upset as Darcie about this situation.

Logan nods. "They did. I was able to make it to that location and tracked you the rest of the way from there."

"Have you been spying on us this whole time?" The thought has me seeing red. I wish I still had my tree branch because I'd be taking another swing at him.

Logan's face falls. "It's not like that."

"Oh really? Care to explain what it is like then. I mean you left me in an Irish hospital without so much as a goodbye, and now you're here telling me you've been spying on me the whole fucking time!" My words come out so loud I'm sure they echo, but I don't care. I'm beyond pissed right now.

"When you say it like that it does sound bad." Logan winces.

"No shit, it does." My arms fold across my chest and squeeze tight against my body to keep me from strangling him.

When I don't show any signs of letting things go, he sighs. "The monitoring of your phone was for protection. Not to spy on you. I swear."

"Is that all?" I shoot him a stern look, knowing there's a lot more.

"No, but we don't have time to get into the rest of it right now. I need to get you girls out of here and to safety before they find you." At least he has enough sense to admit the truth for once. I open my mouth to argue, but he's ready for it and cuts me off. "I know what you're thinking and you can yell at me later. Just know these are bad guys, Ace. If they find us out here, we're screwed."

The dreaded reality of our situation crushes any resistance I had left. "You're right. But don't think you're off the hook. We will be talking later." I point my finger in his face and give him my best 'take no shit' attitude.

"Yes, ma'am." He nods. "When we get out of here you can scream and yell all you want." A grin spreads across his face as he walks ahead, leaving me there staring at his very fine ass. It takes me a minute to realize what he just implied will happen later. That shit. "We're burning daylight, Ace."

With that, I let our discussion go for now. We follow Logan's lead and head off once again in a direction we hope will lead us into civilization. For his sake, I hope it's the right way. I can't handle another night of camping out in the dark.

After a bit, I check on Darcie and she hasn't stopped frowning. "You still mad, Darce?"

"Yes. No. I don't know. I'm mad I've been having hot phone sex with Carter and he couldn't bother to tell me our phones were being tracked." She kicks at the ground as she talks. "Are you?"

I sigh and rub my temples. All of this shit is starting to give me a headache. "I'm not sure what to think right now. I just want to get out of here and shower."

She nods, letting our conversation drop and walking in silence the rest of the way. Both of us are lost in our own thoughts while Jodi is like a kid at the zoo. She's taking everything in like we're on a damn field trip. Then she screams and we stop.

"Check out this bloke!" She runs over to a patch of trees and bends over. Darcie and I slowly make our way towards her, unsure of what to expect. When we peek through the trees we get one hell of a surprise.

"Aw, it's a little monkey." Darcie coos as we watch the little guy hang out on the tree branch.

"How adorable. Look at him." He's the cutest little thing I've ever seen.

"Wait…" Darcie tilts her head to the side. "What's he doing?"

Jodi gasps and smacks my arm. I haven't seen her this worked up since she had her first manually induced orgasm. "He's jacking his little beanstalk."

A closer inspection reveals she's right. "He's spanking his monkey." Then I catch a glimpse of his penis. "It's like a tiny red rocket." I'm not sure why I find this fascinating, but I can't seem to look away.

"You ladies might want to step back and let him be," Logan warns from somewhere behind us, but being the stubborn women we are, of course we ignore him.

"We're fine. Besides, he's a harmless lil guy." I brush off his warning. He's not going to ruin our fun. I mean what's the worst that could happen?

Logan looks like he wants to push the issue, but thinks better of it. Good boy. He's finally learning I'm an independent woman and do what I want. I turn back around and continue ogling over the cute little monkey. He keeps jerking away without a care in the world. All seems just fine. Then it happens.

"Oh fuck! His rocket's exploding." Jodi jumps back, but not in enough time.

We hold our hands out in front of us to protect our faces, but it does little to help. The shit spurts out at us in waves. Who knew these little guys could produce so much spunk? We're covered from head to toe in monkey groin gravy. The three of us stand there in shock as the monkey smiles at us, and then scatters off into the trees. That little fucker!

"I tried to warn you." Logan's mouth twitches as the corners of his eyes crease. He's enjoying this way too much.

"I'm covered in monkey spunk and you're laughing at me!" I wipe at my face, but not in time. Some of it drips down onto my boobs and right between my cleavage.

Logan's blue eyes follow the path, darkening as they land on my chest. "You look better covered in me." The hunger behind his gaze is one I recognize all too well. He's looked at me that same way a dozen times, right before he threw me down on the nearest surface and fucked the daylights out of me.

Part of me wants to jump him, but then I remember he's a lying asshole who left me without a word. There's only one thing to do to keep things from going too far. I lean in and press my chest against him, hugging him so tightly the monkey jizz seeps into his clothes.

Logan gives me a look, but doesn't say anything. He doesn't have to. He knows exactly what I just did.

"Now we're even." A smile spreads onto my face as I turn and walk away. I don't even get a step in before a firm hand smacks against my ass cheek, causing me to jump and my steps to falter. My head whips around as I glare daggers at him.

Logan's mouth lifts into a smile. "Remember I always get even, Ace." He walks off, leaving me there contemplating how much I just screwed myself. There's no mistaking the promise in his voice. Shit.

With the monkey spunk show done, I trail behind him and envision all the ways he might get even. And I have to admit some of them sound damn exciting.

"We know that look." Darcie snorts from beside me.

"What look?" It takes everything in me to keep my face blank, but it's useless because they see right through the act. There's no hiding what I'm thinking because my face always gives it away. I'd be shit at poker.

"The one that says you are totally picturing him gnawing on your muff cabbage." Jodi laughs and skips ahead of us, tossing her head from side to side.

Monkey spunk incident forgotten, Darcie and I share a wide-eyed look and mouth the words 'muff cabbage' to each other. Usually I'm good at understanding Jodi's Britishisms, but this is a new one and I've got nothing. I shrug as Darcie shakes her head, and then we move to catch up to Jodi and her weird skipping.

Logan has managed to stay a few feet ahead and that's fine by me. The distance is much needed between us right now. Him being here is still surreal and I haven't figured out how I feel about any of it. A flutter of emotions crosses my mind. Trust is the main one. Being abandoned in a hospital bed and finding out he lied about who he was when we first met tends to make a girl gun shy of a relationship.

A sudden downpour hits, shocking me out of my thoughts. My hands cover my head, but it's pointless. Rain pounds against the ground so hard everything, including us, is soaked in a matter of minutes. The only positive is that it washes away all the monkey residue.

The rain keeps coming down harder and harder until we can barely see in front of us. We're running around in search of shelter when I hear Darcie scream. I glance up in time to see her slip and slide down the hillside, dickbag and all.

"Oh shit. Darcie!" I limp over to the edge to try to save her, but she's already long gone. This isn't good. "What the hell are we going to do?" It takes everything in me to keep my voice steady. Normally I'm the calm one and Darcie has the breakdown, but since Darcie is lost, a freak out is warranted and I'm going to be the one having it.

In a new twist, Jodi becomes the voice of reason and stands next to me. She peers down and rubs her hands together. "We've got to go after her. Hang on, luv. I'm coming for ya." She plops down on her ass and pushes off with her hands, screaming, "Flick my flaps," the whole way down.

Well, shit. I prepare to follow them when Logan's hands stop me. My eyes glance down at his arm and then up at him. "What are you doing?"

"Stopping you before you hurt yourself. You don't even know what could be down there." Water drips off his chin and I do my best to ignore it and the way I want to catch it with my tongue. Right now is about my girls.

I jerk my arm away and give him my best dick-shrinking glare. "I'll take my chances."

"Ace—" is all he manages to say before I cut him off.

"Don't you start. Those are my friends and we never leave each other behind. Ever. So, you can either stay up here by yourself or you can help me go after them and make sure they're safe." I place my hands on my hips and dare him to argue with me further.

We stay locked in a heated stare down, both unwilling to cave. Unfortunately for him, I'm stubborn as shit and could do this all day. I've had years of practice with my brother, Dusty, and won every single time.

"Shit." He runs a hand over his face and shakes his head. Then his blue eyes flick up to mine with a softness behind them. It's one I recognize all too well. One I've seen right before he makes my panties combust. He's caving. We're going after them. My mouth struggles not to break into a smile at my victory. I can't gloat too much.

"You wind up hurt, I'm going to tie you up and spank your ass. Understood?" His gaze burns into mine with such intensity that if it weren't raining, my body would be on fire.

"Is that supposed to be a threat? Because we both know it sounds more like a treat." I snort.

He leans in so close I can feel the heat of his breath against my cheek. "Take it however you want, Ace." His lips press to my forehead in a quick chaste kiss and then he backs away. He points a finger at me and narrows his eyes. "Careful on the way down."

I ignore the clenching in my gut and nod my head. He's not going to be forgiven so easily. He has to work for it this time. If I keep telling myself that, I might actually stick to it.

"Yeah, okay." I kneel down until my ass hits the soggy ground, and yuck. It's so warm it feels like I've pissed myself, but I ignore the odd sensation and give one last glance at Logan before pushing off to find my Cocksisters. "See you at the bottom." I wink.

Butterflies summersault inside my stomach as I fly down the hill. It's like riding a scary ass rollercoaster with the addition of trees jumping out at you. On the way down it splits off into three separate paths, but I'm going so fast I have no control over which one I take. I just hope it isn't a dangerous one. My screams echo against the trees the entire way down and I can also hear Logan's distant grunts behind me.

When I reach the bottom, I'm spit onto the ground face first. Seconds later, Logan lands right on top of me, knocking the air out of my lungs a second time. He rolls off to the side and I suck in a huge gust of air. "Where'd they go?"

No sooner do I ask than Darcie and Jodi come shooting down, landing off to the side of Logan. I'm not sure how we made it down before them, but at least they're in one piece.

"Bloody hell. That was fun. Let's do it again." Jodi's wearing a shit eating grin, while Darcie and her dickbag are covered in mud.

I open my mouth to check on her when bare feet invade my vision and my words are lost on me. When I glance up the leg of said feet, I find a group of dark-complected men staring down at us, guns drawn and pointed right at us, but that's not what has me pausing. It's the fact they're all naked as the day they were born.

"Bollocks. We're in a real cock up now." Jodi's not wrong. I just hope we manage to get out of this latest hiccup without me getting shot.

13

From the time we get up to the time we follow the naked guys with guns to our unknown fate, Logan doesn't leave my side. Darcie and Jodi bring up the rear and I catch brief bits of their conversation from over my shoulder. A couple of the gunmen struggle behind them. My guess is to make sure none of us runs off. Little do they know I'd rather take my chances with them than come across another monkey cranking his own handle.

The words 'willy' and 'dangling' float up from behind me and I know exactly what Jodi and Darcie are talking about. A laugh escapes free, which earns me a wide-eyed expression from Logan. Not wanting to explain, I just shake my head at him and face forward towards our captors. That's a huge mistake. I catch an eyeful of asscrack. My eyes quickly look away and focus on anything but that.

The guys rest their guns on their shoulders and don't say a word as they lead us to what I hope isn't an untimely death. I'm so glad the downpour earlier washed away all the mud we collected on our way down that mudslide. Having that shit caked on our bodies would be driving me insane. And if we're going to die at least we won't die covered in monkey spunk or mud.

"Where do you think they're taking us?" The panic in Darcie's voice does little to calm my own nerves.

"I don't know," I whisper out of the side of my mouth. A big part of me wishes I could say we'd be fine, but I'm not going to lie and give her false hope. Instead, I focus on not catching my boot on any unseen dangers, which could spring up at any moment out here. I'm pretty surprised this damn thing has survived everything thus far. It's becoming as indestructible as Darcie's dickbag.

"This is a balls-up. It's giving me the collywobbles. I hope I don't shit myself." Jodi rambles, causing her Britishisms to become wilder the longer we walk. "There are still plenty of willies left for this bird to conquer and I'm not ready to die."

"We'll be fine. If they were going to kill us they would have done so already." Logan's hand squeezes my shoulder, giving me a sense of relief as he glances back towards Darcie and Jodi to reassure them. The gesture is thoughtful and sweet, hitting me some place deep. Some place I'm not sure he's allowed into just yet. I shake it off and focus my attention forward. Things between us will have to wait to be hashed out when our lives are no longer in danger.

Calypso music vibrates through the trees, becoming louder with each step we take. Soon after, we're crossing through a canopy of trees into a clearing holding a small village. Dark skinned, naked bodies are writhing and dancing to the beat, lost in their own world. Sunlight glistens off the colorful beaded necklaces of the female villagers, but it's the way they bend and contort to the rhythm that's magical. I'm speechless. It's like watching art in motion. Tops my list as one of the most fantastic things I've ever seen—free flopping tits and all.

All dancing and music ceases the second we enter the center of their village and I don't get a good feeling. My body tenses as all eyes sear through us. The biggest guy in the group steps forward and is met by one of our captors. They bow their heads together and begin whispering amongst themselves.

While they're busy conversing, I take in as much as I can of our new surroundings. There are rows of stone huts with grass roofs spread out as far as I can see. Off to the right, I find a tiki themed bar, which is stocked full of liquor. It's odd and out of place, but who am I to judge? Then again, if I were living in a rainforest I'd be drunk as shit all day, too.

The man who appears to be in charge waves Logan forward to their group. Us three girls aren't even acknowledged. I'm guessing it's because we don't have a penis, which pisses me off.

One of the men catches the evil glare I'm shooting their way and smiles. Never breaking our connection, he says something to them and breaks away from them to move towards us. The movement doesn't go unnoticed by Logan and he clenches his jaw. The guy next to him touches his shoulder, causing him to tear his gaze away from mine, and he's soon lost in their conversation.

The one approaching stops in front of us girls, and his chocolate eyes take me in from head to toe. There's no mistaking the lust lurking underneath his gaze. Then his attention shifts to Darcie.

"Yuh shart." At his words, the three of us share a confused look before we turn back towards him. We must have heard him wrong.

Darcie's face pales as she clears her throat. "Pardon?"

"He thinks you shat your pants," Jodi whispers out the side of her mouth, which in Jodi terms means she shouted it for all to hear.

He laughs and shakes his head. "No. Yuh shat." He holds his hand up to the center of his chest to show us what he means.

"Oh, short. She's short." The three of us join in his laughter with awkward ones of our own. "That she is." Then my gaze skates down his naked body, paying him back for the once over he gave me, and stopping on an important part, which is flopping around like a dead fish— or in his case dead sardine. "And apparently, she's not the only one."

His smile never falters at my comment. Instead, he keeps on talking to us. I guess we're no longer hostages. "Muh name Ross. Ross Small."

No shit he is. I keep that thought to myself, and smile back at him as the three of us introduce ourselves.

It's at that moment Logan comes and joins our little quartet. He stands so close he's practically on top of me. His hand wraps possessively around my waist and yanks me back against his chest. My body stiffens at the sudden contact. I whip my head around to give him hell for it when I find him glaring over at Ross. The two of them are sizing each other up. Tension has become so thick it's hard to breathe. I think I'm about to be in the middle of a cockfight. And not the way I'd enjoy.

"Welcome. Muh name Bembe." My attention goes to the guy I presume is in charge of this village as he finally addresses all of us. He holds his hands out and smiles before gesturing to one of the females and putting an arm on her shoulder. "Dis muh daughter, Mia Aspurn. She tek yuh to yuh hut. Tonight we have party fuh yuh." He claps his hands together and walks off, giving us a perfect view of his bare ass.

Mia steps forward and nods her head. Her smooth dark skin is flawless, while her almond shaped green eyes demand your attention. And that's a good thing because her tits are hanging out for all to see. I side eye Logan, pleased to find that he's keeping his eyes above her shoulders. Another part of me melts at this. Not that I would blame him if he did look. She's gorgeous. If I were a sushi sister I'd be scissoring her later. She smiles and motions for us to follow her, but not before I catch the longing expression she casts towards Ross. Well, shit on a stick, this is an interesting development. And I'll be getting the Cocksister details from her later.

Logan never releases his grip on my waist as we follow her. We pass several rows of huts in an awkward silence. My hands fidget with the need for answers. They're being very hospitable to all of us, but until I can ask Logan what was said between them, I'm not convinced we're safe here.

Mia stops and motions her hand towards the hut. "Dis one fuh yuh girls."

I move to follow Darcie and Jodi, when Logan's grip tightens.

"Hold it. You're with me." My spine stiffens at Logan's command. He knows better than to order me around like this unless we're naked.

"Excuse me?" He opens his mouth to answer, but I'm too pissed to listen and cut him off. "No. I heard you. I just can't believe you think you can demand shit. You know me a hell of a lot better than that."

A muscle jumps in Logan's cheek as he stares me down. I wait him out, ready to push my point when he surprises me. His face softens and his whole demeanor changes. "Fine." He brushes his knuckle against my cheek. Gone is the angry stare, replaced with something else. Something that is my kryptonite. Lust. "I need you with me."

That little move is like a bolt of energy, striking all the way down to my core. I sway on my feet to keep from landing in a puddle at his. Damn this man. He knows how to get to me.

Mia simply nods at our exchange and motions to the hut next to Darcie and Jodi's. My gaze darts to my friends and finds two very different expressions. Darcie's awestruck and biting on her bottom lip to keep from smiling. Jodi on the other hand isn't hiding shit. She flashes me a huge grin and a quick wink. Then she heads inside their hut, never sparing me a backwards glance.

"See yuh tonight." Mia walks off, leaving me alone with the man I've spent this trip trying to forget. The one who has my emotions in a tailspin.

Without a word, Logan leads me into the hut. I glance around at what will be *our* space, something that takes me less than a minute to do because the place is the size of a small box. There's nothing in it besides the bed in the center of the room and a tiny bamboo looking nightstand next to it. It doesn't escape my attention there is no bathroom, which means I will be holding it as long as possible. I won't be repeating the earlier bathroom fiasco unless I have to. My body still cringes when I think of that little snake touching me.

I shuffle my feet against the dirt floor, moving towards the bed, and try not to think of what could be crawling all over it. I plop down and stare back at Logan. He's leaning against the wall next to the flimsy bamboo door with his arms crossed over his chest—a chest I have fond memories of licking. His biceps are straining against the fabric of his t-shirt, and flashes of how good those muscles felt when he would toss me around the bedroom flood my mind. My traitorous body grows warm at the memories. It would be much easier to hate this man if he didn't make me wet on sight.

"You doing okay?" His voice cuts through my cockfog.

Anger rises up, killing my lady boner. I want to know why he left me behind without a word, but if I don't like his answer I'm afraid I'll rip his dick off and feed it to him. A stiff nod of my head is the only response I give.

Logan sighs and crosses his feet at the ankles as his fingers play with the short hairs of his stubble. I'm really digging the muff scruff he's growing and my thoughts begin to drift where they shouldn't when the sound of his voice brings me back to the evil bitch that is reality. "How long you planning on being mad at me, Ace?" He watches my every move, gauging my response.

Honesty is the best way to go, so it's what I give him. "I haven't decided yet. I'm still pretty pissed at you."

His chin tips up in acknowledgement. "I deserve that, but you have to know I had no choice. Chief issued an order and we had to follow it. I would never have just left you like that otherwise."

"I know." It comes out so low I wonder if he heard me. Emotions clog my throat, but I choke them back down. This is something I need to get out of my system. "That doesn't make it any better. I thought you were my permanent cockride and then I'm kidnapped by a crazy nugget and find out you lied to me about who you are."

He says nothing, just watches me, waiting for the rest of my temper to unleash. Part of me wants to, but another part knows now is not the time. A girl needs to pick when to fight her battles, and in the middle of nowhere inside a tiny hut is not it. Not to mention my body still wants to pounce on his dick. Instead, I switch the topic of conversation to something more important.

"Are we prisoners here?"

Logan shakes his head and shoves his hands in his pockets. "No. They thought we were poachers, but once I explained our situation, Bembe offered us a night of shelter. We'll head back out in the morning."

This brings up something else I need to know. "What exactly is our situation? I mean what the hell is Justin involved in?"

"We have reason to believe the cruise is a front for a drug smuggling ring. Agent Rection was working undercover on the ship gathering intel when he went rogue."

"Rogue?"

"He was playing on both sides of the fence until he slipped up and they caught him."

My body shivers as I force away the unwanted images of Rection being shot. "What is your involvement in this?"

He opens his mouth to answer when there's a tap on our door. Bembe walks in wearing a huge smile, but still no clothes. "Come wit muh. I show yuh sumting."

Logan nods, before he casts a glance my way. He tilts his head, letting me know we'll finish our conversation later, and then turns to follow Bembe out the door.

I throw myself back on the bed and attempt to digest what little he's just shared. No wonder the damn cruise was free. It was all a fucking set up. My brain hurts with this information overload. I should tell Darcie and Jodi what I've learned, but my body doesn't want to move. Exhaustion seeps in making my eyelids grow heavy. It isn't long before I'm pulled under into a deep sleep. I'll deal with shit later and tell them when I wake up.

A LOUD SMACK FOLLOWED BY pain vibrating off my ass has my body jerking upright. My eyes shoot open ready to kill when I find Darcie staring back at me with a knowing smile.

"Okay. I get your point. I will stop smacking your ass to wake you up. I promise." I rub away the soreness in my butt cheek. Damn, Darce has some muscle behind her slaps.

"You slept the whole day away, luv. Time to get pissed." I glance over at Jodi and cock my head. Her hair is done in rows of small braids with multicolored beads on the ends.

"What's in your hair, Jo?"

"You like it?" Jodi swings her head around, causing the bundle of small braids to make a clicking sound and whip around like a bedazzled rope. "They're called cornrows." Somehow they work on her.

"While you slept like the dead, we spent the afternoon with Mia." Darcie moves to smack me again, but this time I'm ready and move away before she can.

"And we were willy watching." Jodi bounces up and down on the bed like a little kid.

Speaking of willies, I rub the sleep from my face and realize mine hasn't come back yet. "Where's Logan?"

"Bembe's been keeping him busy and showing him around." Darcie stands up and starts pulling me to my feet. "Come on. Let's go enjoy the festivities."

With Jodi bringing up my rear, I let Darcie lead me outside where I'm met with an explosion of music and laughter. Tiki torches light our path the entire way as laughter echoes around us. It already sounds like my kind of party. Once we pass the last hut, everything opens up and reveals a similar scene to the one we witnessed when we first arrived earlier today. The only difference is the music is coming from what looks like an early eighties boom box. Not sure where it came from, but not to going to ask either. Under the cover of night, the scenery takes on a whole new look. The energy surrounding me is giving off the best party vibes. I'm suddenly ready to give this place the Cocksister treatment.

Scanning the bar area, I find some small tables have been set up. They're made out of tree stumps and bamboo, as are the matching chairs. Not the most comfortable shit to sit on, but it'll work. I just hope I don't end up with a splinter in my clit by the end of the night.

"There's Mia." Darcie leads us to where she's sitting and sipping on a drink from a hollowed out pineapple.

As soon as we sit, drinks appear in front of us. It appears to be the same pineapple concoction Mia has. Darcie takes one look at it and sucks it back like it's water. I guess she's still into pineapples, even after her swinger incident. The smell of it isn't settling well with me for some reason, so I opt for club soda instead.

Mia smiles at us, but then her gaze moves off to the side. I follow her line of sight and find Logan and Bembe with a group of males, laughing and talking like they're old buddies, but it's Ross who has Mia's attention.

"You like Ross?"

Her smile vanishes as she slumps in her chair and nods. " I do."

"Then go get him, luv." Jodi pats her on the shoulder.

"I not pretty like dem girls." Mia jerks her head to a group of girls who are giving Ross the come fuck me eyes.

"No way. You're gorgeous and he'd be lucky to catch you." Darcie places her hand on Mia's arm, giving it a gentle squeeze.

I hate seeing someone as gorgeous as her feel so low about herself. It's time for a Cocksister heart to heart. "You are. If I was into chicks, I'd be all over you." That has the desired effect and her self-doubt disappears. It's time to release her out into the wild. "Now, it's time to go grab that dick by the balls and show him just who's in charge."

"Yuh?" Mia's hanging on every word I say.

"Yes! Ride him into the sunset and enjoy the cockdom, sister." I give her a wink and watch as understanding washes over her face.

"Yuh right." She downs the rest of her drink, wipes her mouth and jumps to her feet. "I got dis." Her newfound confidence is an amazing transformation from earlier and I love it.

"Hells yeah, you do!" Jodi slaps her on the back and nudges her forward.

We shout words of encouragement as she strolls over to Ross with a sexy as sin swagger. She whispers in his ear and his eyes light up as his little soldier rises. Her words score a direct hit. We cheer from the bar as they walk off hand in hand towards the huts.

Darcie turns to me and twists her lips to the side. "Cockdom?"

"Kingdom of cocks." I spin my finger around, gesturing to all of the cocks currently on display. "It sounded good at the time."

We laugh and go back to doing what we do best—drinking. Time passes in a blur after that. Both Darcie and Jodi toss back several more of those pineapple concoctions with ease while I continue to sip on my water. I hope I'm not coming down with a weird infection from being exposed to the shit out here.

I'm not sure how long we sit and watch the dancers, but it's enough for me to become antsy. I jump to my feet and flash Darcie a wide grin. "It's a hard cock life for us." My ass starts to twerk when Darcie puts a stop to my fun.

"Don't start. Now is not the time for you to ruin one of my favorite childhood memories. Or hear you sing 'stay at home and masturbate all day.'"

Jodi's blonde eyebrows pinch together. "I always thought it was 'steada of licked, we get dicked'?"

"It varies, depending on my mood." I take a small sip of my club soda, wishing like hell it was Jameson. Then I spin to face Darcie and stick my tongue out. "Sometimes you are like the blue balls of parties, Darce."

"You still love me." She grins and plays with the lip of her drink.

"I love you both so much. You guys are the balls to my dick and I'd be lost without you." I motion with my finger between the two of them.

"Wait. Why do you get to be the dick?" Darcie leans in, waving a finger at me. It's a sure sign she's getting drunker by the minute. The bartender must have a heavy hand. I should have made her drink water in between. Too late now. I'll just enjoy the show that is a drunk Darcie.

"And why are we the balls?" Jodi cocks her head to the side, looking as trashed as Darcie.

There are so many innuendos I could give, but neither one would get it in their current drunken state so I settle for something simple. "Because I'm taller." My shoulder nudges Darcie's arm while she downs her drink, spilling the last bit of it over her hand. She wastes no time licking it all off of each finger. It's like watching live porn.

Feeling the weight of a stare, I glance over my shoulder to find the group of young cock candy we were lucky enough to catch a glimpse of earlier, watching her every move with apt interest. If I couldn't see the lust in their gazes, the fact they're naked is a dead giveaway because I can see their man rockets standing up at full attention and ready to launch. Oopsie. Time for a distraction.

I grab Darcie's empty glass and set it down on the table. "Time for a refill." I can't help the grin on my face as I head towards the bar. Jodi and Darcie follow behind in a drunken stagger.

My chin juts out to the bartender, asking silent permission to cross his threshold. It's a sign of respect rather than just invading his space like an unwanted dick. He flashes me a wide grin and waves me over.

Excitement courses through me. There's nothing like grabbing bottles of liquor and concocting something that will have someone swallowing with a smile. I walk in behind the bar and feel like a whore in a condom factory.

"What are you doing?" Darcie watches my every move while Jodi takes a seat at the bar and waits patiently.

"What's it look like? It's time to make one of my creations." I flip and toss the bottles like I'm the star of my own version of Cocktail.

Darcie and Jodi snort as they watch me do my thing. They know when I'm in the drink-mixing zone to just roll with it.

The bar is smaller than I'm used to working behind, but it gives off a great island feel. Plus, it's well stocked. "What do we have here?" I pick up a bottle that catches my eye and an idea sparks to life. My hands make quick work, grabbing what I need as I go. I mix, shake and pour, then add the finishing touches of Reddi-wip and a slice of pineapple. I top it all off with a cherry.

Jodi claps her hands together as I slide the light purple concoction towards her. "It's so pretty. I can't wait to swallow it."

Darcie stares at Jodi's drink a beat before glancing down at her own and then back up at me. "You know how I feel about your concoctions."

"Just trust me and taste it, Darce." My finger nudges it closer to her.

She hesitates a second then puts it up to her lips and swallows. "Wow. This is really good. What it's called?" Darcie takes another big sip as I stare at the can of Reddi-wip and think of an answer. It only takes a second for it to hit me and the name is perfect.

"Pussy Whipped."

Darcie spits out her drink at my words, spraying it all over me. I really need to work on my timing. "Why? Just why?"

"What's in it?" Jodi isn't even fazed by our commotion. Then again, she has yet to stop guzzling down her drink.

As a precaution, I take a step back and list off the ingredients to her. I'm just lucky she's not a spitter like Darcie. "Mount Gay Rum, Chambord, Peach Schnapps, and Pineapple Juice."

The more they drink, the more they sway. Both of their eyes have become glossy.

"This is soooooo good." Darcie's words come out in a slurred mess. "I could swallow Mount Gay all day!" She throws her hands up and shouts above the music, bringing everyone's attention to us. I may have made these drinks stronger than I thought. Oopsie.

I'm about to switch her out for some coconut water, when Rhianna's Pon de Replay blares out of the radio. Darcie almost falls out of her chair as she stands and pulls on Jodi's arm. "Let's go dance."

From behind the bar, I watch them bump and grind to the beat, as I get lost in the music and sway back and forth against the bar. Jodi spins in a circle and whips her braids around like a wild banshee. The beads can be heard clicking together from all the way over here. She's seriously going to put someone's eyes out with those things if she isn't careful. The longer I watch them the more I sway my hips back and forth to the music. If my damn boot wouldn't trip me up I'd be out there with them.

Warmth hits my back and I stiffen. Then a pair of familiar hands grips my waist. Lips press to my ear, so close I can feel the heat of his breath and the whispers of his stubble brushing against the sensitive spot where my neck meets my shoulder. "You better be shaking this ass just for me?"

Feeling the need to mess with him, I grind myself against the hardening bulge in his jeans. "Maybe. Maybe not. What's it to you?"

Fingers dig into my sides with a bruising grip. "Careful, Ace. It's been too long since I've been inside that beautiful pussy of yours and I'm seconds away from fucking you right here."

I shudder at his words. Dirty talk is another of my weaknesses and the bastard knows it. Two can play this game. "You're right. It's been so long I forgot what you feel like in my mouth as I suck you hard and deep until you hit the back of my throat."

A groan vibrates against my neck and a smile spreads onto my face. My words blow all his self-control to shit like I knew they would. One minute I'm pressed up against Logan fighting the urge to dry hump his ass, and the next he has me over his shoulder in a firemen's hold, heading towards our hut. My thighs clench together in anticipation the closer we get. This girl needs a good dicking, and she needs it yesterday.

The last thing I hear as we make it inside is Jodi shouting, "Flick my flaps and buy me a poodle. Work that willy, Cocksister!"

I laugh and plan on doing just that.

Game. Set. Match.

14

Logan tosses me on the bed, his body following down after mine. His hands flatten on either side of my head as he glances over my body. I do the same to him and take in every detail of his rugged features. The light dusting of facial hair is growing thicker, giving him the rugged mountain man look, and it's sexy as fuck. As my gaze trails up his face, I'm met with his dark blue eyes. They're burning into me with promise—a promise of all the dirty things yet to come.

He stops staring at me long enough to twist to the side towards a tiny radio next to our bed. I haven't seen a boom box like this since high school. My eyes narrow. "Where did that come from?" It wasn't there when I checked the room earlier.

"Bembe," is all he says, and pushes play. Songbird by Oasis fills the tiny space. Warmth fills my cheeks as a smile forms on my face.

"You remembered our song. How? We were so drunk." Or at least my ass was.

"I remember everything about that night. A man never forgets the best blow job of his life." His nose grazes the underside of my jaw. It's a soft, simple touch and yet it's making my core throb with need.

"I am really good with my mouth." A breathless moan escapes me. "Those bananas really paid off." *Thank you, Mrs. Cummings.* Logan cocks his head to the side, waiting for me to explain further, which is so not going to happen. "A girl never divulges all of her secrets."

He leans down and presses soft kisses against my neck, his lips twisting into a grin against my skin. "I missed you, Ace." The deepness of his voice vibrates against my throat. It's penetrating me rough and deep, better than Henry ever could. He leans back and waits, silently asking for permission. The softness behind his gaze is turning my insides to mush. A few more seconds and I'll be putty in his hands, which leaves me feeling torn. A part of me is still hurt at what happened between us in Ireland. Another wants him as much as he wants me. It only takes a split second for me to decide. I'd like to blame lack of dick for the reason I cave so easily, but the truth is, it's not just my body, but my heart, that has missed every single inch of him. And by inch, I mean several.

My fingers trail along the stubble on his jaw. The lumberjack look is hot as fuck on him. "I've missed you, too." I lean up and press my mouth to his. The second our lips touch it's an explosion of lust mixed with need. He never breaks contact as the weight of his body pushes me down against the mattress. A soft flick of his tongue against my mouth and the feel of his hard bulge hitting my sweet spot have me gasping. He takes advantage of my open mouth and slips his tongue inside. Warmth floods through me as our tongues dance together in perfect tandem, matching the throbbing rhythm of my pussy. The humid air has grown thick with sexual tension. Weeks spent apart have only heightened our desire for one another.

My hands slide down making fast work of undoing his belt and the buttons of his jeans. I give a slight tug, letting him know without words what I want. Hell, what I *need*.

Logan breaks the kiss only long enough to help me rid him of all his clothes. Then he comes back to devour my mouth in another demanding kiss. My face stings from the roughness of his facial hair scraping my skin, but it's a pain I welcome. It's one given to me by my man. This is him claiming me, marking me as his, and I'll wear every scratch with pride.

His hands sneak under the edge of my t-shirt, and slip the cotton material up and off in one fluid motion before undoing my shorts and tossing them over his shoulder. I'm in nothing but my bra and underwear, but the way his eyes rake over every inch of my exposed flesh, I might as well be naked. The hunger staring back at me through hooded eyes is making my panties wetter by the second.

"Fucking perfect, and all mine." Logan licks his lips and cups my pussy. The small movement of his fingers mixed with the friction of the fabric has my body trembling. Slow circles tease my clit against the softness of my damp panties, drawing out an ache from deep inside my core. Logan brings his head down and sucks in my nipple through the thin fabric of my bra.

"Oh fuck." My body arches further into his touch.

He growls, ripping my panties off. I'm so far gone even the slight sting left behind doesn't register. His fingers tease along the edge of my pussy, coating themselves in my juices. "So wet for me already." He rubs my clit, soaking it in my wetness before slipping two fingers inside of me. They curl inward, stroking my inner wall and hitting my sweet spot with each thrust. I cry out as my pussy throbs with need like the greedy whore she is. "You're so sensitive. Has it been a while since you've been fucked properly?"

Guilt hits me at his words, instantly dampening the mood. I can't lie to him. "No." The word cuts like broken glass as it leaves my throat.

Logan's fingers stop and his whole body tenses, making me feel like a complete ass. "No?"

"I hooked up with this guy in a closet at one of the bars on board the ship." I squeeze my eyes shut, hoping by some miracle it also shuts down my feeling of shame. It doesn't. "I thought we were done and broken up for good or I wouldn't have done it."

"Oh." His whole body relaxes at my words as his fingers go back to stroking the fire building inside of me.

My eyes shoot open and burn into him. I'm missing something.

He's letting me off way too easily. "I just told you I fucked someone else and that's all you have to say? You're not mad?"

Logan pulls his fingers from inside me, causing a small whimper to escape. My body aches, missing his touch. He twists to the side and takes something out of his pants. Realization dawns on me as he pulls the familiar mask over his face, causing my temper to flare. I'm going to kick his ass.

"It was you? In the closet of the bar? You motherfucker!" I shove him off of me with such force he falls off the bed. My ass bolts up and wastes no time grabbing for my clothes, which have been strewn all around the room. "I can't believe you. I'm giving you total honesty and you still lie to me. Are you enjoying playing me for a fool?"

When I spin back around to face him, he's still staring at where my butt was with a faraway look in his eyes. "Why is there a Hulk's dick on your ass?" Times like these I'm thankful for my height. Instead of his six-foot frame towering over me, we're eye level. It also doesn't escape my attention he's taken off the mask and still waiting on my answer.

It takes a second for his question to register. "That's my shamcock tattoo. The girls and I all had them done in Ireland before we left."

His eyes dart up to mine. "Your what?"

"Stop distracting me and explain why you snuck on the ship and fucked me." My fingers dig into the material of my shirt as I gather the patience not to strangle him with it.

"That's not what happened."

Right. I'm not buying it and go back to grabbing my clothes when Logan yanks my shirt out of my hand and spins me around to face him. "Will you listen to me for a minute?"

My hands go to my hips as I glare back. "Fine. You better explain everything right fucking now." It doesn't escape my attention I'm in nothing but my bra, and he's standing there buck ass naked. I do my damndest to keep my gaze locked on his, but my natural response is to look down and dickgaze. It doesn't help matters that he's still hard as fuck and aiming it directly at me. He runs a hand through his hair, drawing my attention to the thick bulging muscle of his bicep. Once again, my body hums with desire. I shake my head to gather my wits and refocus on the conversation at hand.

"After we found out Rection was playing both sides, they sent me in undercover. I was supposed to gather the last bit of intel we needed to nail all of their asses, and stay the hell away from you three or else risk blowing my cover. Then you showed up at the bar wearing that fucking skirt and all of my common sense went straight to my dick."

A smile tugs at the corner of my lips at the memory of that night. It also does crazy things to my ego hearing I affect him like this. Sensing he's no longer in danger of losing said dick, Logan closes the distance between us. He wraps me in his arms and pulls me against his firm chest.

"Let me make it up to you." He plants a soft kiss on my shoulder, rubbing his jaw against my neck. The stubble on his chin grazes me, marking my skin once more. "Remind you how good I am with my mouth."

"That's a big challenge." I whimper as his fingers dance along the hook of my bra. I should hold out longer, make him beg for forgiveness, but I prefer actions to words.

"I think I'm up to the task." His teeth graze my ear as he grinds his dick against my pussy. "And something tells me you are, too." He undoes my bra and slides the straps down my arms, letting it fall to the floor. Cool air hits me as his body moves away from mine. He doesn't go far, though.

Logan lowers himself onto his knees, leaving a trail of soft kisses down my body along the way. His fingers grip my waist as his nose rubs along my inner thigh. I should feel self-conscious because I haven't showered in a few days, but I don't. And judging by the way he's inhaling my scent, it's a definite turn on for him. "You smell so fucking good." He presses a kiss on my pussy before spreading me wide open with his fingers. His tongue licks along my slit causing a deep guttural groan to escape him. "But you taste even better." He throws my bad leg over his shoulder and attacks me like I'm his last meal. His tongue thrusts inside me, hitting every nerve ending. He's relentless as he fucks me over and over with his tongue, and I gain a newfound appreciation for beard burn.

Beads of sweat drip down the small of my back, coating the rest of my skin as lust permeates the air. A familiar pull begins to build deep within my belly, one I've been missing the hell out of lately. My hips grind against his face, needing to get closer, chasing the release my body craves. I rock on my toes and bury my fingers into the hair at the back of his head, but it doesn't keep me from falling over. My foot buckles from under me, sending me falling backwards onto my ass. Logan follows, never breaking contact. The new angle causes him to find some new nerve endings that send me over the edge all over again. My body spasms as I continue to ride the high for as long as possible. When I crash back down, I lean up on my elbows and stare back at him. Eyes glazed over, my arousal glistens against his lips and his dick is standing at full attention.

"My turn." Like a cat in heat, I pounce, knocking him on his ass and sliding along his body until I'm eye level with his hard dick. My mouth waters at the sight. It's thick and veiny—perfect for sucking. The angry red head is dripping with precum and begging me to take it in my mouth. My fingers wrap around him, gently squeezing the smooth skin, and pump back and forth. Logan sucks in a gust of air through clenched teeth. Hearing his reaction spurs me on, overcome with the need to taste him. My tongue swipes out, licking the tip in slow taunting circles before taking him all the way into my mouth. He hits the back of my throat and I can't fight the moan that escapes me. Nothing gets me hot like deep-throating my man.

"Oh fuck. Yeah. Just like that." Logan's head falls back as he leans his hips into my touch.

My cheeks hollow out as I continue to suck him, deep and hard. Every growl that leaves him urges me on further. I keep at him, flicking his swollen flesh with my tongue. His hand slides into my hair, gripping it into a tight fist and holding me in place before he starts to pump into me faster and faster. He's getting close, so I keep at him. I can feel his dick begin to twitch in my mouth and I'm prepared to swallow up every last drop, but he slips free and pulls me up to him.

I narrow my eyes at him when he rubs his thumb along my bottom lip, wiping away any remnants of his nut juice. "Fuck me. I've missed this fucking mouth of yours, but this time I want to come inside your beautiful pussy." His arms fall to the side and grab his belt off the floor. He flexes the leather in his hands and eyes me. "You trust me?"

"Of course." I don't even have to think about my answer. He's one of the few people I trust with anything in the bedroom.

"Good." A soft smile spreads over his face. "Then lie back against the bed and put your hands above your head."

I climb to my feet and do as he says. Cold air hits my body as I lie there and wait. He stalks towards me like a hunter ready to play with his food. I watch with rapt fascination as he fluidly binds the belt around my wrists. He's always been good at bondage. The coolness of the leather is a sharp contrast to my overheated skin. He gently tugs on it a few times causing the material to stick to my damp skin. "It's not too tight, is it?"

"No, it's fine." The buckle moves a bit, but other than that I'm not going anywhere.

"Good." He gives me a soft kiss. "You look so fucking beautiful like this." His hands come up and cup my tits. Warm calloused fingers pinch and tease my nipples. My hands jerk against his belt, begging to touch and explore him. "Oh God."

He looks up at me and grins. "Not God, just me." His tongue swirls around my nipple, sucking until it hardens in his mouth, and moves on to do the same to the other one. Fingers thrust inside me, causing my toes to curl against the mattress. "I need to be buried balls deep inside you right now."

"Yes." My hips move on their own, searching for his dick.

He grips it and guides himself inside me. Slowly, I'm being stretched, filled with every single firm inch. My head falls back and my eyes close from the flood of desire pulsing through me. Blood pounds in my ears with every one of his thrusts. I'm getting so close. Judging by the way Logan is twitching inside of me, he is too. Then he does the damndest thing.

"The square root of two hundred fifty six is—" Logan grunts and keeps thrusting into me. "—sixteen."

"What?" My head's spinning and I'm not sure which way is up right now, but I know what I heard.

"I'm trying to keep from coming like a damn teenager. " His pace never slows as he explains.

"By doing math." That's a new one.

"Yes." He groans while his whole body trembles.

I open my mouth to ask him why, but then he hits my magic spot and all is forgotten. Everything inside me clenches as my pussy spasms. My thighs shake while I convulse from the inside. This orgasm hits me hard and deep.

My hands tug and twist against my restraints, demanding to touch him. Other than a small creaking sound, the belt doesn't give an inch. Not to be deterred, I wrap my good leg around his waist and dig the heel of my foot into his side. He gets off on the pressure and hammers into me faster. His fingers stroke my clit as I tug so hard against my bindings that his belt snaps, followed by a dull thump. Logan groans and not in a sexual way. "Are you okay?" My eyes shoot open to find him rubbing at his forehead.

"The buckle came loose and nailed me in the face." Talk about a mood killer.

"Sorry about that. Should we stop?"

"Hell, no." Logan glances down, watching where we're still connected. "Never stopping." He begins to move again and this time he holds nothing back. Watching every muscle of his body flex as he grinds against me has my own throbbing. Wetness coats our skin as our bodies slap together. He thrusts at a punishing pace, marking me, owning me from the inside out. I'm still sensitive from my last orgasm, so it doesn't take long for the next round to hit me. It crashes down on us all at once as we come together this time. His dick pulses as my body milks every last drop from him.

We lie there in the after glow, limp and sated, our labored breaths the only sound floating through the room. Several minutes pass before I'm able to move or even form a coherent thought.

"That was one hell of an apology." I'm flat on my back wearing a big ass smile and nothing else. My body has sunk into the mattress like a dead weight as it hums with pleasure.

Logan's lying on his back as well, a hand tucked behind his head. He's staring over at me wearing a huge ass grin on his face. "I'm not a flowers and candy type of guy."

"Good thing I'm more into oral apologies then." My legs feel like jelly, but he can apologize like this anytime.

"Those I can deliver." His lips trail down my body, raining kisses along the way until he hits my sweet spot. "Lots." Kiss. "And lots." Kiss. "Of those." Tongue swipe.

Moaning from outside catches our attention, stopping Logan mid-lick.

"Yus! It don' tek a big axe tuh cut down a big tree." Mia's groans cut through my cockfog.

"Go, Ross." A laugh escapes me. "I guess size really doesn't matter."

More cries of pleasure erupt, giving me an idea. I prop up on my elbows and glance down at Logan. "Think we can top them?"

A wicked smile dances along his lips. "I know we can." His teeth nibble on the tip of my clit as he gets to work making good on his word.

My body convulses and prepares for one hell of a tongue-lashing. I may end up with clit burn, but this is so fucking worth it. Death by dick is the best way for a girl to go.

15

WARM FINGERS TRAIL SMALL CIRCLES over my bare shoulder, bringing me out of a very deep sleep. My body's exhausted from the all night cockathon and I don't care to move from this bed anytime soon.

"Wake up, Ace." Whiskers tickle the back of my neck, making me groan in protest. Then Logan says the magic words. "I brought you coffee."

My body comes to life as I lean up on my elbows and take the mug. It's been days since I've had a decent cup of coffee. I take a huge sip and can't help the moan that falls out as the warm liquid coats my throat. "This is so good." It's better than good; it's the best damn cup I've ever had. Questions go off inside my head as I continue sipping on my mug of heaven—ones I should have brought up last night, but we were too busy trying to out do Mia and Ross. I'm happy to report it ended up being a tie and I couldn't be happier for Mia or myself. After hours of orgasms, math problems, and sex, we passed out. I lower my mug and purse my lips. "How is it Bembe has all of these perks?"

"What do you mean?" Logan's head cocks to the side, studying me.

"He has radios, a fully stocked bar out in the middle of nowhere, and coffee that's so good I could come from every swallow." My fingers tap against the ceramic mug as I await his answer.

"I could, too," Logan mumbles under his breath, flashing me a devilish smirk.

I laugh, knowing just what he's thinking, but don't let him sidetrack me. "You know what I'm saying."

"He and Ross make trips into the city to gather supplies." Logan presses a soft kiss to my shoulder as I lean away from his touch. He's trying to distract me, but it's not going to work. He's keeping something from me. I know it. The fact he won't look me in the eye when he answers is a dead giveaway.

I set my cup down on the table next to the bed and focus all of my attention on him. "There's more to it than that."

With a blank face, he stares back at me. He thinks if he keeps quiet I'll forget about it and move on. Too bad for him I'm a woman on a mission now. I stare back and wait the awkward silence out. Minutes stretch, and when he realizes I'm not going to let it go, he caves. "In exchange for supplies, he grows." He shrugs and says it like we're having a casual conversation.

"Grows what?" My arms fold across my chest as I continue to stare him down.

Logan runs a hand through his hair. It's longer than when I last saw him and it makes him look sexy as fuck. "Mushrooms."

It takes a second for the light bulb to go off, and when it does I want to castrate him. "Are you shitting me?" I jump to my feet and grab my clothes, shaking off the excess dirt from the damn floor. Sand in my crack is not how I want to start my day. My gaze never leaves his as I slip my shirt on over my head. "You fucking played us. This whole time you knew where we were and you've been keeping it from us." I shove my legs through my shorts sans underwear since the lying dickhead in front of me ripped the only pair I had.

"It's not like that. I swear." The muscles in his throat bob as he swallows, watching my every move.

My spine stiffens as I stand up to my full height, meeting his gaze head on. "Oh really? Tell me what it's like then?"

He opens and closes his mouth a few times, but nothing comes out. It tells me everything I need to know. I shake my head and walk out in search of Darcie and Jodi to distract me, and also to keep from crushing his balls into dust. My nose burns as tears well in my eyes, but I force them back down. This man will not see me cry. I will walk out of here with my head held high.

"Lisa!" he calls to my retreating back, but my steps never falter. I keep walking until my feet take me outside. Every step is pure torture as the rough material of my shorts rubs directly against my sore clit. I wince and squeeze my thighs together, but never stop walking. The combination of pleasure and pain is almost unbearable. Today is going to be a long ass day.

The second I make it out of our hut, I freeze. All eyes are on me and every single person is wearing a knowing smile. Some people would be embarrassed by this, but not this Cocksister. My spine straightens as I stand to my full height. I suck back the uncomfortable situation happening downstairs as I own my shit and do the stride of pride towards Darcie and Jodi.

They're both sitting at a table near the bar, which has morphed into a buffet area since last night. Without a word, I slip into the space next to Jodi and rest my elbows against the rough wood. It takes some serious shifting until I'm able to ease the dull ache happening in my shorts and focus on what they're doing. They're both shoveling food into their mouths and laughing about something when their attention comes to me.

"Looks like Mia wasn't the only one who got lucky last night." Darcie's fork freezes halfway to her mouth when she notices the expression on my face.

"You heard us, too?" A fake laugh escapes me.

"The whole bloody village heard you four shagging." Jodi knocks into my shoulder with a snort as the beads at the end of her cornrows tickle my arm. She stuffs food into her mouth, takes one look at me, and stops mid-chew. There's no hiding that something's wrong from her. "Why do you look like you've got sand in your clit?"

"Because I think I do. Logan ripped the only pair of underwear I had off me last night and now I'm free flapping it."

"And this is why I told Carter no sex on the beach for me." Darcie leans over, waving her fork at me.

"Yeah, well there will not be a repeat performance." The tears I've been fighting finally win and fall down my cheeks.

"Uh-oh. What happened?" Darcie sets her fork down, giving me her undivided attention.

I sniffle and replay my fucked up morning for them. Red colors both their faces when I finish my story. They both share a look before Jodi breaks the silence.

"That fucking twatsicle!" She slams her hand down on the table, wearing a murderous expression. "Where's a broom handle? I'm going to shove it so far up his arse he'll be spitting splinters for a week."

"What an ass. I'm sorry." Darcie reaches across the table and squeezes my hand.

"Thanks, Darce." I wipe away the last of my tears and suck in a deep breath. "And I appreciate the thought, Jo. Really, I do."

"I mean it, luv. Say the word and I'm there." Jodi slings an arm around my shoulder, tilts her head against mine and gives me a one-armed hug.

I nod. "This is why I stick with Henry. He does his job and sits on my shelf until next time. There's no bullshit or drama afterwards, just multiple orgasms." I'm really missing that little blue stiffness of pleasure right about now and the thought has me crying harder.

"We'll get you a better version of him after we get out of this mess." Darcie offers me a big smile and goes back to her food.

"You need to eat. It'll give you the energy you need to go knob chopping." Jodi spins so fast her braids snap around like a whip and damn near get me in the face. My body jerks back in time to save me from a bead to the eye.

"Those things are dangerous, Jo." I tug on one of her braids and force a smile.

She laughs my comment off and winks at me. "Cou cou."

"What?" I wipe the tears off my cheeks and stare at her.

Jodi snorts and gestures down to the plate she's setting in front of me. "The food you're eating. It's called cou cou."

"Oh." I glance down at the pile of sticky white stuff and fight the urge to gag. "It looks like a plate of jizz."

"In that case it's the best plate of jizz I've ever had." Darcie moans and shovels a huge helping of the white sticky substance in her mouth. The three of us break out into a fit of laughter and my troubles get placed on the back burner. I knew if anyone could make me feel better about this craptastic morning it would be my girls.

I stare down at my plate for another few seconds and then dig in. Once the first bite hits my mouth the shit sticks to my tongue. "It's very chewy. Like chunky spunk." I keep chewing and more of the flavor is released. "Not bad though." I dig my fork around, searching to make sure I'm in the clear. It never hurts to be extra cautious.

"What are you doing?" Jodi asks.

"Looking for mushrooms." Given what I just learned, a girl can never be too careful.

Darcie thinks about what I've said for a minute then she shakes her head. "No, they wouldn't do that." She pauses, fork in the air. "Would they?"

I open my mouth to tell her who the hell knows when Mia joins our table, putting an end to our conversation. She takes a seat next to Darcie, setting her plate down in front of her. It's piled high with cou cou and what looks like some type of fish. It's obvious she's loading up on nourishment after the workout she and Ross had last night.

"Good Marnin'" There's no mistaking the shit-eating grin she's wearing.

"Someone enjoyed their trip on the cocktrain." Judging by her glowing skin and radiant smile, I'm not wrong at all.

"De blacker de berry de sweeter de juice." Mia bites her lip and fights a grin.

Darcie chokes on her food while Jodi and I bust up laughing. If there was ever any doubt she just settled it. Mia is our kind of people.

"I guess your name has a new meaning now, Mia Aspurn." Jodi waves her fork in Mia's direction.

Darcie's still recovering from her food mishap, but manages to croak out an agreeing grunt.

After forcing down another mouthful of cou cou, I smile at her. "Welcome to the Cocksisterhood."

"Tanks." Mia dips her head and digs into her fish and jizz.

We spend the rest of our breakfast chatting and listening to Mia explaining the art of cornrows. She offers Jodi some helpful tips on how to make them last and the proper way to clean them. It's a fascinating process.

A few minutes later, Logan and Bembe stroll towards us, smiling like old friends. This morning's revelation flashes through my mind, causing my anger to resurface. I do my best to remain calm while stabbing my fork into my plate harder than necessary. When his gaze meets mine, any sense of calm flies right out the fucking window.

"You ladies ready to get going?"

Jodi nods, while Darcie stands and holds her finger up. "I just need to go grab my bag." He nods his head at her then turns his attention back to me. This time the emotion is so powerful my throat burns as tears threaten to overwhelm me once more. Everything we did last night flashes through my mind, causing my anger to blur into one jumbled mess of emotions, and I have to look away or I'll lose my mind. My hands set about picking up my breakfast mess, as I fight the urge to glance over at him. I will not be cockmatized so easily again.

Darcie comes out with her dickbag in hand, which has seen much better days. The lime green has faded into a dull moss color and the hot pink is more like a shit brown. Not to say my boot's done any better under these conditions. What was once a bright white is now a dingy beige color.

We say our goodbyes to everyone and are greeted with lots of smiles until they get to me. I'm given more smirks and once overs than I've had since Kristyn and I fooled around in college. Apparently, I've made status as the village whore. I'll wear that shit with pride. It's just another thing I can add to my fucket list.

I walk over to Mia and embrace her in a tight hug. Meeting her has been one of the best things about this whole mess.

She sighs against me. "Tank yuh, for everythin'."

"Anytime, Cocksister." And I mean it. She's one of us now.

"De sea ain't got nuh backdoor," she whispers in my ear and gives me one last squeeze before backing away.

"No backdoor. Got it." I nod to myself, assuming it's a Bajan saying for safe anal play.

A familiar warmth seeps against my back as I watch her hug Jodi and Darcie, and I know without turning around who's standing behind me. He's also smart enough to keep his hands to himself.

Bembe nods at him over my head before resting his gaze on me. "Doan be nuh stranguh." The way his eyes are glazed over, I'm thinking he's broken the cardinal rule and gotten high off his own supply.

With those parting words, we set off on our way. Halfway down, I turn back for one last glance at our new friends and smile at what I see. Ross slings his arm around Mia's shoulder and kisses the side of her head. It's safe to say we made an impression on the two of them.

I wave one last time at Mia until they're out of sight, and continue limping on. Then it's just us girls accompanied by one lying jackass, heading towards civilization. And I can't wait to get the hell out of here. The thought of finally being out of this forest has me anxious. Nothing sounds better than a hot shower and being able to use an actual toilet—except maybe some underwear. There is finally some light at the end of this crazy tunnel. I just wish the burning in my crotch would ease up. Between the beard burn and the material of my shorts, my poor clit is thrashed. I'm trying not to wince with each step. Next time I'm stashing an extra pair of underwear in Darcie's dickbag.

For most of the morning, Logan and I keep our distance from each other, but there's no missing the tension that fills the air. He takes the lead, while I hang back with the girls. The less I'm around him the better right now. My temper hasn't cooled and I'm afraid of what I might do.

Darcie, the peacekeeper, strikes up a conversation to ease some of the strain. "Have you been in touch with Carter at all?"

Logan shakes his head. "Not since we lost Agent Rection." His gaze shifts from Darcie onto Jodi. "He and Ryder stayed behind to find out how much of the operation was compromised, but they asked me to keep an eye on the two of you."

Jodi snorts at the mention of Ryder. Clearly, she's still pissed off at him for the Ireland incident. Good to know I'm not the only one who can hold a grudge. "He can sod off."

Logan realizes he's not winning any points with any of us, and stops talking. Silence once again stretches between our group like a rubber band ready to snap, only this time it's his ass getting stung not mine. We walk for a few more miles before he sighs and turns towards me. "How long are you planning on being pissed at me, Ace?"

"A while." I stop and glare at him. I'm not caving so easily this time. He's going to have to work for it. There are too many options to hide a body out here and he needs to remember that. Hell hath no fury like a Cocksister scorned.

Darcie and Jodi hang back in silence, watching our exchange.

"I'm sorry, all right?" He throws his hands out wide. "With my job there's some shit I can't tell you. I just need you to trust me. If I thought you were in any danger I would have told you."

A snort comes from behind us, but I don't turn to see who it is. I'm too focused on the infuriating cocksicle in front of me.

"Sure you would have." My eyes roll back in my head so hard I get a slight headache. He's not pulling this shit on me twice. "And sorry, but right now you're the last person I trust. I understand the need to keep some things to yourself because of your job, but this is bullshit! It's bad enough I woke up in Justin's bed after he drugged me, but you're no better. You've done nothing but lie your ass off." I brush past him and stomp away. It would be a more dramatic exit if my damn boot didn't slow me down.

He reaches me a moment later and grabs my wrist, spinning me around to face him so fast my boot catches in the dirt. "I'm sorry, could you repeat that."

"You heard me. He drugged all three of us and when we went to confront him, we saw him put a bullet in your friend's head." It isn't until the words are out I realize I should have kept that shit to myself.

Logan's face grows hard. The muscle in his cheek twitches and his jaw clenches. I've never seen him so angry. He turns around and storms off.

"Bollocks," Jodi mumbles from behind us, followed by an, "Oh shit," from Darcie.

This is not good. I traipse after Logan when something flies through the air. His steps falter as he cups the side of his neck. Seconds later, his legs buckle from underneath him and he's collapsing to the ground.

Our argument is shoved aside as fear grips me. "What's wrong?" I bend down and check him over when Darcie and Jodi's shouts of pain register next. They do the same as Logan and fall to the ground into a lifeless heap. "Shit on a dick!" This is bad, very bad. I stand and run back towards the village in search of help. Thanks to my damn boot, I stumble along the way and end up resembling a free flopping dildo.

A sharp pain stings my ass after a few steps, but it doesn't deter me. I'm a woman on a mission. I reach back and feel a dart sticking out of my right ass cheek. My fingers tighten around it and yank it free in one quick motion. Needles are like one-night stands. It's best to pull the fucker out fast.

I toss the dart aside and keep moving, but I don't make it very far because my legs become heavy, like anchors dragging me down. Coolness floods my body as my steps falter. Tingles course through my limbs and numbness takes over. My vision blurs while I sway back and forth. There's a solid mass next to me, which resembles a tree, and I raise my hand to brace myself for balance. Too bad I miscalculate the distance. My hand misses and I end up face planting into the ground. My head lands to the side, saving me from ending up with a broken nose, but the dirt scrapes my skin, stinging like a bitch.

Footsteps move near me, and the last thing I hear before I pass out is a familiar voice taunting me. "Told you I'd find you, Coxy."

16

SHARP SHOOTING PAIN ALONG THE side of my neck is the first thing I feel when I come to. Cold metal digs into my spine as the itchy burn of a rope digs into my wrists and ankles. There's also a sharp stinging sensation coming from my ass cheek. *What crazy ass situation did we find ourselves in now?*

My eyes crack open, but I can't see shit. Whatever was in that damn dart has made my vision blurry. After blinking a few times, things begin to come into focus and that's when my heart stops. I'm inside some room I've never seen before. When I glance down my body and do a once over for injuries, I see red. They took my fucking boot off. "Those giant dickholes!"

Groaning from my left catches my attention and halts my screaming. Jodi's moving around and finally waking up. Behind her, I hear but can't see Darcie begin to stir as well. They're pressed back to back with a band of rope wrapped around their midsections, and Jodi is the only one facing me. Other than looking like she's been thoroughly fucked outside with a few scrapes and dirt stains, she's fine. Even her cornrows managed to survive the kidnapping in one piece.

I lean around her to check on Darcie with my own eyes and relief washes over me. She's in pretty much the same condition as Jodi. Even her dickbag has made the trip in tact as it sits next to her feet. I sag against the metal pole holding me up and take a minute to absorb everything. The good news is all of us are in one piece. I just hope it stays that way and none of us ends up shot this time.

"Why does my mouth feel like a dog's dirty arsehole?" Jodi smacks her lips together and shakes her head.

"It's probably the after effects of whatever they gave us." Anger courses through me at the thought of us being drugged—again.

"Where are we?" Darcie slowly takes in our surroundings. Then her nose scrunches up and she sniffs the air a few times. "And why do I smell chocolate?"

"I don't know." My head falls back against the metal, hoping to alleviate some of the tension running through my body. My efforts are in vain. Everything from the top of my head down to my toes is beginning to ache. The longer I'm stuck in this position, the harder it's going to be for my ass to get up.

"Willies!" Jodi's shouts out of nowhere, her finger waving around the room like a wild dick.

Darcie snorts and glances in the same direction, but in her position I'm not sure she can see much. "They must have given you some strong stuff, Jo. I think you're hallucinating."

My neck cranes and I find exactly what has Jodi so excited. There are rows and rows of stacked boxes. Some are torn open and have big chocolate dicks spilling out the top, while others are sealed shut with strips of red tape. But it's the chocolate dicks that grab my attention and give away our location. A burst of excitement surges through me. "I know where we are now. We're in the Erection Confection candy factory."

"Why would they bring us here?" Darcie asks. She doesn't wait for an answer before she's talking again, suffering one of the worst cases of verbal diarrhea I've ever seen. "Unless they're planning on killing us and putting our dead bodies in the chocolate. Oh my God! We're going to die and become chocolate dicks. We're only thirty-five. That's too young to die. And even if we do die, I don't want my final resting place to be inside a chocolate dick." Her voice rises an octave with every word. If she keeps this up she's going to cause a major scene. And the last thing we need is for our captors to know we're awake, at least until we've had a few minutes to come up with some sort of a plan.

"At least we'll melt in your—"

"Don't even say it. You are not going to ruin my favorite candy for me."

"Seriously, Darce? Screen writing for all those pornos has rotted your brain. I'm sure they'll kill us at sea. It's much easier than hacking our asses up into tiny pieces." It's meant to be reassuring, but judging by the way Darcie's body shakes I may have made it worse. I really need a damn filter. Something about this whole conversation niggles at my brain, but for the life of me I can't figure out what.

"Not helping." Darcie groans and hangs her head.

"Where's Logan?" Jodi changes the subject and I could kiss her, but then guilt hits me at her words. I've been so preoccupied with dicks and Darcie, I forgot all about him.

"I don't know." Images of what they could be doing to him make my stomach churn. The thought of him meeting a fate similar to Agent Rection has fear coursing through me, just the thing I need to light a fire under my ass. "We need to get out of here and find him before something bad happens."

"How?" The uncertainty in Darcie's tone doesn't go unnoticed. If she could see my face right now, I'm sure she'd be staring at me like my tongue's turned into a dick. Lucky for me, she can't.

My gaze dances around the room until they land on a door not too far from us. Then I glance down at the rope binding my legs together and my lack of boot. Even if we somehow manage to get free, my limp would slow us way down. I shake my head and form a plan because I refuse to let it deter me. It will be difficult, but not impossible to do.

All thoughts of escape disappear when weighted footsteps echo from outside and stop just in front of the door. Hinges creak and my whole body tenses up as Justin, Kristyn, and two other guys walk into the room. These guys' arms are the size of my thighs and they're both built like brick shit houses. One has a giant mole in the center of his forehead, while the other has a crescent shaped scar that runs down the entire side of his neck. The one with the scar looks oddly familiar, like I've seen him before, but my mind is racing so fast I can't place where.

Both of the guys are tall and mean looking motherfuckers, but it's who they're holding that has me gasping. An unconscious Logan is being dragged to the center of the room. His face is marred with cuts, and dried blood mars his brow bone and along his bottom lip. It looks like he was involved in some BDSM gone wrong.

Justin grabs a chair from around the corner and sets it in the center of the room before motioning the guys holding Logan forward. "Put him here and use these." He pulls a pair of cuffs out of his back pocket and tosses them to the one with the mole.

They plop his unconscious body in the chair and mole-man handcuffs his hands behind his back. Once he's secured, they step back, fold their arms across their massive chests, and stand guard by the door like a couple of pit bulls.

Kristyn strolls towards us, wearing a plastic smile and once again dressed in a business mixed with pleasure outfit. She has on a black leather corset, a matching pencil skirt, and those same thigh-high fuck me boots I saw her wearing at The Wicked Tuna. "You're awake and just in time to join the fun." Blank eyes stare back at us waiting for our reply and that's when I see it. I'm not sure why I haven't noticed it before, but it's flashing like a red neon sign now. She's one testicle shy of a full set. Her chin tilts forward in a silent command.

The big guy with the mole steps forward and slaps Logan in the face. Logan doesn't stir, so he does it harder. The sound of skin slapping together in a non-sexual way has me cringing.

"Easy, Clamshank. I don't want him dead before we can get what we need." Kristyn glares at him.

Jodi and I share a look at the mention of the poor bastard's name. We thought our last names were bad, but nope. He wins, hands down.

The one I now know is Clamshank hits Logan once more and this time he finally comes around. Logan coughs as he comes to and slowly lifts his head. The cut above his right eye doesn't appear to obscure his view any. His eyes narrow as he glares daggers at Justin. I don't think I've ever seen Logan look so pissed off.

"I'm going to kick your ass." He fights against his restraints, struggling to break free.

"From where I'm standing, you're the one whose gotten their ass kicked." Justin laughs, but it's forced. The skin around his phallic-shaped mole grows pale and sweat builds on his forehead, giving him away. His bravado's all an act. The truth is he's a weasel with a tiny dick and a porn star mustache, and he's all talk.

"No, you just need to drug women to get laid." Logan clenches his jaw so hard I can hear his teeth grind together from where I'm sitting.

"Is that what she told you?" Justin shoots me a look and shakes his head at me. "I told you, Coxy. Nothing happened."

"And destroying our rooms?" I shouldn't be encouraging him to keep talking, but I need to know more. I know there's more to the story than what he said before.

"Like I told you earlier, it was to make sure they weren't keeping tabs on you and that Agent Rection didn't hide anything in your rooms."

"And waking up naked in your bed was just a bonus?" The more I think about that part of the evening, the more pissed off I'm getting.

"What the fuck? You forgot to mention that part." Logan's whole body tenses at that little bomb. Oopsie.

Justin ignores him and gives me his full, undivided attention. "You really need to work on your trust issues."

"Says the lying asshole with the gun." I mutter under my breath, surprised he's explaining anything to me at all. Then a thought occurs to me. Tamping down my fear, I continue to push him for more information. Maybe if I can keep stalling it will give Logan or the girls time to come up with a plan on how to get us out of here alive? "Why didn't you take me back to my room?"

Justin shrugs as his lips curve into a smile, causing the handles of his mustache to move. "I may have enjoyed the view of you in my bed.

You know, like old times." His hazel eyes travel all the way down my body, stopping at my legs. "You remember, don't you?"

"I take back what I said. I'm not going to kick your ass. I'm going to fucking kill you," Logan threatens. A vein throbs on the side of his head as he thrashes against his bindings. It's like he's gone into Hulk mode.

Justin's cool gaze lands on Logan and he laughs. "Again, you're the one who's in the chair with a busted lip."

"Only because you outnumbered him. You wouldn't last in a fair fight, you cuntmuffin." I probably should have kept my mouth shut, but I've never been good at doing what I should.

"Good thing I don't fight fair then." Justin grins at me as he pistol-whips Logan, causing the three of us girls to gasp.

"Enough." Kristyn rolls her eyes. "I can't handle anymore of this pissing contest." She points to a stack of boxes. "Clover, take those boxes out to the front and prepare the rest for delivery."

The one with the scar in his neck, who I know now as Clover, nods his head and grabs an empty box from the far corner of the room. He disappears through the door, but not before I catch a small glimpse of the hallway. Flashbacks to when we took our tour come to me and I know exactly what part of the factory we are in.

"The whole task force is aware of your drug smuggling operation. You might as well cut your losses and give up now." Logan continues taunting them. I really hope he knows what he's doing and not trying to get us killed.

"Doubtful." Justin comes to stand next to Kristyn and crosses his arms over his chest. Of course, it's nowhere near as hot as when Logan does it. Then again, everything he does seems like a cheap knockoff in comparison, even his facial hair. "We have friends in much higher places than even you know."

Logan snorts as if he knows something they don't. "That's where you're wrong."

"Enlighten us then?" Kristyn puts her hands on her hips and cocks her head to the side.

"Agent Rection found all of your contacts and managed to send them to my superiors before you took him out." Logan's tongue licks at the cut on his lip, taking a dramatic pause. "I must admit it was pretty smart of you to use a cruise ship as your cover and smuggle the drugs inside the chocolates. You have unlimited access to ports all over the country. Too bad for you, we're smarter. We have everything we need to take you down. All your suppliers, contacts, and accounting info is in the hands of the FBI as we speak."

Kristyn isn't shaken by his confession. If anything, she looks turned on. She leans down until she's a hair's breadth away from Logan's face. "We'll have to call your bluff, won't we?" Her tongue darts out and licks up the side of his cheek, groaning as I assume the hairs of his beard tickle her tongue. "Damn, you taste good—salty and toxic, my favorite combination. Such a pity I can't keep you. You'd be a great toy."

"Hey!" Justin whines like the little bitch he is. I can't believe I ever let that fucker punch my v-card.

"Don't worry, babe. You're still my number one." She pats him on the cheek like he's a toddler.

Logan opens his mouth to keep taunting them, but Kristyn isn't listening. She shimmies her panties down her legs and balls them up in her hands. Then she shoves them in Logan's mouth, letting her fingers linger against his lips. "Shh. Too much talking. I prefer my men like my vibrators—silent."

The bitch! The only panties ever going in his mouth are mine.

Kristyn's gaze flicks to me as a wicked smile curves her lips. I guess I said that out loud. Oopsie. She moves to step towards me, but stops and takes her phone out from between her boobs. Her face lights up as she glances at the screen.

"Bembe's here. Let's see what he has for us and then we'll come back and deal with them later." Kristyn waves the guys ahead of her. The last thing I see as the door closes is her wink as she blows me a kiss.

If we don't find a way out of here soon, we are going to be so fucked and not in a good way—more the 'I'm going in dry' type of way.

17

WE ARE NOT GOING TO sit here waiting around for them to kill us. No way. Cocksisters never go down easy unless it's on a hot dick. I glance at Logan, letting him know without words we're getting him free and all of us the hell out of here. His gaze holds mine as he gives me a slight nod of his head. It's all the encouragement I need.

My arms twist against the rope over and over, but it's no use. These knots are tight as shit. "I can't get free. Can you two stand up and untie him?" I jerk my chin in Logan's direction.

"On it." Jodi nods her head so hard the ends of her cornrows click together.

"How the hell are we going to do that?" Darcie's not feeling as optimistic as Jodi about this, but since they're tied together she has no choice but to go along with it.

"Push against my back and we'll counter each other's weight, luv." Jodi sits up straighter and takes charge of the situation.

After a few attempts and a lot of grunting—mostly from Darcie—they're finally up on their feet. They manage to get a few steps in, but then Darcie's foot catches and they fall forward. Jodi takes the brunt of the impact, headfirst into a pile of sealed boxes.

"Shit, sorry." Darcie presses her lips together in a firm line and thinks for a second. "On the count of three, rock forward with me and I'll pull you up."

The second they're back on their feet, Jodi inhales a deep breath. "Thanks, luv."

It takes Jodi and Darcie a second to collect themselves and keep upright until they move again. They're able to take a couple more steps before they teeter from side to side, almost tripping once again. Darcie sighs. "I told you I can't do this." Her frustration is getting us nowhere. It's time for some Cocksister love.

"You got this. It's just like dancing, Darce." Encouraging her is the only thing keeping me from going insane. I hate sitting here watching. I'm like a limp dick at a whorehouse—completely useless.

"I'm not a good dancer. You know this." Darcie's voice wavers as she leans against Jodi.

Images of our high school talent show fiasco flash in my head and I do my best not to cringe. "That doesn't count. You were wearing my cousin's clothes and they were two sizes too small."

"She's right, luv." Jodi bends over so fast to emphasize her point that it causes them to almost lose their balance again. "Besides, it's not your fault you weren't wearing any knickers that day."

Darcie lets out a fake laugh. This isn't working like I hoped it would. She's going to need more convincing.

"You're a legend, Darce. They still talk about what happened to this day." She just doesn't need to know exactly what they're saying.

"They do?" Darcie's face lights up at the thought.

"Yup." I press my lips together and give her a stern nod. Her features soften as I see her confidence building. "And legends can do anything. Keep a steady one-two rhythm in time with Jodi's steps and you'll be just fine." I keep her focus on me and not on the thought of her ass being flashed to our entire school.

Darcie takes a deep breath and nods. "Okay. I can do this." Her lips move as she counts and keeps tandem with Jodi's steps. They shuffle the rest of the way across the room at a steady pace, only tripping a couple more times before they make it to Logan.

Jodi pulls the bunched up panties out of his mouth and wipes away the dried blood from his nose with them before she drops them to the floor. "There we go. All better, luv."

"Thanks." Logan clears his throat and stretches his mouth around. "There's a back way out of here. Untie me and we can sneak out through there and grab one of their boats." He gestures towards his hands and the slight movement causes him to sway. His eyes blink a few times as he shakes his head, and something doesn't seem right. They must have hit him harder than I thought. We might be carrying him out of here.

"You sure you can walk?" I take in the dried blood on his face and fight the urge to pluck the hairs out of Justin's mustache one at a time.

"I'm good, Ace." He'd be more convincing if the bruising around his cheek wasn't puffing up.

"Hold tight. We're going to walk around to see if we can untie your arms." Darcie hobbles forward, dragging Jodi behind her. This time they've gotten the hang of it and manage without any issues. They don't get very far when a door outside slams followed by footsteps coming from down the hall. This is not good. If they catch them, we're going to be fucked up the ass without lube.

"Shit! Somebody's coming." My heart lodges in my throat. Darcie and Jodi shuffle back towards me, but I stop them. "Wait! The underwear."

"No!" Logan protests, but it falls on deaf ears.

"You have to. They'll know something's up if they see them on the floor." My gaze bounces from him to Jodi. A slight tilt of her head lets me know she agrees with me.

As one, Jodi and Darcie lean to the side. Jodi swipes the underwear off the floor with the tips of her fingers and eyes Logan. "Sorry about this, luv. I truly am." She sighs and raises her hand back to his lips. Logan opens his mouth to protest, but Jodi shoves them inside his mouth before he can make a peep. He glares my way and I shrug. He's not happy about this and I don't blame him, but there's no other choice. We can't risk them catching us trying to escape.

Darcie and Jodi hobble back towards me, falling back down against the metal railing into a sitting position in a matter of seconds. They land so hard I can hear the air being knocked out of them.

"You two okay?"

Jodi groans and squeezes her thighs together. "I think I bruised my flaps."

"I'm good." Darcie pants like she's just had an all night sex marathon from behind her. "That was close."

Justin chooses that moment to come strolling through the room with Clover and Clamshank behind him, wearing a smug smile. Anger boils up inside me. When we get out of this I'm going to punch the fucking dick shaped mole off his face and cut off his tiny dick. "Time to go."

My spine stiffens. "Go? Go where?"

Justin ignores me and motions a silent command with his head to both Clover and Clamshank.

Clover frees Logan, pulls him to his feet, and aims a gun at his head. "Try anything and he puts a bullet in one of the girls."

Logan spits Kristyn's underwear of his mouth and glares at him, but doesn't say anything. His hands ball into fists at his side, anger radiating off of his every pore. He glances towards us, sucking in a deep breath, and studying the shit show that is our situation. His jaw clenches as he walks out the door with stiff movements. There's no doubt in my mind it took everything he had not to knock Clover out, and he did that for us, which makes all the small shit he did to me seem insignificant.

Clamshank unties Darcie and Jodi, and orders them to their feet. He curls the side of his mouth up in a lopsided grin as he holds his gun on them. "Follow him."

Darcie clutches Jodi's hand as the two of them trail behind Logan. My stomach twists as I watch them leave. Then Justin's ugly face is right in front of mine, cutting off my view.

"Up we go." He grabs my arms and drags me to my feet in one quick motion and then he tosses me over his shoulder like dead weight. The overpowering stench of his cheap cologne punches me in the face and a wave of nausea hits me. I have to fight the urge to puke all over him.

"Put me down. If you untie me I can walk." My hands pound against his back, but he ignores it and keeps walking. Each step causes the material of my shorts to ride up further and rub against my lady bean. Since I'm still going commando, it's giving me one hell of a clit burn.

"No can do, Coxy. Besides, I like you all tied up like this." Justin's boney ass shoulder digs into my stomach as his mustache tickles my thigh. When we walk out into a hallway, I push my hands against his back for leverage and glance around. Through one of the windows I see a familiar face with the same forehead skin sagging over his eyebrows. John Thomas stares at me with a knowing look as we pass by and then continues on with whatever he's doing. I guess he remembers our sparkling personalities from the tour.

Sunlight blinds me as we make it out into the open air. We're shoved into the back of a couple of golf carts and driven off in silence. The tension-filled ride doesn't last long before I feel us slow down to a stop.

The sound of waves crashing hits my ears as the smell of the ocean washes over me. Maybe we will be buried at sea after all?

Justin grabs me, throws my body back over his shoulder, and starts walking again. His steps change from soft to hollow as they clunk against the wooden deck. He only makes it a few feet when a female voice stops him.

"Not so fast, Justin Bush."

"FBI, dickhead! Drop your guns." I'd know that Australian accent anywhere. My hands push against Justin's back to keep upright and get a better look. Tre and Kate are aiming their guns in our direction, looking like total badasses. My jaw drops. This is a twist I never saw coming.

"Is anyone on this bloody cruise who they say they are?" There's no hiding the confusion in Jodi's voice.

"Who cares? We're saved." My body sags against Justin's with relief, but it's short lived. One minute Tre and Kate have their guns drawn on them and the next they're on the ground with darts sticking out of their necks.

Kristyn slinks out of the shadows wearing a cavalier expression with Darcie's dickbag slung around one shoulder and a gun in her other hand. "I knew those two were fishy."

"What should we do with them?" Clover tilts his chin towards the unconscious women.

"Put them in the golf cart. We'll come back for them later." Kristyn waves her gun in our direction. "We'll toss them overboard with the rest."

Clover nods his head and tosses Tre over his shoulder like a sack of potatoes. Clamshank does the same with Kate's body and I watch helpless as they dump them inside the back of the golf cart.

Justin's shoulder digs further into my stomach as he pushes his gun against Logan's head. "Don't even think about it." His body leans forward and he plops me down on the dock. "Stay," he orders like I'm a damn dog and then waves his gun at Darcie and Jodi. "You two sit next to her." He waves them over with the tip of his gun. They shuffle until they're next to me and slide down until they're seated on their butts.

Justin and Kristyn break off and have a private conversation, while we sit there and watch. Judging by the way Justin's thrashing his arms around it's an intense one.

From my position I can make out the outline of our cruise ship and something that has been niggling in the back of my brain finally clicks into place.

"That's what she meant," I whisper out loud, mostly to myself.

"Who?" Darcie stares at me like I've lost my mind, and I probably have.

"Mia. Before we left she said something to me and I wasn't sure what she meant."

"What did she say?" Jodi asks.

"*De sea ain't got nuh backdoor.* I thought she just meant anal." I shrug, causing the rope to dig into my wrists.

"Of course you did," Darcie snorts.

"Now, I'm thinking she was trying to warn us about this."

Kristyn chooses that moment to break away from Justin and strut in our direction, gun aimed at us while he heads off towards Logan. She tosses Darcie's dickbag down by her feet and stares at me. "I'm truly sorry about this, but don't worry. I'll make your death quick." She rattles on, but movement from the floor catches my attention, causing her voice to become background noise. It's subtle, but there's no mistaking that something is alive inside it. My eyes switch between Kristyn and the bag, wondering if I should even warn her. Then a small snake—much like the one that crawled on us days ago—pokes through the top, flicking its tongue out. Judging by the gasps next to me, Darcie and Jodi see it, too.

"Um, I hate to interrupt you, but—" Darcie attempts to cut off her rant, eyes glued to the same slithering thing mine are.

"Be quiet." Kristyn never takes her focus off of me as she ignores Darcie entirely.

"But, luv, I really think—" Jodi tries once more to catch her attention, but fails.

"Shut up!" Kristyn swings her gun towards Jodi. "I'm talking now and you aren't going to distract me."

"But, I really think you should—" My mouth snaps shut as I watch the tiny snake slither up her leg and disappear under her skirt.

This time Kristyn shifts the gun to my head. "Stop talking. Or I'll..." She freezes mid-rant. Her mouth hangs open at the same time her eyes grow wide. It's obvious what's happened the second she screams and drops her gun. "What the fuck is that?"

We remain quiet and watch with horrified fascination as Kristyn starts jumping all over the place, waving her arms around. "This is worse than crabs!"

Darcie's face pinches together as her color pales. I don't blame her. Having something slither up in one's cockpot is the equivalent to a man having his balls snipped.

Jodi breaks the silence. "That looks bloody awful. It went inside her undercarriage."

Justin rushes over, gun raised. "What the hell's going on over here?"

"Something just slithered inside my honey hole." Kristyn lifts up her skirt and bends over, exposing her ass. Since she's still commando from earlier, everything is on display for all to see. "Help me get it out!"

Clamshank and Clover watch from the sidelines, their faces pulled tight. Not sure when they came back, but to be fair I've been slightly distracted by the shit show in front of us that I'm dubbing as Vaginageddon. Even Logan is staring and turning a light shade of green. I don't blame him; it's not something you see every day.

Justin is kneeling down with his face buried between Kristyn's legs, the ends of his mustache peaking out the sides of her thighs. "It's caught on your piercing." He turns his attention to Clover. "I need more hands in here."

Clover sighs and comes around to help. Clamshank hangs back with Logan, but his gaze stays transfixed on Kristyn's crotch and I swear he's going to either puke or faint.

"Don't tug on it that way!" Kristyn screams, making me cringe. "You're going to rip it out."

"Bloody hell, her poor flaps. It's caught on her bean bling." Jodi winces next to me and fidgets with her hands. I nod my head, thankful it isn't my lady lips that are in trouble this time.

Seeing two men with their faces buried up in Kristyn's shit is not how I envisioned this day going, but this is just the distraction we needed. I nudge Darcie with my shoulder and give her the signal. A slight nod of the head is the only sign I get she's understood. She nudges Jodi with her elbow and passes along the plan.

Once Jodi's on board, she wastes no time jumping to her feet like a rabid ninja, springing into action. She swings her head around so fast I'm amazed she doesn't get whiplash. Her cornrows look awfully similar to what just crawled up inside Kristyn's crotch and that thought alone has my thighs clenching together. From that point on, complete chaos ensues.

Logan takes advantage of the distraction we created and tackles Clover. They fall over and begin to wrestle for the gun. Punches are thrown as they roll around the deck battling for dominance.

"Shit!" Justin moves to intervene, but Kristyn stops him.

"Clamshank can handle them. Get this fucking thing out of me or I swear I'm going to shoot you in the dick."

Justin goes back to what he was doing while Clamshank strolls towards Jodi. She whips her head towards him, but he jumps out of the way before she can nail him. He takes off his jacket and cracks his neck back and forth. "You want to play?" Smirking, he crouches down and waves her forward. "Let's play, blondie."

"Um, Jo, I don't think you should do that." Darcie attempts to be the voice of reason, but Jodi's lost on her own planet right now and has become the British version of La Femme Nikita.

"I've got this, luvs. This wanker is going down. He's made a huge cock up messing with us." Jodi's blue eyes have gone black at the same time as her body twitches back and forth. She looks feral as she stares him down. It's safe to say our British Cocksister is pissed off.

"This is not going to end well," Darcie sighs. I'm not sure if she's too tired to freak out, but it's unnerving how calm she is right now.

"Untie me so we can stop her before something bad happens." As soon as I get the words out, Jodi launches herself at Clamshank. She must catch him by surprise because he jumps back a few steps. Her legs wrap around his waist, as she clings to him like a spider monkey. The movement causes her braids to whip the shit out of his face in the process.

Darcie scoots closer and works at untying me, while Logan's grunts echo from behind us. But, it's the show that is our Jo I can't look away from. Darcie's fingers struggle to loosen the rope and after a few failed attempts, my wrists are finally free. I move to work on freeing my legs when movement from over her shoulder catches my attention.

"Look out, Darce!"

Clamshank's right behind her, dodging and weaving away from Jodi and heading straight for us. I'm not sure how he managed to scrape her off of him, but he did and looks ready to kill. Before he can reach either one of us, Jodi intervenes once again. She spins her neck around and whacks him in the head with her hair. The force behind those braids is like a heavy rope and knocks him out cold. He falls to the ground, but Jodi's so cranked up she keeps going. She's like a wind up toy of destruction, knocking anything out of her way. I'm amazed she isn't dizzy yet.

"Take that you bloody arsehole!" she screams at no one in particular.

Darcie and I stare after her with our mouths hanging open. "Fuck me in the ass with a spork! Did that really just happen?"

"It did." I work the ropes the rest of the way off my legs and roll up onto my knees, but get stuck halfway. My bad leg is seriously cramping my style. Darcie grabs my arm and helps me the rest of the way.

"I got it." Justin holds the snake in his hand and scrunches his nose. I don't even want to know how he managed to get that thing out of her.

"Good." Kristyn pulls her skirt down and composes herself. "Now take care of them!"

Justin throws the snake over his shoulder and it slithers away into the unknown. Pressing his lips together into a firm line, he aims his gun at us. "I'm really sorry about this, Coxy."

"Sure you are." I hold his gaze and straighten my spine. If he's going to shoot me then he'll have to do it looking me in the face. I grab Darcie's hand for moral support and together we brace for death.

A commotion draws our attention and we twist our heads in time to see Jodi come flying back our way and right into Justin. Her braids whip the gun out of his hand and then she does another wild swing of her head. This time the beads at the ends of her hair clank together so hard a few break off. Pieces fly everywhere.

Justin screams and clutches his face, as one nails him right in the eye. He trips and falls back against the edge of the dock, waving an arm around for balance, but Jodi hits him again and this time he falls right into the water.

"Take that, you blimey arsehole!" Jodi shouts out into the night air. It's the last thing I hear her say before a shitload of guys and one very short blonde woman, led by a pissed off Carter and Ryder, swarm the dock from all sides.

"Drop your weapons," a man blares from a megaphone. I smile. I'd know that voice anywhere and this time it's welcome.

"Cuntie!" I wave my arms over my head. Never have I ever been as excited to see this man. I'm so lost in my excitement at being rescued that I'm not paying attention and get tackled from behind, face planting into the wooden floor.

"No! You ruined everything." Kristyn straddles me and pulls out fistfuls of my hair. I try to twist out of her grip and throw her off, but it's no use. She has thighs of steel. This crazy bitch is much stronger than she looks.

Then I hear Darcie scream like a wild banshee followed by a muffled thump. Kristyn falls to the side in a lifeless heap, and I'm no longer pinned to the floor.

I roll over to find Darcie cradling her bag in her arms, looking like a total badass. Blonde strands of hair whip around her face and she's panting like she just ran a mile. "Don't fuck with a Cocksister. Especially one armed with a dickbag, you cuntsicle."

I laugh and stay on my back, watching as Clover and Clamshank are cuffed. Exhaustion is starting to take over and I just want to lie here forever. Jodi and Darcie must be feeling the same because they both fall down next to me on their backs. We lie there like dead fish, panting and tired. This adventure has taken one hell of a toll on us. I might sleep for a week after this.

A pair of men's Timberland boots invade my vision, stopping all train of thought. My eyes follow them up the dirt covered jeans, which cover a moose knuckle I know so well and lead up to a face that has my body melting into the floor. Logan's standing with his hands on his hips, staring down at us like we have balls for chins. "If I didn't see it for myself, I'd never believe this just happened. You three are insane."

The three of us share a look and shrug. What can we say? We saved ourselves and nobody was shot this time.

18

LOGAN'S STILL STARING DOWN AT us when he's joined by Carter and Ryder. Both of them look similar to the last time I saw them. Gone is Ryder's sandy blonde mohawk, replaced by a cropped cut that closely resembles a buzz cut. Carter's brown hair is a touch longer than when we last saw him, but it's the only difference. Both of them have grown full beards, but it does little to detract from their strong pronounced jaws and muscular physiques.

"You girls okay?" Carter's deep blue eyes inspect Darcie from head to toe.

"I am now that you're here." Darcie's face lights up at the sight of her man leaning over us. He rewards her with a bright smile, revealing a deep dimple on each cheek.

"We're good." My body grows heavier the longer I lie on the wooden dock. I'm not sure I'll be getting up any time soon.

"Howdy, Sugar." Color spreads across Jodi's face as Ryder's southern accent washes over her like a warm glass of bourbon on a cool night. His baby blue eyes do a once over, stopping at her cornrows. He grins. "Digging the new look."

She snorts, but other than that remains quiet. I think he's done something no other person has before—stunned Jodi into silence.

Logan pulls me to my feet and against his side. Groans from next to me signal Ryder and Carter are doing the same with Darcie and Jodi. He holds me at the waist and puts my arm around his neck. "Lean on me for support." The fact he says this without me ever uttering a word is another reason he's a keeper.

Together we hobble off the dock and back onto solid ground. The sound of footsteps, followed by Darcie and Carter's voices, let me know they're following close behind. The second my feet hit the soft sand it takes everything I have not to drop to my knees and kiss the ground. Being on solid ground has never felt so good.

Off to the side, Tre and Kate are being tended to by paramedics, as Chief Cunterson watches from the side.

"Are they okay? I feel bad they were hurt trying to help us."

"Yeah. They'll be fine." He wedges me into his side and cups my ass. Something tells me the guys won't be letting us out of their sights for a while after this. "And don't feel bad. Those two are as tough as they are smart. Chances are Agents Felterbush and Widerbox will be back out in the field tomorrow."

"Are they really even sushisisters or was that just a cover?"

Logan chuckles. "It's true. They're together."

I nod my head and watch Carter and Darcie approach us. As they stop a few spaces in front of us, it isn't lost on me that we're a Cocksister short. I glance over to the docks and see Jodi and Ryder in deep conversation.

Carter slings his arm around Darcie and pulls her up flush against his chest, drawing my focus to them. He tilts his chin in my direction. "Cox."

"Haddick." I almost leave my greeting at that, but it's not my style. And where's the fun in playing it safe? If I haven't found a filter in thirty-five years, no sense in starting now. "Played with any catfish lately?"

He shakes his head at Darcie. "I can't believe you told her that story."

Darcie shrugs. "We're girls. We tell each other everything."

"Sure do." I wink. "So, how you lost your nut isn't that far of a stretch."

The hand on my ass tightens as I feel Logan's lips brush against my temple. "Please tell me you're kidding?"

My answering laugh tells him all he needs to know. "Shit," he mumbles next to my ear.

Yelling halts our conversation and draws our attention back to the docks.

Jodi and Ryder are not done having it out. She looks ready to castrate him, while Ryder isn't looking much better. He tugs at the blonde stubble along his chin and keeps his sky blue eyes transfixed on Jodi. At the moment he looks like a lost puppy, which makes me feel a bit sorry for him.

"Come on, Sugar. Don't be like that." Ryder reaches for Jodi, but she backs out of his reach.

"You're a bloody areshole!" she shouts back.

"You think they'll work it out?" Darcie asks the same thing I'm wondering.

"I don't know. Jodi can be pretty stubborn." I sigh and study her body language. The way she's waving her arms around would have me worried for Ryder's dick if I didn't see the need for him in her eyes. She can deny it all she wants, but it's there plain as day. Like any good Cocksister, though, she will not make this easy on him.

"They will in their own time," Carter assures us, but right then Ryder must say something stupid because Jodi shoves his ass off the dock and into the water.

"Or not," I mumble.

Logan sighs. "I'm not sure my blood pressure can handle another Cocksister adventure."

"Hey!" I elbow him in the stomach. He grunts, but doesn't take his arms away from me.

"Lisa!" I turn at the sound of my brother's voice. "Thank fuck you're okay." He yanks me out of Logan's arms and into a tight hug. My body's too stunned to reciprocate, but it doesn't stop me from inhaling a giant whiff of his hair gel. He really needs to stop shellacking his head with that shit. "You scared the shit out of me. Don't ever hang up on me like that again." When he pulls back, his light brown eyes take in my face.

"What are you doing here?" As happy as I am to see him, I stare back like he has a vagina for a nose.

"I called him," Logan interjects and shakes my brother's hand like they're old friends. "Glad you made it, man."

"Thanks for the heads up." Dusty glances in Logan's direction and nods.

My head whips back and forth, trying to figure out how my man has a sudden bromance with my brother. One I wasn't aware of. "When did this happen?" I point a finger towards the two of them.

"We're guys." Logan grins, repeating Darcie's earlier words back to me with a twist.

Then someone speaking in rapid Spanish followed by another person with a very thick British accent hits my ears. My gaze burns into the side of my brother's face. "Please tell me you didn't call all the parents?"

Dusty's face reddens against his olive skin. "What was I supposed to do? Ma heard me shouting your name into the phone."

"You could have lied." I fist my hands at my sides and beg for the strength not to junk punch my brother.

"And risk the wrath of the *chancla*? Hell no. That woman's got a bullshit detector that out does the CIA. No way I'm risking my ass for yours."

I cringe at his words because he's right. Mexican moms are known for two things: making sure no one goes hungry and loving you like no one else, but the second you step out of line they'll be the first to beat your ass. Still, he could have at least tried.

"You're such a pussy." I roll my eyes and nudge his shoulder.

"You are what you eat." Dusty licks his lips with a loud smacking sound. "And eat a lot of *panocha* I do." His light brown eyes gleam as he continues to lick his lips.

I'm about to slap him, but luckily for me my mom comes up behind him and whacks him on the back of the head with said *chancla*. She may be four-foot nine, but my mom isn't one to be messed with.

"*Cochino!*" Her dark eyes burn a hole in my brother's face as her dark brown hair whips around with each bob of her head. She looks ready to rip Dusty's nuts off and I almost feel bad for him—almost.

"Ouch. *Córtele*, Ma!" he screams as she drags him away by the ear, chastising him in Spanish the entire way.

"He never learns." Darcie throws her head back and laughs.

"Nope. He sure doesn't." I lean back against Logan's chest, watching the shit show that is my family with a smile on my face.

"Willy." My head twists to the side at the sound of Jodi's mom shouting to her husband. "I found her." Her platinum blonde hair is teased up in a giant ass pompadour on top of her head—that may be bigger since we last saw her—while a cigarette dangles from her hooker red lips.

"Mum, Dad." Jodi rushes over and wraps her parents up in a tight hug. That family is always one to go overboard with some serious PDA.

"About bloody time, Elise. I was about to get a bit cheesed off if we didn't find her soon." Mr. Cummings is rocking his typical outfit of a bow tie and suspenders with a kick ass beard like only he can. Flecks of silver reflect the light in between strands of his dark brown hair and it's safe to say we could find him in the dark.

"Darcie Olivia Badcock!" Darcie hangs her head at the sound of her mom's voice. Other than her loud tone, there's no other movement on her face. It's like a relic, frozen in time. The only thing that does move on her is the bald dog in her arms.

"Is your mom mad or happy? I can't tell." All of her botox injections make it hard to decipher what that woman is feeling.

"I don't know. Her face never moves anymore." Darcie shrugs and drags Carter off towards her mom. "Let's go introduce you to the alien that is my mother, and the dick with hair known as her dog, Martini."

"Word of caution, Haddick. He likes to chew on *toys*. I'd hide your nut if I were you." Darcie's eyes spit fire at me for saying it, but I can't help myself. It comes naturally. I turn my attention back on my mom and brother as they walk off. She's still going at him like a raging bull with no sign of stopping anytime soon.

"She always so intense?" Logan arches a dark eyebrow, looking slightly terrified.

"Yup, but don't worry. She's going to love you." I reach back and pat the side of his face. "We'll just let her get out all of her stress on Dusty before I introduce you." I tilt my head back and wink.

"Fuck! It's got my dick!" Justin's shrill screams cause everyone to stop what they're doing and focus on him.

We glance towards the docks and I have to do a double take because I'm not sure of what I'm seeing. There's a crab dangling between Justin's legs and its pincers are clenched around his dick. Behind him is a drenched Ryder doing his best to usher him to shore.

"Haddick, Cochran! Go help Sorenson take care of that while I help Agent Spitzer," Cunterson barks out from over my shoulder before he walks off to help the tiny blonde female with a cuffed Clamshank.

"On it, Chief." Logan gives me a quick peck on the lips before he and Carter jog over to assist Ryder with Justin.

Darcie and Jodi leave their parents and come stand next to me as we watch the entire scene unfold around us.

"That has to hurt." Darcie shudders.

"His poor knob." Jodi winces and lets out a small laugh.

"I'm just surprised the little guy found something to latch on to." My lips curve into a wide smile at the thought of the little crab inflicting justice for me.

More commotion from behind has our heads turning around in time to see an angry Clamshank break free of his cuffs and charge straight for us like a rabid bull. It all happens so fast there's no time to react. One minute he's there, rushing our way, looking ready to maim us. The next he's on the ground being pummeled by a five-foot nothing blonde.

"Nut him!" Jodi shouts like she's watching a real live wrestling match.

"What do you want her to do?" Darcie cocks her head to the side, but doesn't take her eyes off of the pint-sized package of badassery that is Agent Spitzer.

"I don't think she wants that close to his nuts." I cringe at the thought myself.

"No, not the twigs and berries. On his head." Jodi motions with her head, giving us a visual demonstration of what she means, her cornrows swaying back and forth as she does. "Nut him good, luv!"

"Oh," Darcie and I share a look before turning our attention back to Agent Spitzer.

We watch in fascination as the two of them wrestle. If I thought Jodi was rocking killer moves earlier, she ain't got nothing on Agent Spitzer. This girl must be Ronda Rousey's nugget-sized twin. She flips and spins Clamshank onto his back like he's a weightless bag of dicks. Her fist connects with his face and the crack that resonates has me cringing. Clamshank is knocked out cold, but Agent Spitzer's still going.

"Agent Spitzer!" Chief Cunterson's voice slices through her cockdown. When she doesn't appear to hear him he tries again. "Lacey, he's down."

"Sorry, sir." Agent Spitzer—aka Lacey—brushes the stray strands of blonde hair out of her face and stands up, her blue eyes wild as she composes herself.

"I think I'm in love." Dusty sighs next to me.

I roll my eyes at my brother. He's definitely twatstruck.

"I'll just go see if she needs some assistance." Without a backwards glance, he jogs off towards Lacey.

Cunterson shakes his head when sees us. "Why is it whenever I see you three I develop an immediate case of indigestion?"

Without missing a beat, Darcie fires right back at him a question of her own. "When are you going to wear a decent tie?" She still hasn't forgiven him for arresting her in Ireland and I can't say I blame her.

My eyes cast down to the bright material in question and wrinkle my nose. Someone needs to have an intervention with that man. A multi-colored tie covered with tiny oysters is not something that's pleasing to the eye. "Seriously. What's with the vagina tie?"

Rather than respond, he shakes his head and directs his gaze above mine. "We're finished here. They're all yours."

"Thanks, Chief." Logan grunts and interlaces his fingers with mine.

"How do you put up with that guy?" Darcie shakes her head.

"You learn to appreciate his non-bullshit approach." Carter kisses the side of her head and leaves it at that.

"Can you guys excuse us for a minute? I need to have a word with Lisa." Logan nudges me forward. He doesn't stop tugging me along until we're covered by some nearby bushes. At least, I think they're bushes. It's hard to tell because I've never seen any as tall as me before.

"What's so important you had to drag me away from our friends and all the way over here in these shrubs?" My hands go to my hips, waiting for a response, and I get one—just not the one I was expecting.

"This." Logan's lips crash down on mine, swallowing my surprised cry. One of his hands fists my hair at the nape of my neck while the other kneads my ass. "I know you've been mad at me and you've had every right." His lips trail down my neck, leaving a blaze of fire along my skin in his wake. The stubble of his beard tickles the sensitive area where my neck meets my shoulder, and my knees damn near buckle. "But we'll work through this. No more fighting unless I get to fuck you into oblivion afterwards." He lifts his head and the promise in his eyes leaves me of all people speechless.

"Make up sex is hot." Nothing better in my opinion.

The hand on my ass lifts, coming to rest against my heart. "I want in here." His hand moves, cupping me between my legs. "And here." My body quivers at his words. If he weren't holding onto me I'd be on the floor. His words are hitting me in all the right places. Then he speaks again and my core throbs. If I were wearing any underwear they'd be disintegrated into a pile of ash.

"This is the only pussy I'll ever want." His blue eyes darken with a hunger that matches my own.

Coming off the earlier adrenaline high is making me horny as fuck. I need his dick and I need it yesterday. "You have such a way with words." I laugh, but then his fingers find my clit and I lose all train of thought. "Is that like a proposal or something?" I sigh against his lips.

He cups my face with his free hand and rubs small circles against my cheek, his gaze transforming into something warmer. "I'm not the—"

"I know." I cut him off because I know what he's going to say and I don't need to hear it. He's already shown me exactly what type of guy he is and actions are more powerful than any words could ever be.

He dips down and sucks the skin where my shoulder meets my neck a few times before giving it a light tug with his teeth. His lips move further down my body until he's kneeling on the ground in front of me. He looks up at me and smirks. "I promise you'll never be unhappy with me." He buries his head between my legs and groans against the material of my shorts. "Both of you." His fingers continue stroking me, playing me like a violin before being joined by his tongue. He flicks at my clit, soaking the seam of my shorts with a mixture of his saliva and my pussy.

My head falls back. "Oh fuck." I grind myself against his face. Everything around us fades into the background. It doesn't matter that we're out in the open and could get caught any second. Or that I can hear my friends and family calling my name. Nothing matters except what this man and his talented tongue are doing to me. Each thrust of my hips causes the material to rub tighter against my clit. The friction is becoming too much and yet not enough all at the same time. Beads of sweat drip down my body, causing my shorts to hug me like a second skin. I may never wear underwear again if this is the reward.

"I need more." He hooks a finger through the crotch of my shorts and tugs them to the side. "That's better." His tongue swipes through my folds, lapping at me like I'm his last meal.

"Lisa! Where did she go?" Darcie's voice barely registers through my cockfog.

Logan curves his fingers and increases his thrusts, hitting me in the sweet spot. Everything intensifies times a thousand and I can't control the loud moan that escapes me.

"You hear that?" Jodi isn't far behind her. I love my Cocksisters, but they have real shitty timing.

"People are coming." Logan stops mid stroke and my insides ache for more. Muffled footsteps echo near us, but I don't care.

"The only one who better be coming is me." I grab the back of Logan's head and beg him to keep going. I'm so close to the edge and I want to fucking fall. Then I hear a familiar gasp followed by Jodi's voice.

"Flick my flaps and buy me a nugget. He's muff diving."

"What's with all the noise?" And then my dickbuzz is finally killed by my brother's voice. "Did you find—"

My eyes shoot open to find two Cocksisters, one brother, and a mortified looking mother. It takes a second for the scene unfolding in front of me to fully register. Logan's still on his knees, hand up my shorts, and we freeze like two teenagers who were just caught. I guess this might look bad. Oopsie.

Dusty blinks a few times before he puts his hands over our mother's eyes and backs away, disappearing from view without uttering a single word. Darcie and Jodi, on the other hand, are still staring.

"We'll just um...yeah." Darcie walks back from where she came, but when Jodi doesn't move to follow her she grabs her arm and has to practically drag her ass away.

My gaze darts back to Logan and the hunger in his gaze is waning. He looks ready to bolt. "What's wrong?"

"I don't think that was the best first impression to give your family."

"They'll learn to love you like I do." The words are out before I can stop them. Damn me and my filterless mouth. My eyes bulge out of their sockets as I try to backtrack. "Uh, what I meant was..." My words falter as Logan's face spreads into a shit-eating grin. "What's so funny?"

"You love me?" He presses his lips to mine in a slow lingering kiss. "I love you too, Ace."

And that is how another Cocksister fell under the spell of a permanent dick. He doesn't always say the right things, but he sure does them, and even comes with a full set of balls.

Dicks are like rocks—always hard and come in all shapes and sizes, making it a challenge to find the perfect fit, but when you do, he becomes your penguin and you lock that shit down. Screw riding off into the sunset. This girl rides off on her trusty dick named Logan.

EPILOGUE

Four weeks later...

Things have returned to normal since our eventful trip, but they're anything but quiet. Logan took a short leave of absence from work to spend time with me and help at the family restaurant. I think it's his way of trying to make up to my mother for what she saw in Barbados. Little does he know she was just happy her daughter found a man who knew what he was doing in that department.

I'm wiping down the bar top when Darcie walks into the restaurant and straight towards me.

"Logan looks happy." She tilts her head to a smiling Logan as he disappears into the kitchen. As soon as her ass lands in a seat I'm sliding her favorite drink, a Cumdrop Martini, in front of her.

"Now that my leg is fully healed we've been fucking like rabbits." There's no stopping the smile from spreading across my lips —both sets.

She holds her glass up to her mouth, but pauses and lets out a long sigh. "Must be nice. Carter had to leave on another assignment, so I'm back to self-serving Saturday nights."

"What can I say?" My shoulders shrug. "I'm like a fortune cookie. You split me open the right way, we both get lucky." I wriggle my dark eyebrows, ignoring the damn nausea that's been plaguing me lately.

Of course my words come out right when she has a mouthful of her drink. She chokes and spits cumdrop everywhere. I swear I don't time that shit. It just happens.

"Spitter," I tease, but then my stomach gurgles, killing the humorous mood.

Darcie narrows her eyes. "You okay?"

"Yeah. I don't know why, but lately I can't stand the smell of alcohol." Which sucks, because I love me a good stiff drink.

She studies me a minute and opens her mouth to say something, but her words are cut off by the sound of 'Me So Horny' playing from her phone.

"2 Live Crew?" I prop my elbow against the cool tile and cast her a suspicious look.

"Damn, Carter. He thinks it's funny to change my ringtone all the time." She shakes her head, but when she sees who it is her whole face lights up. Her finger clicks on the answer button as she leans over so we can both see the video call. "Hey, Jo! We miss you."

"I miss both you twats, too, but I've got great news." Jodi's smile is so big it looks like she's about to burst.

"What's that?" I lean in closer to the bar to keep from losing my breakfast. This damn nausea better hurry up and go away. I want to get my drink on.

"I'm coming to your side of the pond." Jodi drops the best news I've heard all day.

Darcie and I scream our heads off in excitement. We're so loud Logan comes rushing in. "Everything okay in here?" He has his gun out, looking ready to fuck someone up. It's so damn hot when he goes all badass like that. If I didn't feel so sick I'd jump his ass.

"We're good. Jodi's coming to visit." I wave him off.

"Nothing is ever boring with you, is it?" Logan shoves his gun back inside his holster and stares at me like I've just told him to pierce the tip of his dick.

"This place isn't called *Casa De Locos* for nothing." I gesture towards the western decor and giant stuffed horse that's center stage in my parent's restaurant. He studies me for a second before heading back into the kitchen and my attention sweeps back over to Darcie's phone.

"How long are you staying?" Darcie asks.

"I'm not sure. I have a work thing to do in Vegas and then I thought we could do some sight seeing." It all sounds good, but she's being a bit cryptic, which isn't normal for her.

"Hells yeah," Darcie shouts. Judging by her excitement she hasn't picked up on Jodi's vagueness.

"Everything okay, Jo?" I study her face for any tells.

"Fine, luv." She smiles, but it doesn't reach her eyes. I'm ready to do some more prodding when she changes the subject. "Did you give it to her yet?"

"No. I was waiting for you to call." Darcie bounces in her seat so hard I'm afraid she's going to tip the damn thing over.

"Give me what?" My gaze bounces back and forth between my two crazy friends. The last time they bought me a gift I was in the hospital with a gunshot wound.

Darcie bends to the side and grabs something from the floor. "This." She slides a hot pink bag across the counter to me.

"A present? It's not even my birthday." A smile brightens my face as I toss the white tissue paper aside. When I pull out my *gift*, I don't know whether to laugh or scream. To say I'm surprised is an understatement.

"It's Henry 2.0," Jodi shouts through the phone.

"I love it. This is why you're my BBFL. First I get a box of tampons after Darcie shoots me and now this." I study the blue phallic shaped toy of dick perfection. There's something about it I can't quite place, something I swear I've seen before. "Wait, why does it look familiar?"

"Because Henry 2.0 is really a mold of Logan 1.0." Darcie holds up her martini glass in a mock toast.

"Thanks, you guys." Only my girls would get me a vibrator molded from my man's dick. Excitement courses through me as I bounce up and down. All the jumping isn't a good idea, though. The nausea becomes too much for me to handle and I drop Henry 2.0 on the counter before running off towards the bathroom to bring my breakfast back up. Once I feel like my stomach isn't going to turn in on itself anymore, I head back out. Darcie's still video chatting with Jodi, but both of their gazes land on me the second I'm back behind the bar.

"You still fighting that bug?" Darcie asks.

"Yeah. It's been worse the past week. I think I either ate something bad or picked up a virus during our night in the jungle." I swallow a small sip of water and take slow deep breaths.

Jodi and Darcie grow quiet as a knowing look passes between the two.

"What?" I'm not liking the strange look they're giving me.

Then it's like a light bulb goes off inside Jodi's head and she gasps. "Are you up the duff?"

"Up the what?" My nose crinkles.

Jodi laughs and rolls her eyes. "You know. In the club, pea in the pod, up the pole?"

I stare at her, shaking my head. My friend is finally losing her mind. "No idea what the hell you're talking about, Jo."

Darcie starts shaking with laughter in her seat and if she doesn't stop I may just push her ass off it. The shit. "She means do you have a bun in the oven?"

"I'm not even cooking." A faint understanding is clicking into place, but I'm keeping deniability as long as I can.

"Not that oven." Darcie's eyes flick to my belly and everything inside me stops.

"No. NO. Noooooo. I can't be. Can I?" I mentally calculate the date of my last period and want to throw up all over again. Add in the fact that we haven't used condoms and, "Shit!" I scream and bang my head against the bar as Logan comes back around.

"Everything all right?"

"Welcome to adulthood." Darcie's enjoying watching me squirm way too much.

"Adulting sucks dick and doesn't even swallow." My throat grows dry at the thought of there being two of me.

Jodi's laughter vibrates through the phone. "A wee Cocksister is coming."

"Or a Cockmister." The alcohol is getting to Darcie and making her loose lipped. I may gag her with Henry 2.0 if she's not careful. Then she holds up her glass and smirks. "To Lisa. Soon she'll be trading dick for diapers."

Logan's eyes widen on me as they both drop the news like a bomb. "This true, Ace?"

I open my mouth to answer, but words fail me. Shock is causing my basic motor functions to cease up. I swallow the lump in my throat and force out a low, "Maybe."

Logan moves so fast I'm dizzy. One minute he's across the bar and the next he's in front of me on his knee. He places his hands on my stomach and looks up at me wearing a huge grin. "I'll look after you both." Figures. He's treating this like the best oops ever, while I'm freaking the fuck out.

A Cocksister pregnant? Cock help us all.

THE END OF THIS
COCKSISTER RIDE

Up next is our favorite dirty Brit in
Badcock Tour 3: Cummings to America

Keep reading for a sneak peek at Badcock Tour to
see where the adventure began.

Present Day
Los Angeles

"Fuck yeah! That's it! Fuck me harder!"

"You like that, don't you, you dirty slut?"

"I am a dirty slut. Put your big cock in my ass."

Both actors pound away at the blonde as a group of us watch on the sidelines. Years of this shit, and it never changes. The chick fakes an orgasm, long enough for one of the guys to pull out and give her a pearl necklace. Another day, another money shot.

"And cut!" Richard takes his headphones off and gives them a thumbs up. "We got it this time." Then he turns his head towards me, holding his hands out and smiling. "Darcie, baby, we make one hell of a team." He gestures towards himself and then points a short stubby finger at me. "Beaver and Badcock have another hit on our hands. This script you wrote is the shit!"

"Thanks." You'd think I'd cured cancer with the amount of praise I'm getting.

"Mr. Beaver, there's an urgent phone call for you in your office." One of his very young, very tan, and very plastic receptionists hands him a slip of paper, eye-fucking him the whole time. The only difference between us is that my carpet, if I had any, would match my drapes, and my big tits are real. I woke up on the morning of my seventeenth birthday with them practically falling out of my shirt. They may have come in overnight, but I've been thanking the boob gods ever since.

Richard is hot, so I can't blame her for staring. But, she doesn't have to be so obvious about it. A little tact would go a long way. Unfortunately, I don't think she has the brain cells for it.

"I have to go take care of a few things. I'll meet you in my office." Richard's toffee eyes gleam down at me like I'm walking candy. He grabs me by the collar of my shirt and plants a wet kiss on my lips. It's so deep his tongue practically hits the back of my throat. My fingers grab onto his short, dark hair to keep from falling on my ass. The kiss can't end fast enough.

When he finally pulls away, it takes me a minute to wipe his spit off my face before I answer. "Yeah. That's fine. I have a few things of my own to take care of."

He smiles, pats me on my ass, and then heads off with blondie in tow. My eyes glare into the back of her head, hoping she falls on her face in those fuck-me heels she's wearing. No such luck, though.

The two male actors walk off the set, their limp dicks swaying in the wind as they pass me, each giving me a playful wink that has me grinning. Sometimes I'm glad I don't work in a regular office.

The actress is still on the bed covered in their jizz. "Can someone get me a towel?"

Usually we have a towel boy for this, but he didn't show up today. I glance around and everyone is wrapped up in their own stuff, not paying her any attention. Well, that or they're ignoring her on purpose. I'm not a big enough asshole to do that, so that means it falls on me. *Fan-fucking-tastic!*

The heels of my shoes clank against the concrete floor as I stroll over towards the cart and grab her the biggest towel I can find. She's going to need it because let's be honest, that's a lot of jizz to soak up. When I hand it to her, she smiles and pops her gum. "Thanks, doll."

"Don't mention it." I turn around and wipe my hands on my black skirt as I debate on going to my office to finish writing the scene I was working on, but now I'm not in the mood anymore. So, I skip it and head up to Richard's office. On the elevator ride up, I'm mentally making plans for us for dinner. I'm really in the mood for some Thai food.

When I get to his office, the door is shut, and weird noises are coming from behind it. Then I hear him in an all too familiar tone.

"Oh, yeah. I like hearing my balls slap against your ass."

Against my better judgment, I twist the knob and shove open the door.

Asses greet me. Naked asses. Richard pounds into his blonde receptionist from behind on his massive oak desk. The fluorescent lighting really isn't doing him any favors right now. His skin looks all yellow and jaundice.

I'm so mad I see red. "Are you fucking shitting me right now?"

Richard freezes mid-thrust and whips his head towards the door. He's wearing a deer in the headlights look—one that clearly says he's fucked. And he is, in more ways than one.

"Darcie, baby." He pulls out of her and twists towards me, pants around his ankles. His dick is wet and semi-hard, but at least he's wearing a condom. That's something.

"Don't you Darcie me, you lying, cheating asshole!" I don't know why I'm surprised. There have been a shit ton of rumors about his onset "activities". I heard them all before we even started dating, but like an idiot I tried to be the better person and see the good in him. "And will you fucking cover up that shriveled cock of yours?" I'm so pissed I debate shoving the heel of my shoe up his ass, but he'd like that too much.

Blondie tugs her dress down, and skirts past me. It takes everything I have not to cold-cock her ass before she makes it to the door. When she's gone, I cross my arms over my chest and give Richard an angry, hard glare.

"You have every right to be upset with me." He holds his hands up in defense, making me want to vomit.

"You think? For fuck's sakes, your fingers are still wet from her!

And you're what? Going to play it off like it's not a big deal?" This is such bullshit!

"It was a moment of weakness. You know I love *you*. Come on, Darcie baby. Don't let this one little mistake ruin what we have. We're so good together." His words are making me gag.

"First of all, you can't tell someone you love them when you've had your cock buried in someone else's pussy only seconds ago. That's a total dick move! What we have obviously doesn't mean as much to you as it does to me. And secondly…" I struggle to find my next words, but once they come I know they're the right ones. "I quit!" I don't need this job. He can shove it up his ass!

"Darcie!" He pulls up his pants and moves towards me, but I'm quicker.

I reach the door before he can stop me. The same time I twist the knob, it's pushed open from the other side, causing me to stumble back a bit. Two large men are waiting in the middle of the doorway. Both of them are African American. One is about three inches taller than the other, but the shorter one has freckles dusting the tops of his cheeks and a scar under his right eye. They both have arms the size of my thighs and that's saying something, since I work out six days a week.

"Can I help you?" My words tumble out in a squeaky rush. Their blank expressions are a bit intimidating.

"We're looking for Dick," the larger of the two demands.

I open the door wider and jerk my thumb back in Richard's direction. "The asshole is right behind me."

His eyebrow arches at my comment and then glances over my shoulder. He nods his head to the freckled one. They both move forward through the door, causing me to take a step back and to the side.

"Hello, Dick." The larger of the two crosses his arms over his chest.

"Terrence would like a meeting," the freckled one adds.

Richard's demeanor changes. I'm no longer a concern. His face pales as he starts to break out in a sweat. If I didn't know any better, I'd say he was about to shit his pants. Too bad I don't care right now.

They both look down at me with an expectant glare. I swallow the lump in my throat and take that as my cue to get the hell out of there.

"I'll just be leaving now." I spin around towards the door when Richard attempts to stop me.

"We're not done."

I whip back around to face him and point my finger in his face. "Done. Finished. Never want to see you again. Ever!" With that parting line, I haul my ass out of there and never look back. I have a date with a gallon of ice cream to eat my feelings away.

As soon as the door shuts, I hear scuffling noises. My temper is still fuming so I don't pay them much attention. Instead, I go straight to my office and clean it out. It's a good thing I don't have a lot of stuff. I'm in and out in less than ten minutes.

In my car, I sit and stare out the windshield. Now that I have time to think, it's all hitting me. Not only am I single, but now I'm unemployed, too. I scream and bang my hands on the steering wheel. "Shit!"

The ringing of my phone cuts into my breakdown. I don't even look at who it is before I answer. "Hello?"

"How's it hanging, Cocksister?" Lisa's cheery voice blares in my ear.

"Awful." Tears spill. Why am I crying over this dick? "I just caught Richard banging his receptionist over his desk."

"That fucking cuntsicle! I'm going to shove a tampon up his dick and hope it falls off from gonorrhea!" she shouts, so loudly that I have to hold the phone way from my ear to avoid going deaf.

"As much as I appreciate that, I don't think you'd want to get that close to his junk." I sniffle.

"I'd do it for you." And that is why she's still one of my BFFs.

"Thanks, but I just want to go eat my weight in ice cream." My finger traces along the seam of my steering wheel as I fantasize about a big tub of cookie dough covered in caramel.

"No way. Come by the restaurant. I'm working the bar and you could use some alcohol therapy."

I sigh. "You're not going to make me drink one of your weird concoctions again, are you? Last time I was hung over for a week."

Lisa snorts into the phone. "They weren't that bad. You're just a lightweight." When the silence stretches on the line she adds, "You know you want to." There's a muffled voice in the background that's hard to make out. "Dusty says to get your ass over here or he's coming to get you. And the drinks are on the house."

"Who can turn down free alcohol?" She knows me so well.

"Exactly. See you in a few."

I hang up and shake my head. Alcohol is better than a solo ice cream binge any day.

Fifteen minutes later, I'm walking through La Casa de Locos, Lisa's family's restaurant. It's decorated like it sounds—crazy. There's a mixture of Mexican and western decor throughout. Each booth or table even has its own special name. Off in the left corner is a giant stuffed horse. I've never asked if it was once a real one or not. Truth is, I don't want to know. It's creeped me out since I was little. This is what happens when dad's a huge Roy Rogers fan.

"*Hola, mija.*" Lisa's mom comes storming out of the kitchen and wraps me up in a tight hug, giving me a mouthful of her salt and pepper hair. She doesn't speak much English, but that's never stopped us from communicating.

"*Hola*, Dolores."

She's tiny but strong. One thing I learned as a kid is to never piss her off. Shoes will become weapons if you do. Beware of the *chancla*. Her black eyes glisten at me as her round face smiles. Dolores has some laugh lines showing on her face and crow's feet around her eyes, but she's still a knock out regardless. She's short and curvy with a heart of gold. Lisa's dad scored with her. He may be American, but he speaks perfect Spanish. You'd never know he learned it from his wife.

"*Lisa está en el bar.*" She gestures towards the back of the restaurant.

"*Gracias.*" That's about the extent of my Spanish. I pass a group of guys downing beer by the pitcher, and take a seat at the end of the bar.

Lisa's with a customer, but she sees me and nods her head in acknowledgement. She finishes up their order, turns back and makes another drink before coming over to me.

"Here." She shoves what looks like some type of martini in front of me. It's light pink with a mixture of white, blue, and purple stuff stuck to the rim of the glass. There's also a blue toothpick with three cherries on it.

I lean forward and sniff it. It smells fruity. My eyes dart up to hers as I wrinkle my nose. "Am I going to like this?"

"Just drink it." She nudges the glass closer.

I cave and take a sip. I'm pleasantly surprised. It's sweet and salty. There's a mixture of pineapple along with something bitter. "It's good. What's it called?" I'm mid-sip when she answers.

"A Cumdrop Martini." She winks.

I choke, spitting Cumdrop everywhere. "Why? Just why?" I'm going to kill her.

Lisa tosses me a pile of napkins. "Relax. It's not made with real cum." She puts her finger to the side of her face. "Well, at least not yet."

It's the stupidest thing I've ever heard and yet I can't stop laughing. "Yeah, I'm just gonna let that go."

"Got you to laugh, though, didn't I?" She claps her hands together and grins.

"You did. You shit." I throw a balled-up napkin at her. She puts her hand up and it ricochets off to the side. Still laughing, she throws back a shot. "Patrón?"

She slams the shot glass back on the counter and shakes her head. "No way. It's Jäger. You know what happens when I have tequila."

"The whole fucking town knows what happens when you have tequila." I laugh and take another small sip of my Cumdrop. It's growing on me.

"That was one time." She holds up a finger.

I hold up two. "Twice. And security was called both times."

She shrugs. "At least it was a night to remember."

"Yup. Being arrested with my BFFs is definitely my favorite memory. Loved it when Jodi used her accent to try to seduce the cop out of his pants." My mouth curves into a grin.

Lisa's eyes gleam. "Being handcuffed by a hot as shit cop is always a good time."

I lick the rim of the glass and the taste of salty and sweet hits my tongue. "What's on here?"

Lisa's eyes light up. "An awesome mixture of colored sugar and salt that's like an orgasm on your taste buds."

I nod in agreement. There's no denying that she's a genius when it comes to making drinks.

"Yo, Lisa! You gonna make me a drink or what?" A customer shouts for her attention from the other end of the bar.

"Duty calls." She smacks the counter in front of me. "I'll be right back so expect a grilling on all things Dick related." She walks off to the other end of the bar. I swallow back more liquid courage to prepare to divulge the details of my horrible afternoon.

A head of dark brown hair catches my eye as he approaches. His dimpled smile hasn't changed since we were kids. It screams mischief, just like his big sisters. "Hey, Darcie. Looking good."

"Thanks, Dusty. How you been?" My fingers toy with the stem of my glass.

"Good. Turns out an all access pass to alcohol means an all access pass to free sweet pussy." Dusty may be two years younger, but he's so far behind in the maturity department. Not that we're that mature to begin with.

"That's great." Maybe I should have stayed home and indulged in a cookie dough rush after all?

"Dusty Cox! Are you bothering her again?" Lisa shouts from across the bar.

Dusty sets his elbows on the bar before leaning in towards me. "Don't trust anything she gives you to swallow," he whispers. Then his eyes travel down my face and land on my chest. "Nope. I'm just admiring the view, big sister."

"Thanks. I think." I take another big gulp of my Cumdrop. With this family, I'm going to need at least four more.

"Think you can introduce me to a porn star or two?" His lips spread into a wide grin, showing off his dimples.

"Oh my God! You're an idiot!" Lisa comes up behind him and smacks the back of his head. "Get out of here before I tell Ma you're trying to molest my friends."

"Don't be such a cock blocker. I'm working on my game here."

Instead of admiring my tits, he should have been paying attention to what's behind him. "Seriously, hook me up with some of that hot on-set pussy." His eyes are now up on my face, but mine are on who's crept up behind him. Dusty's too into trying to sample porn pussy to realize his mother is even there. She's standing behind him and, by the look on her face, understanding every word.

Dolores mimics her daughter and slaps Dusty on the back of his head. The loud *smack* that echoes is the best sound ever. "*Cochino, Dustin!*"

Lisa and I bust out laughing. Her brother will never learn.

"Ouch. Ma! *Ya parele*. Damn." He runs his fingers through his hair, attempting to fix it, like it could move from all that gel. His teeth sink into his bottom lip as he jerks his chin in my direction. "See you around, Darcie." He walks off with his mother following the whole way, ripping him a new one in Spanish.

Our laughter fades and Lisa's attention shifts to me. She slides another Cumdrop in front of me. "Spill it. What happened with fuck face?"

"What usually happens when I meet a guy and things seem like they're going great? His inner asshole appears. Or in this case, his inner cheating slut. I caught him fucking his receptionist on his desk when he knew I would be in my office right down the hall."

Lisa sucks in a deep breath and shuts her eyes. When they open, the fire behind them is scary. "The tampon offer still stands."

"Thanks, but I'll pass." Frustration over this shittastic day boils over. "What's wrong with me? I'm surrounded by dicks all day, and I can't even get a decent one. I'm thirty-five. I thought I'd have my shit together by now. I still feel like an immature kid pretending to be a grown up."

"Just because we're thirty-five doesn't mean we have to have our shit together. I'm still figuring out what the hell I want to do with my life. Some people want the white-collar job with the white picket fence and a dozen little ankle biters running around. Fuck that. I want orgasms, plain and simple. And maturity can suck it. I'm mentally thirteen and plan on staying that way. Besides, I don't know anyone we went to school with who has their shit together. As far as the dick situation goes, nothing's wrong with you. It's them. Some guys are just clueless." Lisa swigs back another shot.

I stare at my drink and sigh. She's right about everything. "They think they can shove their dick into anyone they want, and we're supposed to be okay with it because it was a moment of weakness. We have needs, too, damn it! Some couldn't find my moan button if I drew them a fucking map." It's hopeless. "I want to be wined, dined, and sixty-nined. Is that so hard for guys to understand?"

"Seriously. I'm tired of having to show them how my shit works. I want a man who eats me like I'm a steak and treats me like I'm caviar. I'm so tired of being fucked like he's having a seizure while I lie there and hold on, waiting for the scary ride to end." Lisa plays with the rim of her shot glass. Then she jumps like she shit her pants and pulls her phone out from her back pocket. "Yeah?" Her hazel eyes brighten, and not just from the alcohol. "Hold on!" She pushes a button and holds her phone out. "Go ahead. You're on speaker."

"Hello, my gorgeous American cunts!" That cheery voice is the best thing I've heard today.

"Hey, Jodi. How's it going on your side of the pond?" I miss her crazy ass.

"Fucking fabulous, but I miss you bitches and your flaps."

"We miss you too, Cocksister." Lisa eyes me for a second, which never ends well. "Darcie just caught her latest man-friend stuffing his sausage into someone else."

Yup. Just as I thought. I'm going to kill her. I lean over the bar and reach my hand out to grab the phone and shut her down, but she's quicker. Her long-ass arm holds it up out of my reach. There's no retrieving it unless I hop over the damn bar and pounce on her. The thought crosses my mind, but I'm not in my twenties anymore and will probably land face first.

"WHAT? That fucking twat stain! Do I need to fly over and bury his ass for you, luv?"

"No. I'm good. I swear." I do my best to calm the storm that is Jodi.

"You are not. You're drowning in Cumdrops." Lisa snorts and I toss a napkin at her face to shut her up. She ducks to the side and laughs.

"In what?" Jodi asks.

"Nothing," I say to her before I address Lisa. "And I will be."

"You need to stop dating these players and turn the tables on them." Lisa keeps going, ignoring me.

"You need to get back on that meat stick and pound your problems away on the next bloke or five. Works for me every time." Jodi's the queen of advice, whether it's good or not.

Lisa's whole body perks up. "That's not a bad idea."

"What's not?" I don't know if I'm going to like where this is headed.

"Guys do it all the time. Why can't we?" Lisa shrugs. "We're single, not to mention better at playing games than they are."

"So, what? We travel and fuck any guy we want to? Like what? A Badcock Tour?" I tease. I'm not serious at all, but my comment backfires.

"Hell fucking yeah!" Lisa's eyes sparkle.

"I was joking." Fuck me. What did I just do?

"So? Guys here are shit. Maybe we'll have better luck tasting all the flavors the world has to offer." Once Lisa starts, there is no stopping her. "Think about it. Curing you of your problems one international cock ride at a time." She's way too excited about this.

"Oooh yes. I fucking love it. It's like the muff diving Olympics." Jodi is always the one to encourage Lisa and her crazy ass ideas.

"Come on. It'll be like old times, when the three of us used to let our crazy flags fly. Besides, you're unemployed. You have all the free time in the world right now. And Ma will let me have the time off." Lisa sticks her bottom lip out and pouts. "Please?" She knows I can't resist when she does that.

I stare at my friend, not knowing whether to slap her or kiss her. She'd probably love both. The idea starts to sink in and my vag gets very happy. You only live once. "Fuck it! Let's do this. I've always wanted to take a trip to pound town with an Irishmen. If they can talk like that with their tongues, imagine what else they can do with it."

Lisa jumps up and down like a little kid. "Hells yeah! What's hotter than being balls deep in Irishmen in June?"

Jodi's screaming can be heard through the phone and in the whole damn bar. "I'm so bloody fucking excited I think I just pissed myself. You twats fly to London and meet me. Then we'll take our muffs to Ireland and get our willy wrestling on."

"It's a plan. Booking our flights now." Lisa claps her hands together.

"Leave the Ireland flight to me. Our girls' holiday will be the tits. My flaps are clapping they're so happy right now. See your faces in a couple of days." Jodi's crazy, but she's the best kind of crazy there is.

"Bye, gorgeous," I call out, feeling a bit excited myself. Despite the crazy ass trip we've just planned, seeing Jodi will be amazing.

Lisa shoves the phone back in her pocket and makes me another Cumdrop. Then she does the same with the Jäger for her. She holds up her glass, ready to do a toast, and I mimic her movement. "To wine in the glass." I smile and sip my drink. Then she decides to add more. "And cocks in the ass!"

I choke again, spitting Cumdrop everywhere. Maybe I should rethink this Badcock Tour?

ABOUT THE AUTHOR

CHRISTINE BESZE IS A WRITER, reader, mother, wife, and lover of all things wine. She lives in her own world of crazy most days, because the voices inside her head hold some great conversation. When she does have to come back to reality and act like an actual grown-up, she spends her time with her handsome hubby Z, their two gorgeous gingers and their mini-herd of German Shepherds. Born in sunny Southern California, she now lives with her family on the East Coast and couldn't be happier. You'll still find her in flip-flops—with a full glass of wine—all year round.

If you enjoyed this story and would like info on future release dates, or just want to see what kind of shenanigans she's up to follow her here:

FACEBOOK READERS GROUP:
CHRISTINE'S CRAZY CREW

facebook.com/authorchristinebesze

twitter.com/Cbesze

instagram.com/christinebeszeauthor

amazon.com/author/christinebesze

bookbub.com/profile/christine-besze

ALSO BY
CHRISTINE BESZE

BADCOCK SERIES:

Badcock Tour

FIRE AND WATER SERIES:

Leo Rising—One

Aries Fire—Two

ANTHOLOGIES:

Brothel: The Magnolia Diaries

COCKSISTER APPRECIATION

OH BOY. WHERE DO I START? There were so many people that inspired me for this book.

My brain is all over the place and I'm like a squirrel snorting cocaine off a strippers ass, so before I lose it completely, I need to give a huge shout out to you, the reader. Thank you. Thank you. Thank you. Without you, the voices in my head would remain just that. You were brave enough to take a chance on my crazy world and for that, I am forever grateful. I hope you enjoyed reading about these crazy ass characters as much as I enjoyed writing them.

To my husband Z and our baby gingers, thank you for putting up with all of the crazy shit that is constantly running though my head. Without your love and support, I wouldn't be able to do any of this. Babe, you're a trooper for helping me with any questions I have. I love you all so much.

Darcie, my blonde Scotty with the great rack, I'd have been a mess without you. Who knew that what started out as a simple joke between us would turn into this? Thank you so much for all of our crazy conversations and being such a kick ass inspiration for this Darcie. No matter how wild my ideas were you always encouraged me to write that shit down. Without you, my British would have made me sound like a giant bawbag. Love ya, Cocksister!

My book sister from another mister, Lisa. We did it boo! There are no words to describe what you mean to me. Our constant texts from sunup to sundown (time difference be damned) mean everything. You were always there to kick my ass and keep me writing. You encouraged me to let go and just let the words flow. You are the Monica to my Rachel and I seriously love your face to Uranus and back.

Jodi, my amazing, filthy, flap happy, Brit who loves her some bum fun, thank you for not running away screaming when I first messaged you about this idea. You've been such a great sport about all of it and one hell of a muse for this Jodi. It was a blast to get inside this character's head and become British for a bit. Hopefully, I didn't come off as a giant knobhead.

My beautiful bad ass Betas: Kate, Lacey, Naomi, Tre, and Shelby, thank for all of your feedback. Love y'all as much as Lisa (from BT) loves dick.

Christi Anderson, you are one of my most favorite twisted and crazy friends. Thank you for putting up with all of my questions and helping me get my shit together.

Lastly, Heather, my amazing editor, thank you for always being so supportive and enjoying every crazy thing I send you. I promise I'll learn where the hell to put a comma eventually.

Made in the USA
Columbia, SC
16 March 2023